Kathleen Rowntree grew up in Grimsby, Lincolnshire, and studied music at Hull University. She has written seven previous novels, *The Quiet War of Rebecca Sheldon*, *Brief Shining*, *A Prize for Sister Catherine*, *Between Friends*, *Tell Mrs Poole I'm Sorry*, *Outside, Looking In* and *Laurie and Claire*. She and her husband live on the Oxfordshire/Northamptonshire borders.

Also by Kathleen Rowntree:

THE QUIET WAR OF REBECCA SHELDON
BRIEF SHINING
A PRIZE FOR SISTER CATHERINE
BETWEEN FRIENDS
TELL MRS POOLE I'M SORRY
OUTSIDE, LOOKING IN
LAURIE AND CLAIRE

and published by Black Swan

MR BRIGHTLY'S
EVENING OFF

Kathleen Rowntree

BLACK SWAN

MR BRIGHTLY'S EVENING OFF
A BLACK SWAN BOOK : 0 552 99733 1

Originally published in Great Britain by Bantam Press,
a division of Transworld Publishers Ltd

PRINTING HISTORY
Bantam Press edition published 1997
Black Swan edition published 1998

Set in 11/12pt Melior by
Phoenix Typesetting, Ilkley, West Yorkshire

Black Swan Books are published by Transworld Publishers Ltd,
61–63 Uxbridge Road, London W5 5SA,
in Australia by Transworld Publishers (Australia) Pty Ltd,
15–25 Helles Avenue, Moorebank, NSW 2170
and in New Zealand by Transworld Publishers (NZ) Ltd,
3 William Pickering Drive, Albany, Auckland.

Reproduced, printed and bound in Great Britain by
Cox & Wyman Ltd, Reading, Berks.

To Tony Hill

Three women, who have never exchanged a word and are not in every case aware of the others' existence, sit alone in their separate homes and watch the same television programme with very nearly the same emotions. Dread is what they feel, and embarrassment; also regretfulness and sorrow.

'How did you feel?' the interviewer asks a succession of interviewees, the majority of whom are female and appear in dark silhouette to prevent their being identified. But two of the three watching women actually feature in the programme, and when their own silhouettes appear they have no trouble recognizing them. 'Vicious,' snaps one of them now on screen. 'Fit to do murder. I mean, how would you've felt, duckie?' The interviewer's answer is not transmitted. When the question is put to the other, there is a long hesitation. 'Well I . . . I felt bad,' she gets out at last. 'Like it was the end. Like . . . Well just for a bit I can honestly say I wanted to die.'

This answer seems more to the interviewer's taste, so much so that he repeats it. 'Wanted to die. You really and truly wanted to die?'

The silhouette remains perfectly still; there is only the merest quiver as she agrees that yes, briefly she had wanted exactly that. 'When, you know, I thought of the consequences, and what the future would've been if I hadn't . . . hadn't been so pathetically stupid.'

The eldest among the three watching women, and the only one not interviewed for the programme, now guesses the identity of this women who has talked about dying. 'For God's sake, let her be,' she growls – uselessly, of course; the torture was recorded weeks ago.

'So, what would you say to him now if you were given the chance? If you happened to bump into him today: how would you respond?'

Another long silence. When she begins to answer her voice is lighter, her speech quicker and edging towards recklessness. 'Probably I'd . . . Well if I suddenly saw

him, I mean if he was there . . . you know, close . . . I bet
I'd . . .'

'Yes?' prompts the interviewer.

'Give him a hug,' she cries, and her two shadowy arms
shoot out. 'Give him a hug and a great big kiss.'

Alone in her room, the woman whose frank admis-
sion has gone out to the nation buries her head and
rocks back and forth: 'Oh, Christ,' she moans. But her
recorded words have driven a shaft of recognition into
the hearts of the other two. The senior woman claps a
hand to her breast, then rises up and turns off her television. The third, having allowed the escape of an
involuntary sob, is angry with herself, and reaches to a
box and snatches out a tissue.

1

Mrs Parminter opened her eyes and, squinting a little against the brightness, took note of the sky overhead without the least feeling of surprise. In the milky blue, large white clouds were apparently stationary. So too, she sensed, were the trees and shrubs just beyond the scope of her vision; though she declined to turn her head and make certain of this, her head and neck being comfortably cradled by something cushiony. This cradling was a piece of luck considering the nature of the ground beneath the rest of her. She was aware, not of discomfort exactly, but of hard knobbyness pressing into her shoulder blades, buttocks and calves. (And no wonder, with not a drop of rain on the garden these past five weeks!) It occurred to her that her mode of lying here in the parched rose bed might be described as *to attention*, for her palms were clamped to her sides, her ankles were touching and so too were her gardening shoes. And the further thought occurred that this was exactly how she would be arranged in her coffin before too many years elapsed, though minus the clothes of course. *Laid out*, she told herself. Which seemed so wildly funny that she laughed out loud. It was a pleasant feeling, the easy eruption from her throat. And its sound was heart-warming, seeming to mingle naturally with the twitter of birds in a nearby almond tree and the closer hum of insects.

Minutes went by before her present position struck her as strange. After all, she had been attending to a lurching berberis on the far side of the narrow path. She recalled driving in the stake, arranging a length of twine round the shrub, then removing her gauntlets in order to tie a knot. What happened next was a complete mystery. But somehow or other here she was, flat on her back in the rose bed, her head in a clump of soapwort, her toes turned up and her heels propped (now she came to think about it) on the gravelly path. Perhaps she had taken a dizzy turn. Perhaps even fainted. (She recalled the prolonged bending down that had been necessary during her struggle with the berberis.) In which case she ought to take her time before attempting to right herself. The wisdom of this comfortably matched her inclination.

Her eyelids drooped, and she visualized the odd sight she would present to anyone happening to come into her garden. What a shock it would be. What a shock to Mrs Everett in the house next door should Mrs Everett happen to glance out of her back bedroom window. 'I've just spotted a pair of legs sticking out of Mrs Parminter's rose bed,' she would cry over the phone to one of her cronies. 'Unless I'm very much mistaken they are Mrs Parminter's own; I believe I recognized the shoes. Ought I to go round there, do you think? You know me, never one to interfere, a person can do as they please in the privacy of their home has always been my motto. But it did look peculiar, my dear, two stockinged legs sticking out like that between . . .' (here Mrs Parminter raised her head and peered down her body) 'between the Lili Marlene and the Ballerina. What dear? No, no movement. Not even a twitch, far as I could tell. Oh my goodness, you don't think Mrs Parminter's . . . *passed on*?' Triumphantly, Mrs Parminter came up with the euphemism, for unlike herself, Mrs Everett would be too delicate to say *dead* with reference to a known and respected person. 'What a terrible thing! Oh, I shall miss her! I wouldn't say we were close. She was not the sort to pop in, always a little aloof. But as a neighbour one couldn't have wished for a pleasanter person. Poor, poor Mrs Parminter,' Mrs Parminter, with a chuckle, allowed Mrs Everett to wail to a succession of intimates, foreseeing (if she were dead indeed) how the story would pep up her neighbour's contribution to chat in the town.

Mrs Parminter was *Mrs Parminter* to almost everyone these days. Indeed, generally speaking she was so to herself. She had begun life as Clara Millicent, but had always disliked her given first name, hearing in it a cold ring of finality, like a door shutting. Her parents had said *Clara* she supposed, and her teachers and other relatives and her parents' friends. But at school she had rapidly become Milly ('Come on Milly!' and 'Well played, Milly!' were cries that were heard regularly during games of lacrosse). Marriage to her best friend's brother settled her in the name. Sadly, all the dear voices saying Milly nowadays did so only in her head, for the speakers were no longer living (and nor was the one who said Mother): save for the one who tacked the name on to Aunt, of course, and of whom she was not over-fond. No, Mrs Everett might be a woman of unreliable taste in some areas, but Mrs Parminter could not imagine she would designate her other than Mrs Parminter; at least she could have faith in that.

It would be about a decade ago, she thought, screwing up her eyes in an effort to remember, when the terrible fashion for using everyone's first name arrived in Chedbury – arrived with the new influx of smart young people with plenty of money and startling confidence. Incomers had for years outnumbered those born and bred in the small market town or the surrounding villages. She herself had been an incomer, arriving with her husband when he retired from his practice in Edgbaston. It was usually retirement that prompted people to settle here. Chedbury was considered a perfect place in which to spend one's declining years, large enough to possess all the vital amenities – obliging shops, cosy cafés, pubs, a good hotel, an impressive church, a handy cottage hospital and access to all the important professional services – yet small enough to

11

retain its old-fashioned air of friendly gentility. Among the retired, clergymen figured prominently; and there were people who had made a success of their businesses, and ex-headmasters and their wives, and several former members of the armed services. They were a cultured lot in the main, people who formed book-discussion groups and record-listening groups, who put on plays and joined the church choir, and became Friends of the Angela Symmonds Memorial Hospital, and members of the Royal Horticultural Society, and opened their gardens to public view once a year in aid of the nurses. Intimacies were doubtless formed in which first names became appropriate, though in general people stuck to the courtesies, were neighbourly to one another but discreetly so.

Then in the early eighties a different type of person began to buy property in the town, young married persons of a totally different sort from the young marrieds raised in and around Chedbury. These new people had ties to London, Birmingham and Coventry, to which cities the menfolk commuted. Suddenly (that is, in retrospect it seemed to have happened suddenly, no doubt because it was discomfiting) Mrs Parminter found herself accosted after church or in shops or during coffee mornings by young women loudly proclaiming themselves to be Kate or Libby or Jenny and somehow divining that Mrs Parminter was Clara. Mrs Parminter blamed a certain young clergyman for making free with the information, a newly ordained man sent to Chedbury around this time to assist Canon Rawsthorne whose health was declining. But whoever was at fault in giving her away in the first place, the upshot was that Clara she now was to a score of acquaintances many years her junior. Happily it remained the practice among her long-standing friends in the town (those who still survived) to address one another by title and surname.

Canon Rawsthorne had recovered sufficiently to continue in the living (depending heavily on the assistance of the lay reader, Mr Brightly) until a few months ago when he retired to a nursing home close to his sister's house in Shrewsbury. With the Church of England strapped for cash, no young curate was sent to mind the parish during the interregnum. An incumbent had yet to be appointed, and for the time being Chedbury Parish Church was relying on the retired clergy living round about to administer the sacraments, and on Mr Brightly for everything else. However would people manage without Mr Brightly? Indeed, how dull would her own life be without Mr Brightly's visits! He was too generous for his own good; his kindness begged to be taken advantage of. Once, she remembered, she had worried whether she were guilty in this respect, and had rehearsed a speech in order to test the ground.

'You are a very busy man. I fear I take up too much of your time. It is always a great pleasure to see you, but please never feel obliged,' she had finally said to him one evening as she charged their whisky glasses, her voice gruff-sounding, her ears warm.

He had seemed genuinely surprised, as if the idea of obligation had never entered his head. 'My dear Mrs Parminter, of course I don't feel . . . No, no, the pleasure is mine. To be able to sit here quietly, in this lovely house with such congenial company . . . In my hectic week it's a veritable oasis of peace. I only hope I don't trespass too frequently on your hospitality.'

'Never, Mr Brightly. You are welcome any time. I was merely thinking of your many commitments – your wife and family, your work in the parish, your business affairs . . .'

'Exactly. So I think you will agree I am owed a little recreation. Wednesday, you see, when my wife is at choir practice, is my evening off.'

Of course he was teasing her. That twinkle in his eyes gave it away. It was one of the things she found so attractive in him, that hint of amusement, of a readiness to laugh at life which would sometimes dance in his eyes even at solemn moments, for instance when he was preaching. Of course he couldn't seriously mean that a handsome and successful man with untold demands on his time would choose to spend his single evening of recreation per week in the company of an old woman. Though evidently he had spoken the truth to an extent, for he continued to visit The Gables most Wednesdays, sometimes for just the half-hour before dinner, but more often arriving after dinner for the remainder of the evening. He really did appreciate the peace and quiet, she supposed. And for herself . . . Well, going against a lifetime's practice she had rather come to depend on him: not for practical things, she was perfectly capable of managing the affairs and chores of her life; but as a friend. A dear, reliable, trustworthy friend. One to take the place of those who had gone. How unusually fortunate she was! She would wager not many eighty-two-year-old widows without living issue could boast of the same.

A sudden breeze brought her to her senses. She wondered how long she had been lying here wool-gathering. The air carried a hint of evening. How completely mad of her. It would serve her right if she had grown too stiff to move.

She rehearsed what she must do: onto her hands and knees she must go; and therefore, because her left knee and hip were swollen with arthritis, her right knee must come over to take the strain, to act as a lever against the ground. With a great heave she thrust over: only to discover that she had neglected to take into account the proximity of the Lili Marlene. She shuffled her bottom closer to the Ballerina and tried again. This time her right arm was caught by the over-grown Madame Isaac Pereire, and it proved quite a job to unhook her sleeve from its thorns. These shrub roses at the back of the bed were a mistake; she had begun to suspect this for some time. They had been all very well when she and John planted them, and in the ensuing years had presented no problem to a woman who single-handedly raised and turned her ailing

14

husband several times a day. However, lately they had started to get the better of her, threatening to thrust outwards and skywards beyond the scope of her secateurs. No point in struggling on out of sentiment. In the autumn she would tell her odd-job man to root them out. She'd plant a lilac tree in their place, and if there was room a lavender bush . . .

Good grief, if she hadn't gone off on another tack! What was the matter with her today? More to the point, how was she to extricate herself, given the obstacles? 'Hello?' she called out experimentally, having taken a moment or two to steel herself to do so; for she did not relish being discovered in the rose bed by Mrs Everett and could not for the life of her imagine why a moment ago she'd found the prospect amusing. 'Hello?' she called again, reluctantly but with more force. If no-one heard she might lie here all night and in very truth be a goner by morning. She drew in breath, preparing to invest every ounce of strength in a third cry.

Then, before she uttered it, she recalled what day it was. Wednesday. 'Oh, oh,' her relief bubbled out. So she was safe. No need to worry. For without fail he would come, she would wager her life on it. She imagined him: knocking at the front door, receiving no answer and coming round to the back, anticipating that he would discover her sitting in her garden or doing a little dead-heading as was often the case when he called on a warm summer's evening. 'Coo-ee,' he would call.

And just as she imagined, so it was.

'Over here, Mr Brightly,' she called. 'In the rose bed. Really *in* it, I'm afraid.'

'My dear Mrs Parminter! Are you all right? Whatever . . .? Let me . . .' Then he hesitated, vaguely recalling certain principles of first aid. 'But I wonder if you've broken something. Are you in pain? Perhaps I should call for an ambulance; it might be better if you were raised by professionals.'

'No pain at all. Nothing is broken. Look.' She raised

each of her limbs in turn. 'It's just that I'm stuck. This wretched shrub rose, and my arthritis . . .'

He hurried forward, stooped down beside her and slid an arm under her shoulders. There were a few false starts, but at last she was hauled to her feet. On the path she clung to him, made dizzy by blood seeping from her head. She took a cautious step, and was immediately obliged to renew her grip of his jacket. 'Oh dear me.'

'Just take your time. Take it gently.'

'Yes, that's better. Yes, I think . . . Oh dear, such a silly.'

'You're doing splendidly.'

An age it took to cross the lawn, to cross the paving, to mount the step through the open French windows, finally to reach her armchair. And all the time his strong right arm was about her and his left hand clasping hers. They were so close she could smell his lemony fragrance (cologne she supposed, or after-shave lotion). When he braced her as she sank into the chair and then promptly removed his arms and stepped backwards, she wanted to cry out to him not to relinquish her, to please keep holding her. Instead, in order to gather her composure, she put her hand to her face.

Before the arrival of the hand he noticed her chin's sudden wobble. She must be in shock, he told himself, for she was uncommonly self-possessed, and though kind and sensitive was rigorously unsentimental. Dismayed for her though he was, he decided against a sympathetic squeeze of her shoulder: during their many conversations (which had grown cosier and more intimate over the years and sometimes bordered on the gossipy) he'd detected a hint of scorn in her at any report of self-indulgence. Smothering his initial impulse, he directed concern for her into practicality. 'It's shaken you up,' he said gently. 'I really think I should call your doctor.'

'No,' she declared, then raised her head and smiled. 'Absolutely no need. Now, will you please pour us a drink?'

He got up at once.

She watched him take the bottle and glasses from their place in the sideboard. It soothed her to see him handle her possessions so knowledgeably. She was gladdened by any evidence of his being at home in her house. 'This will put me right in no time,' she promised, accepting the crystal tumbler he brought her.

He sat where he usually sat on the far side of the fireplace. When they had sipped their drinks he said conversationally, 'Keep it under your hat, but I do believe we've got a taker for the living. An offer has been made, and the prospect has duly inspected the vicarage, together with his wife and four young children.'

'Children! That will make a change.'

'It's not entirely settled. But the omens are good. They paid visits to the schools which met with approval. And the size of the house didn't worry them, apparently.'

'Well I suppose it wouldn't. A large family would be glad of the space.'

'So much space, and a lot of it unheated, has certainly put off one or two. The church council's been chewing over the pros and cons of building a new vicarage, perhaps reserving a plot on that new development near the hospital; and selling off the old place.'

'Oh, never!'

'If this chap's really interested it needn't come to that.'

'Then let's hope he is. And I'm sure *you*'ll be glad of the chance of a let-up.'

He smiled quizzically. Made no comment.

What a foolish remark, she scolded herself. As if there were ever limits to parish work. 'I heard from Mrs Everett that the Players are to put on a farce,' she remarked, changing the subject. 'Quite a change for them.'

'Indeed. And my own dear wife has landed the female lead, no less.'

'Aha!'

'Yes, the past week has been rather tense. But the

suspense is over, and we are now an ecstatically happy household. As you can imagine,' he added, darting her a look of rueful amusement before turning aside to take up his glass.

Mrs Parminter and Mrs Brightly could not be said to know one another. The most that had been exchanged between them was 'Good morning, Mrs Brightly,' (or afternoon, or evening) on Mrs Parminter's part and 'Good morning, deah,' on Mrs Brightly's who could never remember Mrs Parminter's name. But then, as Mrs Parminter had had occasion to observe, Mrs Brightly was fond of calling the elderly *deah*, and also shop assistants and doctors' receptionists. She had also observed her with other sorts of people displaying a manner that was far from grand; gushing with excitement, perhaps, or wistful, or flirtatious. Whatever her mode, it was calculated, Mrs Parminter sensed. The mystery was why Mr Brightly of all people, a man of sensibility and impeccable taste, had married her. Presumably because he had once fallen in love with her. This was not too hard to believe, for Mrs Brightly was pretty, with fluffy hair, large blue eyes and a small snub nose – perhaps *kittenish* would be an apt expression. Certainly he always spoke of her with complete loyalty and evident affection. But from reading between the lines, Mrs Parminter had decided his wife was not a pleasant person. She recalled her friend's misery when his daughter failed the entrance exam for a prestigious girls' school in Warwick. Mrs Brightly had reacted as if it were the end of the world, principally because the school's rejection of her daughter coincided with its acceptance of two other Chedbury girls. To regain 'face' in the town, she'd insisted on packing the poor child off to a famous boarding school for which a great deal of money was the qualification rather than academic prowess, and had prevailed in this despite the qualms of both daughter and husband.

Only once had Mrs Parminter observed Mr Brightly resist his wife. This had happened in church, when Mr

Brightly first became a lay reader. After the service his wife had hurried to the door to share the congratulations of departing members of the congregation. 'Good evening, good evening,' she'd cried. 'Yes, wasn't it a lovely service? So glad you found it inspiring.' After a moment or two Mr Brightly had drawn her aside: and presumably spoke plain, for, pink of countenance, she had returned down the aisle to wait meekly in her pew. So he did have it in him to be firm with his wife, Mrs Parminter deduced. Just very seldom chose to.

His voice broke into her thoughts. 'Er, sorry,' she mumbled. 'Didn't quite catch . . .'

'I asked whether your nephew had returned from his trip.'

'I've no idea. There's only been that postcard from Washington.'

He asked out of politeness, of course – probably wanting to impart news of his own family but allowing her to get in first. He knew she saw very little of Julian (who was in fact not her own but her dead husband's nephew) and also that she was largely indifferent. Six or so years ago she'd spoken frankly to Julian about her intentions and had not from that day to this set eyes on his wife or their children. He occasionally telephoned, or dropped by when a business engagement brought him within striking distance of Chedbury. But she was not his closest relative and he had in any case other expectations, and Mrs Parminter, being resolved in her mind, could not feel regretful. Once, when Julian and her only son Robert had been fellow students at medical school, she had felt more warmly. The cousins had been climbing enthusiasts and often spent their vacations together as members of a climbing party. Then on one of those expeditions Robert was killed by an avalanche, and for several years afterwards Mrs Parminter heard nothing from Julian. But it seemed a very long time ago . . .

She recollected with a start her companion, who, having anticipated an enquiry as to his own family and had his expectation dashed, was turning his whisky glass round in his hand.

'Do please top us up,' said Mrs Parminter, giving her own glass a nudge, and as he rose to do so asked, 'How are the children? Have you heard from Giles?' Giles, their son, was a university student; a clever lad who gave his mother complete satisfaction.

'Oh Giles is all right. But Harriet now is in tip-top form.' He brought over her replenished glass, and she saw how his eyes gleamed at this mention of his daughter. 'She's just heard from that singing teacher I told you about – the one who's so choosy about which pupils she'll accept. Well, she's agreed to take on Harriet.'

'Oh, I am glad. That's wonderful news.'

'Isn't it? It'll mean travelling up to London once a week. Which will present no hardship to Harriet: she loathes school and will be glad to get out of it; and singing does at least allow her to shine at something.'

He took a sip from his tumbler. Mrs Parminter repeated how glad she was. She pictured Harriet, whom she had often spoken to after church: a tall, lumpy girl, as plain as could be and burdened by thick spectacles. Apparently she was not over-bright; at least, she was not in her brother's class. Mrs Parminter guessed that she brought pain to both her parents – the pain of annoyance to her mother, the pain of an often thwarted desire to protect her to her father.

'I must say she has a glorious voice,' he went on. 'Deep, and remarkably mature for a sixteen-year-old.'

'She got that from you,' Mrs Parminter declared.

He seemed surprised. 'Well you know Ginny, my wife, sings.' Then a frown came to his face. 'My only fear about these lessons is that Ginny will read too much into them. Harriet has a lovely voice, but little aptitude, I suspect, for a musical career. The career she has set her heart on, nursery nursing, hardly meets with my wife's approval, and I dread her spoiling Harriet's pleasure by setting too high a store on her singing. Well' – he smiled and shrugged – 'we shall see. I confess Harriet's voice is rather special.'

But so was his voice special, insisted Mrs Parminter to herself, thinking how pleasurable it was to listen to him in church. That voice was uttering now; but because of her train of thought, instead of registering its message, she began confirming her opinion of its mellifluous sound. Then his silence jolted her, and she saw he was studying her quizzically. 'I do beg your pardon. I seem bent on wool-gathering this evening.'

'I mentioned the Reece case.' He nodded towards her copy of the *Daily Telegraph*. 'There's a column about it in the paper.'

'Oh indeed, I think I read about it. What an unfortunate young woman she has been, one way and another.'

'Let's hope this time she enjoys a happy outcome.'

Scrupulous though he was never to confide one parishioner's affairs to another, he felt able with Mrs Parminter to relax this rule. He could tell her things he wouldn't dream of telling his wife. And in all this time she had not once let him down. Nor did she overstep the mark: only when he introduced a person's name into their conversation would she venture a comment or make an enquiry.

'I think I saw her once,' said Mrs Parminter. 'She was pushing the boy towards the square. I was in my front garden at the time. We smiled but we didn't speak . . .' Her voice, its reminiscent tone, trailed off. Abruptly she said, 'I think I told you that before.'

'Yes,' he admitted.

She laughed. 'I knew it. Usually I manage to stop myself in time. But I always know. It's a mistake to imagine old people don't know when they're repeating themselves; what happens is they lose their will to resist. As soon as I detect that cosy feeling when I'm holding forth, I become suspicious and close my mouth. A bit feeble, I'm afraid, this evening. Not quite myself.'

'No,' he agreed gently, 'I don't think you are. Can I ask . . . Did you trip over something out there in the garden?

How did you come to be lying on the ground?'

She hesitated. 'I'm not sure. I don't seem to remember.'

'In that case, my dear friend,' (just now and again, usually during the course of a shared confidence, this degree of endearment felt appropriate between them) 'will you promise to phone your doctor tomorrow and tell him about it? If there's a danger of its happening again, then we ought to know. After all, you were quite out of earshot lying there.'

'Yes, I was,' agreed Mrs Parminter, looking down at her lap. She thought for a moment. 'Very well, I'll phone in the morning. Though on past experience I doubt Dr Page will be terribly interested. But thank you. Yes, thank you,' she repeated, raising her eyes. 'If it had to happen, what a mercy for me it was on your evening off.' She invested a roguish emphasis in these last three words, for she still had his wife at the back of her mind.

'Indeed,' he responded gravely, while his eyes glinted with merriment. But his amusement was not for the same reason as hers. Simply, it tickled him the way she pronounced certain words: *off*, for instance, like a haughty duck. He heard her again in his head: 'What a mercy for me it was on your evening orff.'

2

Usually when he left her on a Wednesday evening –
closing the front gate and beginning the walk along
Sheep Street towards Market Square – Richard Norris
Brightly had a spring in his step, a tune on his lips;
newly conscious he would be of the satisfaction that
follows upon shared blessings. But tonight he felt differently. He was worried for her. He also had doubts as to
his own behaviour. Ought he to have phoned her doctor
anyway? After reflection he thought not. To have done
so would have gone against his understanding of her
character; it would have given offence, their relationship would never again be the same. She was mightily
independent, would consider any advice proffered but
only days or weeks later indicate whether she intended
to act on it or not. He was not altogether sure whether
his anxiety was purely unselfish. Certainly he would
miss these Wednesday evenings when, as must
inevitably happen, Mrs Parminter of The Gables was no
longer equal to visitors or even there to receive them any
more. At this thought his spirits dropped further. He
pictured her: a strong upright old girl, always direct
without a trace of artifice. Her boniness fascinated him,
– her large hands gripping her knees when she was
animated or lying in her lap when she dozed. For, yes,
she did sometimes nod off on him. When this happened
he would endeavour to bring her round after a while
without giving away that he'd caught her napping. He'd
reach for the *Telegraph* (always folded by her chair
with the day's completed crossword uppermost: 'Keeps

my brain ticking over,' she said) and while pretending to read it would give the paper a vigorous shake; or he'd lean forward and poke the fire, or take their tumblers into the kitchen and noisily rinse them. But sometimes she awoke before he could manage his device, in which case she would widen her eyes at him and break out with her frank and surprisingly girlish laugh. He loved the sound of that laugh – like a spurt escaping to the surface from the deep hidden well of her youth. He felt rested in her company, but also pleasantly stirred. For without a shadow of doubt his presence gave her pleasure. Simply by being there he enhanced her life. Acknowledging this to himself made him feel emotional; it was satisfaction beyond price.

Turning into Market Square Mr Brightly noticed a huddle of youths in the newsagent's doorway: grey shapes in the dusk, jeaned legs jutting out over the pavement, the glow of cigarette tips stabbing on and off. He frowned and crossed to the other side. It was a great problem for Chedbury shopkeepers and hoteliers, the way disaffected youth from the estates larked about in the town centre by day, chucking down their empty beer cans, playing transistors loudly, jostling shoppers and tourists; and then in the evening hung about the square in menacing groups, causing visitors on three-night breaks at the Brown Bear to think twice before taking an after-dinner stroll. Leaving the square he turned right on the High Street and walked in the direction of Framley Lane. Passing the George and Dragon he bumped into Tom Jessop of Jessop the butcher's who was coming out of the bar.

'Good evening, Tom.'

'Oh, g'evening, Mr Brightly. Been a grand day.'

'Indeed it has.'

For some reason this banal exchange left Mr Brightly feeling reassured. Probably, the day being so pleasant, Mrs Parminter had stayed outside too long. Jobs in the garden had lured her to exert herself for longer than was prudent for an eighty-two-year-old. She'd become over-tired and then, stepping from the flower bed, had very likely tripped on the raised edge of the path. He could be perfectly certain of her ringing her doctor tomorrow. Once she had given her word she honoured it.

His customary cheerfulness was fully re-established as he turned west into Framley Lane. After half a mile the cottages gave out; the lane broadened, became bordered by the lawns of half-acre gardens. Half a dozen substantial homes were positioned here, built twelve or fifteen years ago, each in a different style – mock Georgian, mock Tudor, mock Gothic, vaguely Alpine, vaguely Dutch, vaguely Spanish. And one of these, the mock Tudor, was his and Ginny's own. 'Sub Lutyens' was how he half apologized for it to a couple of friends – a chap he'd known at school, and an ex-colleague in the firm. But to Ginny the house was perfect and would remain so for as long as it had the edge over other houses in Chedbury – regarding the number and size of its rooms, the grandeur of its garden, and its possession of the latest addition and amenity. It was fortunate, he sometimes reflected, that she did not take it into her head to compete with Framley Hall.

He reached the porch of his house, and a car swept into the drive. It went speedily to the garage door which opened in response to a signal. Putting his key in the lock, he heard the garage door descend and the car's engine die, and, as he stepped into the hall, heard the door between kitchen and garage slam shut.

She came running through the house. Her lips were bunched, she emitted an urgent humming noise, until – 'Mmm*uh*!' – her kiss exploded against his cheek. She always was a human whirlwind, gusting with speedy non-stop chatter, darting from one subject to the next, irrepressible. But tonight she appeared even more than usually excited, he thought, unconsciously bracing himself.

'Darling, I've had such a lovely evening. People were *so nice* about me getting Cynthia. Even Maria, who must have been secretly disappointed. I told her: Darling, I

25

said, I almost didn't try for it when I heard you planned to audition – I'm still overawed by your amazing Hedda. No Ginny, she said (honestly Dick, she was *so sweet*), you'll make a perfect Cynthia, Ginny, everyone thinks so. Of course I had to warn Pamela that later on I may need to give choir practice a miss. I mustn't over-tire my voice.' She had been hanging on to his arm as they went into the kitchen, and now disengaged to fill the kettle.

'Go on with you,' he told her. 'Your voice can take any amount of punishment.'

'Now, now! Anyway, Teddy being so strict about rehearsals and so forth . . .'

The local evening paper lay folded in half on the table. Glancing at it, his eyes focused on a face that was well known to him. LOCAL WOMAN AWARDED the headline began, its continuation hidden on the underside. His heart quickened; he lifted the newspaper and laid it out flat to discover the award's precise sum.

'Oh, if I'm boring you,' Ginny said.

'Of course you're not.' He took a backwards step, and willed her last phrase to sound again in his head (he hadn't registered it as it was uttered but long practice had made him adept at this exercise). 'Teddy's always been a stickler,' he commented, 'as Pamela must be aware . . .' The award was a substantial sum, an attention-grabbing sum. But not altogether sufficient, he considered when he had rapidly computed the likely return from its investment.

'Well yes; everyone knows Teddy won't tolerate cast members having other commitments. In any case, there's nothing huge coming up for the choir before Christmas.'

Insufficient if invested *conventionally*, he corrected himself.

Ginny's voice ran on. By absently recognizing the signposts of her favourite words, *sweet, lovely, horrible, ghastly*, he was able to make small interjections – mm, good, oh? tch! – to satisfy her as to his rapt attention.

In fact, he was engaged by a memory. It ran through

his mind like a film sequence: Cressida Reece pushing her disabled son in his invalid chair along the busy part of Stratford Road; the sudden onset of heavy rain; Cressida Reece stopping in her tracks to unbutton and take off her raincoat (more a thin cotton coat than a proper waterproof), then draping the coat over the boy in the chair; the boy making some sort of protest, trying to push away the covering; the mother quickly prevailing and resuming her pushing of the chair, her head bent over her son's. All this he had witnessed several weeks ago from his car while he was held up at the traffic lights. She had hurried by, but though her head was lowered he'd clearly caught her expression; and so startling had he found it that for a second or two he'd missed the lights changing to green. That wide and rather blank face of hers had been darkened and livened by fierce passion. A passion to protect, he'd understood as he finally drove off, raising a hand in apology to the car behind. He set this in his mind against the impression he'd hitherto gained of her, of a passive sort of person, pale, somewhat overweight, hopelessly self-deprecating. At least she'd had the spirit to seek compensation through the courts for the dreadful thing that had been done to her, but he sensed she had hardly expected to win – not because she didn't have a clear-cut case, but because of a fatal inability to conceive of herself as one of life's winners. She'd confided that her true reason for proceeding with the action was the hope of gaining money to secure her son's future – as if the notion of achieving justice for herself left her deeply lethargic and only her maternal urge was sufficiently sharp to be galvanizing. A parishioner and near neighbour of the Reeces had brought Cressida to his attention; had reported that she was depressed and alarmed by the interest of the news media. 'She's not much of a church-goer, Mr Brightly, but I think she needs someone to talk to – someone who'd know the right things to say, if you get my meaning.' Naturally, he'd agreed to call, and had been moved as any visitor would be by what he'd observed: it was painful to watch the boy hump himself about, and to listen and respond to his reedy voice and receive his mother's gratitude for doing so. But it was that sighting in the rain from his car that had made him burn to help her.

'You'll have a cup?'

Ginny was holding out the instant coffee jar. He didn't actually want a drink, but to be sociable nodded.

'So how was *your* evening? Been buttering up your old ladies?'

'I visited Mrs Parminter,' he conceded, secure in the knowledge that she would not find this interesting.

'Mm, how is she, darling? Oh by the way, we're invited to the Thompsons' three weeks on Saturday. I said that'd be OK. We've nothing on, have we?' She went to peer at the wall calendar. 'No, nothing. So please don't get tied up with a business call. And *don't* let one of your lame ducks muck it up, however desperate. Maggie's still furious with you, you know, over that time . . .'

Laughter rang out overhead muffled by distance and thick carpets. It bought a hiatus to Ginny's sunny mood and a frown to her face. 'Harriet's got someone with her up there. Don't say it's that Chapman boy. Honestly, Dick, I did ask you to say something. Whatever's the point of spending all this money educating her with nice people, if she wastes time in the holidays with ghastly kids like that?'

'He's not at all ghastly. He and Harriet have been chums since primary school.'

'And wasn't that a mistake! Heavens, it's not as if there aren't plenty of young people here we're perfectly happy for her to see . . .' She stopped abruptly, as feet came pounding downstairs.

Ahead of Harriet, a tall, dark-haired girl in jeans arrived in the hall. 'Oh *Polly*,' Ginny cried. 'How lovely, darling! I'd no idea you had a friend with you, Harriet. How are you, dear?'

'Fine thanks, Mrs Brightly. Oh hello, Mr Brightly. I

just called to ask Harriet to play tennis tomorrow. We're having a sort of party . . .'

'Lovely! She'll adore to, won't you darling?'

'Er, actually,' said Polly, turning to Harriet.

'I told Polly I'm hopeless, Mum.'

'Nonsense, darling. It'll be fun.'

'Well, come if you feel like it,' Polly told Harriet. 'You don't have to play. You can just hang out.'

'Yeah. Thanks.'

'How are your parents, Polly? I haven't seen them for ages.'

'No. They've been in the Dordogne for six weeks – you know, at our holiday place.'

'Holiday place? I didn't know you have your own . . .'

'Yeah – just a beat-up old farmhouse.'

'But how gorgeous! It sounds lovely!'

Beyond his reply to Polly's greeting, Mr Brightly took no part in this exchange. I must help her, he vowed, looking into the serious eyes of Cressida Reece as depicted on the front of the *Evening Argus*. Perhaps this award provided a chance. He'd ring her from work in the morning, offer his congratulations and suggest calling round. She always seemed pleased to see him.

The door closed on Polly. Ginny hurried back to her cooling coffee.

'Oh Dad, I've just remembered,' Harriet called from the stairs. 'While you and Mum were out a woman rang. A Mrs . . . Reece, would it be?'

He put down his coffee mug. 'Yes?'

'Said she might ring back later. Sounded sort of flustered.'

'Thank you, Harriet,' he called, and heard his daughter continue upstairs.

'Gosh yes, Cressida Reece,' said Ginny, her eyes going to the newspaper. 'That woman in the papers. That unmarried mother.'

'Divorced.'

'You know what I mean, Dick. She's won all that money, and she used to char for the Rawlins.'

'Did she? I didn't know that. If you'll excuse me, I think I ought to phone her back.'

It was difficult not to see God's prompting behind her call, he reflected as he entered his study and closed the door. God perceiving Cressida Reece in need of help and knowing the very man to provide it. It had always appeared self-evident that God's purpose for Richard Brightly lay beyond the obvious one of requiring a well-tuned voice and sympathetic manner to do service in church. God had a use for all his talents, and the most significant of these was a proven feel for the productive deployment of money. It was his unshakable belief that when it came to being creative with matters of finance and investment, his was the touch of genius. He held this belief not in any boastful way, but humbly, mindful that failure to acknowledge his gift would be to fly in the face of the evidence (witness the rich and wonderful things he had got with his talent) and insulting to God who had made him as he was. The right course was to rejoice and to use his endeavours wherever possible to further God's will.

'Good evening, Mrs Reece, my daughter tells me you phoned earlier. First, let me congratulate you on your well-deserved victory.'

'Oh, thanks,' replied Cressida Reece. 'And thanks ever so for ringing back. The thing is, I wondered if you could come round some time soon, if it wouldn't be too much trouble. I've had a bit of bother. It's the publicity that's done it. I knew soon as they put the amount in the paper it was bound to happen.'

'Have you been pestered, Mrs Reece?'

'Well, yeah, sort of.'

'How would tomorrow suit you – about eight o'clock?'

'Oh, it'd be fine. I'd be ever so grateful.'

'My pleasure. Try not to worry. I'm sure we can sort it out.'

'It's really kind of you. Goodbye then, Mr Brightly.'

'Until tomorrow, Mrs Reece.'

He returned to the kitchen to collect the newspaper, which he tucked under his arm.

His wife read the sign. 'Are you going up already?'

'I feel in need of a good long soak.'

Coffee mug in hand, she followed him to the stairs. 'You know, Dick, I've often thought it'd be jolly nice to have a holiday place somewhere. I've often thought it'd be convenient: being able to stay as long as we liked, have our friends join us, and the children have their friends.'

'Isn't this a bit sudden?'

'No, no. I've often thought . . .'

'We'll discuss it some time.'

'Dick, I wish you wouldn't walk away when I'm talking. It's not very nice of you, Dick.'

He was halfway up the stairs, but with a sigh of resignation paused and looked down at her.

At which she relaxed against the newel post, her face taking on a dreamy expression. 'Can't you picture it? Endless summer days, lovely rustic old place, getting to know the locals. I'd mug up my French . . . And we could always let it when we weren't using it ourselves. It'd be an investment.'

'Mm. Can we talk about it when I'm less tired?'

'Tomorrow?'

'Soon as I get back from the office tomorrow I must call on the Fieldings; I've some papers for them to sign. (The Fieldings, who lived in the sprawling Spanish-style house opposite, were also clients.) 'Then after dinner I've agreed to call on Mrs Reece.'

'That's right,' she cried, 'put your lame ducks first! Anyone, in fact, before your wife. So when *can* we discuss it? Perhaps I'd better make an appointment.'

'I'm sorry, dear, but Mrs Reece is under a strain. Someone has to advise her . . .'

Ginny's face, which had darkened, now cleared. 'Oh, I see. You mean about the money. Yes, she'll be needing advice with that little lot. Better get to her double quick – before some wide boy beats you to it.'

31

'I'm not sure that's the problem exactly. It's possible she simply needs a friendly ear. The past few weeks have been quite an ordeal for her.'

'Well thank heaven she's got someone like you on hand. Honestly, the number of people in this town who have reason to be grateful to you, my love.' She craned her face up, pouted him a kiss. 'Sowwy, Dickie. Sowwy to be cwoss. We can chat at the weekend about the holiday thingy.'

He continued upstairs. Only when he had his back to her did he indulge in a weary smile. Once his wife had seized on an idea she did not lightly let go.

'No, no damage,' said Mrs Parminter the next morning into the telephone's mouthpiece. 'No ill effects whatever. I'm not even stiff. Merely, I am reporting to you what occurred because the friend who helped me to my feet prevailed on me to do so. For some reason or other he thought you should know.'

There was a short silence. Mrs Parminter imagined the unseen practitioner – thoroughly bemused and with a patient waiting who was actually sick.

'Perhaps you'd better pop into the surgery in the next day or so. Then we can take a look at you.'

'You mean make an appointment,' said Mrs Parminter testily: she was always irritated by figures of speech which distorted the facts of the matter. 'Very well. Unless you think it'd be a waste of your time.'

'Not at all. Thank you for putting me in the picture. I'll just put you through to reception. Hang on, Mrs Parminter. Goodbye now.'

'Thank you. Goodbye.'

She made an appointment for the following Monday morning. There were none to be had earlier except for urgent cases, which was more or less as she had foreseen. Usually when she thought of Mr Brightly it was with affection and thankfulness, but in this moment of replacing the receiver and walking out of the hall into her kitchen she felt quite cross with him. She wished she had not acceded to his request and reported her fall to the doctor who clearly wondered, as she now did herself, what was the point of the information since no harm had been done. She made herself a second pot of tea then took it into the sunny sitting room to begin the day's crossword.

Soon her annoyance vanished. She reflected that Mr Brightly had not made a song and dance over discovering her flat on her back in the rose bed (she could imagine the to-do there'd have been if she had succeeded in rousing her neighbour). He had merely asked for that one small piece of reassurance. Why should she care two hoots for Dr Page's opinion of her? Let him think she was a silly old bat. It was the feelings of her loyal friend that she ought to care about.

Having settled the matter she put it out of her head and bent her entire attention on the solution to One Across.

3

Forty or so identical semi-detached houses stand on the east side of Chedbury in a close off the Stratford Road, each with an integral garage, a small rear private garden, and the frontage laid to lawn and unfenced. They were built around fifteen years ago by the local builder Frederick Reece, who retired soon afterwards with his wife to a spacious villa on the Costa Blanca. In one of these houses on Thursday evening, Cressida Reece – who bore the builder's surname because she was once briefly his daughter-in-law – awaited the arrival of Mr Brightly.

Her son, Alex, had retired to his room. There was no need to go up so early, she'd told him. Nevertheless he had wheeled himself to the chair lift, and there, declining her assistance, had used his relatively well-developed arms to heave his pitifully undeveloped lower half out of one seat and into the other. She was still labouring the point – 'Won't it look funny, a fourteen-year-old in his bedroom by eight o'clock?' – when he pressed the lift's button and ascended away from her. Meekly she had followed after and hung around to give him a hand with this and that. Now he was seated in front of his computer, already engrossed.

'I'll bring you a mug of coffee later on.'

'Thanks.'

On her way to the door a thought occurred to her. 'Alex, don't you like Mr Brightly?'

'Of course I do, Mum. I just think, you know, it's great you've got someone coming, someone you can talk to.'

34

He didn't turn and look at her when he said this; in fact his eyes failed to leave the computer screen. But this was as usual; that screen had a power over him; once switched on, it held his eyes captive. 'OK, then, love. After all, this isn't just a bedroom. I mean, your things are in here, it's more of a study.' Having herself satisfactorily answered her query, she left him in peace.

Alex's room was the largest of the house's bedrooms. It was the one she had once shared with her former husband. Three years ago, when her brother Jonathan bought Alex his computer, it had made sense to move the double bed and her wardrobe and dressing table into the back bedroom, and put Alex's single bed, wardrobe and desk and his shelves of books and his TV and radio and computer paraphernalia into the front. There was also a tiny third bedroom, but that, owing to its situation over the garage, was inclined to be chilly. In this she stored her second-hand sewing machine and cartons of household stuff and lumber from her past, and also a fold-up bed which she would unfold and sleep on when a guest came to stay, preferring to put the guest – her mother, usually, or her friend Julie from schooldays – into her own room. She took deep pleasure from Alex's bedroom being kitted out handsomely. Often in passing she found cause to refer to the fact.

The first thing she would do when she finally got hold of the money, Cressida decided as she squeezed past the chair lift at the top of the stairs, was pay her parents back. A charity had provided half the cost of the chair lift, her parents the rest. It would be good to see them take a holiday or buy something they'd long wanted. Her parents were both retired teachers. When Cressida and her brother were growing up things had always been tight at home, and even now her parents were by no means flush with money. Jonathan sometimes provided them with treats, though Cressida only knew this because his wife let the information drop: her brother and her parents would naturally keep the matter a secret from her for fear of hurting her feelings. Not that she had ever been in the least bit jealous of her brother's success. She was only glad that one of them had fulfilled their parents' hopes. Jonathan had gone to university then to dental school and was now a partner in a flourishing dental practice. She on the other hand had wasted her chances (her mother's words) by falling in love and going to live with a guitarist in a rock band. She and Baz were in Germany, touring the clubs during the winter months, when it occurred to her that she was probably pregnant. At the end of the tour they'd flown home to marry in a register office, and Alex was born four weeks later – and prematurely, according to the doctor's estimate. After the birth her mother observed that had Cressida been in England and receiving proper care and advice during her pregnancy (or in other unspoken words, not been so feckless), the trouble with the baby would have been spotted before it was all too late. She'd meant too late for an abortion, Cressida belatedly understood, and had never since managed to expunge the remark, nor the pain it caused. The memory of it was worse when Alex was tiny. Sometimes it leapt into her mind when she was nursing him: and possibly made her flinch, for always the baby would pause in his suckling and open his eyes and widely stare – as if suddenly doubting his place in the world. Years later Cressida wondered whether her mother was so good to Alex and stout in his defence – extolling his high intelligence and lovely nature – because she herself remembered the remark and knew Cressida did.

From the window of her small front sitting room, Cressida watched for a sighting of Mr Brightly. She imagined the route he would take: a thing she was well able to do from her own knowledge of it, for when Alex was small she had gone three times a week to clean the large mock-Georgian house next door but one to the Brightlys' mock-Tudor. Outside the brightness was fading. Nevertheless she would not switch on the sitting room light until it was dark enough to draw the curtains:

probably there were no reporters or photographers lurking in the close, by now they'd have moved on to a more newsworthy topic than the case of Cressida Reece versus a certain gynaecologist; even so, the way she'd been pestered these past weeks made her cautious. There was no need either to advertise her visitor to the neighbours – although it was one of these, Mavis Hutton at three doors down, who had passed on the news to Mr Brightly (there being no vicar at present in Chedbury to pass it on to) that a parishioner and near neighbour of hers was under a particular strain. That was some months ago, when Cressida's case first hit the newspapers. On Mr Brightly's initial visit, when Cressida learnt that its nature was pastoral, a large red blob developed in each of her pale cheeks; she felt she scarcely deserved the term 'parishioner', not being a churchgoer but having simply made use of certain church facilities. When Alex was small she'd wheeled him regularly to Sunday School with the prime intention of improving his chance to make friends with ordinary children. Later, because he enjoyed music and could sing in tune and the doctor said singing was good for his lungs, she'd asked if he could attend choir practice (although Alex steadfastly refused to sit in the choir stalls for Sunday services) and had wheeled him to St Peter's every Thursday evening for four or five years. Nowadays, with Alex's voice taking its time over the breaking process, the church had practically ceased to play a part in their lives. However, Cressida soon forgot to be embarrassed by this. Mr Brightly was wonderful at putting you at ease. He was the nicest, the most charming man you could meet: patient and kind, brilliant at grasping what could hardly be put into words. Also he was incredibly good-looking. She meant, of course, for his age. Furthermore it was the most amazing feeling to have a man in the house.

When her imagination had him only just turning into Stratford Road, he surprised and delighted her by in fact turning into the close. Instinctively, she stepped

37

backwards (unnecessarily, for net curtains were masking the windows), but continued to study his progress: the long easy stride along the curving pavement, splotches of sun and shadow playing on his elegant silvery hair. As he drew yet closer she was able to register further detail: the briefcase swinging from his hand, the smile of a man plainly at peace with himself and the world (did he derive this quality from his religious practice, she wondered, or was it simply part of his nature?). And what she couldn't see, she recalled: the intent way he would look at her, his blue eyes twinkling with humour and sympathy; and the way he would nod encouragement when she got into difficulties expressing herself. He managed to convey that visiting her was a pleasure as well as part of his Christian duty. She hoped very much this was indeed the case, that he truly liked her.

When he stepped onto her short asphalt drive she raised a hand to lift and spread her newly washed yellow hair, then hurried into the hallway to open the door to him.

'I was not detained, you'll be pleased to hear,' he reported as she led into the sitting room. 'There was no cameraman lurking when I turned down your path.'

'I think that part of it's died down,' she said, as they sat opposite one another in easy chairs. 'It's other people ringing up now that's the bother, people who've heard about the award, people I used to know.' She hesitated. 'Well, Baz actually.'

'As in former husband, I take it?' He stretched his long legs over the carpet and crossed them at the ankles and smiled across at her.

'Well and truly "former". He's been married again since he was married to me, and left her too. Now I hear he's living with a woman in Scotland.'

'Ah, so you do hear?'

'From his mother. She drops me a line from Spain – that's where they live, her and Mr Reece. They send things for Alex – money mostly. They're very kind, considering Baz is their son and everything. Mrs Reece gets to know what he's up to from his second wife.'

'Sounds like a busy fellow.'

'He's phoned me twice; says he wants us to meet. It's a bit unsettling.'

'I'm sure. But might it be Alex he'd like to see?'

As Cressida snorted, he watched colour seep into her face. She was given to blushing; it was one of the first things he'd noticed about her. Otherwise he'd thought her very plain: pale and plump and drably clothed, her flaxen hair drawn back from her broad face and clasped by a rubber band and looking in need of a stiff shampoo. But lately, perhaps because of all the publicity she'd received and her court attendances, she'd begun to take trouble with her appearance. It had struck him at once that she was looking quite pretty this evening: her hair gleaming and fanned out over her shoulders, and the flattering cut of her soft summer dress making her figure appear rounded and comely rather than merely large, and its shade of blue very kind to her colouring. These were excellent signs, he told himself. Her victory in court had boosted her confidence. And just possibly the interest he himself had taken in her – on the Lord's behalf – had contributed to this growth in her self-esteem.

Cressida was working herself up to tell him something, something it was hurtful to remember and would certainly be hurtful to recount.

'Do you know what Baz said to me once?' she blurted. 'It was when he was gearing up to leave us, looking for an excuse. "I can't hack it," he said. Meaning Alex being different, of course.'

Mr Brightly moved not a muscle, but his eyes told her he was listening intently. So she admitted that her reaction to this had been violent, although in fact it was later on in her altercation with Baz that she'd actually lashed out. '"Hack it"?' she'd cried scornfully. 'You can't talk about hacking it with your own son!'

'Well, he wouldn't be, would he, if you'd . . .'

'What the hell d'you mean by that? Go on, say it!'

'I mean it's *your fault*, you stupid slag. No-one asked you to keep hanging around. Like your mum said, you should've gone home.' (When Alex was still an infant, in a moment of weakness and needing comfort, she'd repeated to Baz her mother's comment. At the time he'd been properly sympathetic – put an arm round her and hugged her and told her to forget it. Her ears scorched hearing the confidence rebound on her.) 'You could've had a scan,' Baz continued. 'Then you'd have known and you could've got rid of it.'

It was at this point that she drove her fist into his face.

'You see,' she told Mr Brightly, looking down at the knuckles that had once broken her husband's nose, 'people can say what they like about me, but I can't put up with . . . Alex being . . . rubbished.'

'And I'd say you'd be quite right not to.'

'Thanks.' She threw up her head, sending the mane of hair flying out. 'Let me get you some coffee.'

'Ah now . . .' He motioned her to wait and leaned down to open his briefcase. 'As you've a victory to cele-brate, I thought this would be in order.'

It was a bottle of Chablis he brought out. He'd thought carefully before making this choice of wine. Champagne must be drunk in one go, and there would only be the two of them present to drink it. To keep on the prudent side (and he strove always not to be im-prudent) one glass apiece taken in the other's company would be quite sufficient. He'd imagined filling the glasses himself, then replacing the cork and putting the bottle away in her fridge to be enjoyed later. And in case she hadn't got one, he'd brought along a corkscrew.

'Oo, lovely,' said Cressida. 'I hope I can lay hands on some glasses.'

This little problem he hadn't foreseen. He followed her into the dining room and watched her fall onto her knees and grope to the back of a sideboard cupboard. He hadn't been in this room before. So far he was acquainted only with her sitting room, hallway and kitchen. There was no indication of the dining table's being used for its purpose; it was piled high with books, open notebooks lay on it and biros and an old typewriter. He recalled that she was halfway through an access course at the local college. If she completed this satisfactorily she'd been promised a place at Warwick University. It was her ambition to qualify as a teacher.

'Will these do?' she asked, holding up two chunky glasses with squat stems.

'Admirably.'

He went ahead of her into the kitchen to carry out the planned operation with corkscrew and bottle.

She lounged against the sink unit, watching. 'I'll get some decent glasses when I get my money,' she declared. Then laughed at herself. (As he'd noticed before, she had a most appealing laugh – frank, full-throated.) 'Actually I probably won't,' she confessed. 'There's a list as long as your arm of things I *might* spend money on, but only a very short one of things I *will* – like paying back Mum and Dad for what they put towards Alex's chair lift. But the bulk of the money's going into the building society, I'm clear about that. To take care of Alex's future.'

'May I put the bottle in your fridge?'

'Mm? Sure, go ahead.'

'Now . . .' He picked up the two filled glasses and handed her one. 'Here's to you. Well done!'

'And to you, Mr Brightly.'

'Call me Richard,' he said, and tried his wine. 'Mm, not bad. Shall we?' He led back into the sitting room and settled again in his easy chair. 'Yes, we've known each other long enough not to be so formal, I think. May I use your beautiful Christian name?'

'All right,' she giggled, and sank her nose into her glass.

'Thank you, Cressida. You were saying you wanted to invest your money?'

'That's right. God, it's terrific knowing that come what may Alex's future's secure. It's almost worth losing my womb – if you'll pardon the expression, Mr, er, Richard.'

'It's a perfectly proper term,' he smiled. 'However, I'm sure you were speaking in jest.'

She laughed. 'I wouldn't be too sure. I wouldn't admit it to just anyone, but I have actually thought that it's a bit like those cases you read of sometimes – you know, when people sell a bit of themselves – like a kidney. I wonder: if I'd known I could make Alex's future safe, would I have said "Sure, doc, go ahead, just help yourself, and that'll be a hundred grand, ta very much"? No, of course I wouldn't, not really. Hell, I was only twentynine when it happened, I hadn't exactly lost hope; I still thought I'd meet a nice guy some day and have more children. Even now, three years later . . . Well I'm not exactly past it.'

He made no comment, but his eyes twinkled at her as if to say of course she wasn't. She ducked her head bashfully and took several sips of wine. As she did so, an urge developed to confide a very serious idea she'd had, an idea she'd never so much as hinted at during all the consultations with lawyers – for the pressing reason that if Alex got to hear of it he'd be devastated. Why not? She would speak very low. Broaching it aloud would be quite a relief.

'Shall I tell you what really hurt about what he did to me – the gynaecologist?'

He remained silent, but his expression encouraged her.

'It wasn't the shock, I got over that. It was the thought of maybe *why* he'd done it that wouldn't go away, that burned me up. You know he claimed it was because he'd found a dodgy-looking growth, and when we finally got a look at the lab report it showed he was lying, that there'd been just an innocent little fibroid, nothing calling for drastic measures? Well, I figured he must have had a genuine motive for whipping out my womb when he was only supposed to remove an ovarian cyst. And do you know what I finally came up with?' She held her breath for a second before coming out with the answer: 'Knowing about Alex put it into his head. He'd met Alex, you see. I can still remember him weighing him up. Usually people go out of their way to be kind; in fact some people overdo it, which can be awkward. But this guy just sort of *observed*, like Alex was, you know, a specimen. Thinking about it afterwards, after I'd had the op, I wondered if maybe he's the sort of bloke who holds views about bringing people into the world to be a so-called burden. Once I got the idea, it wouldn't go away. It made me determined to screw the bastard – um, sorry.' But Mr Brightly seemed not to mind her language, and continued to regard her with an absorption she found encouraging. 'I'm pretty soft really, a bit of a push-over – as certain friends and relations just love to point out. But not over this. Because I can't help thinking . . . what that surgeon did . . . it was like his verdict . . .' – she gulped – 'on *Alex*.' She gulped again and grabbed her glass.

He allowed time to elapse before commenting. Then, 'Thank you for sharing that with me,' he said. 'I'm glad you felt able to. You know anything you tell me will always be in the strictest confidence?'

She nodded.

'Good. As a matter of fact, I may be able to help you in another direction. Perhaps you know that I run a financial consultancy?'

She shook her head absently, still warm from confessing her darkest thought.

He put down his glass and lifted his briefcase onto his knees. 'I have some details here of a pet scheme of mine. If you like, I could leave them for you to mull over. You see, while it's an excellent plan to put a portion of the money into a building society so that you can get at it easily for Alex's immediate needs, it would be a waste not to use the larger proportion to secure the very best return. To take care of the more distant future, you understand.'

She blinked and returned to him her full attention.

'Oh yeah that's right: I remember Mavis saying you only work for the church in your spare time. I thought she said you were a lawyer.'

'That's quite correct, I am. But lawyers specialize, you know. And my expertise lies in matters of finance – loans and investments, probate – boring things like that,' he said, smiling at her.

She laughed. 'Well, it's ever so kind of you, Richard, but it sounds a bit out of my league. I bet advice of that sort comes pretty expensive.' The moment these words were out she felt flustered, wondering whether they could be taken for rudeness or as a hint she was seeking a favour. 'I mean, of course it'd be expensive. People'd be glad to pay lots for expert advice,' she hazarded, trying to improve matters.

'People are,' he said simply. 'But for close friends and family, and for St Peter's of course (the Church Building Fund is very close to my heart), I've devised this excellent scheme.'

Close friends, eh? So he really must like her. God, but he was a lovely bloke. 'It sounds wonderful,' she said, clasping her hands over her waist to calm a fluttery excitement.

'Well, you're welcome to study the details. I'll leave them with you till my next visit.'

'Er, I suppose you wouldn't,' she began, bumping forward onto the edge of her chair, 'you wouldn't like to come and eat with us one night next week? I mean, I don't know if that'd be OK with Mrs Brightly, but I'd really love to cook you a meal. You've been so kind,' she added, by way of excuse. 'Not, er, that she wouldn't be very welcome to come too if she wants, only I don't actually know your wife . . .'

'I'd be delighted. And I'm quite sure Ginny would have no objection. As a matter of fact she's awfully busy at the moment. She's landed a part, you know, in the forthcoming production by the Chedbury Players.'

'Right. Which night, then?'

'How about Friday? The Players meet on Fridays,

whether or not they're rehearsing; so Friday, you could say, is my evening off.'

'Oh,' she said, and in her imagination gathered to her all his forthcoming Fridays.

'And that will give you plenty of time to digest this,' he added, indicating the notes he'd placed on the coffee table. 'And of course if any other ideas come to your notice in the meantime I'll be more than happy to look them over.'

'Thanks,' she said, resolving to search the financial pages of her newspaper for ideas to be taken Friday by Friday. And tomorrow she'd start on a strict diet. Eight days hence she'd be thin.

'And about your ex-husband getting in touch,' he said, reverting to their earlier topic. 'If you don't wish to see him I see no reason why you should. He has no claim on you, I take it. This house . . .'

'It's mine. Mine and Alex's. Baz's father built it, Frederick Reece. He built the whole close.'

He nodded to indicate he was aware of this, and silently rebuked himself for failing to connect her surname with that of the builder (it was his business to make connections). 'So Mr Reece, your husband's father . . .'

'He let us have this house, yeah. Because when we got married and Alex was born, Baz was out of work. The band he was playing with folded. Mr Reece had always wanted him to join the firm – which Baz did for a while, till he got restless. Then another band asked him to join and he just cleared off. His parents were furious, specially when he said he was finished with me and Alex; so after the divorce they said the house could be mine and not Baz's. And my brother told them we'd like it in writing. (I'd never have dared myself.) But Jonathan explained that I needed to be sure how I was placed, and in fact they were good as gold about it.'

'Jonathan,' repeated Mr Brightly. 'Does your brother often advise you?'

'Used to. Not so much these days. Well, he's married

now with kids of his own. And he's terrifically busy. He's a dentist, a very clever one; he's done crowns and bridge work for famous people – models and pop stars and people on telly. Trouble is, Myra – that's his wife . . . I seem to rub her up the wrong way for some reason. Maybe that's why we don't see them all that much. Tell you one thing though, Jonathan's a fantastic uncle. He's keen on computers, and it was him who got Alex interested. Jonathan must have spent a fortune over the last few years, setting Alex up, adding the latest stuff – Myra'd go mad if she knew how much. Alex and Jonathan can actually send each other messages – you know? I'm not very up on computers myself. But it's so nice they have that in common. It's good for Alex.'

'You couldn't ask Jonathan to deal with Baz?'

'I could but I wouldn't. Definitely not. Jonathan was really proud of me fighting my case – I can just hear him saying to Myra, "Proves Cressida's not as wet as you think." No, I want to show them I've stopped messing up, that I can stand on my own two feet.'

'Then perhaps if Baz persists you should ask your solicitor to write him a letter.'

'Yeah, I thought of that. And I'll tell you another thing: I'll phone his mum. He hates her getting on to him. And she is absolutely disgusted with him now he's deserted two more children.'

'You mean children from his second marriage?'

'That's right. He's utterly bad news, is Baz. I shall tell him straight if he rings again – I would've yesterday only his money ran out: "Baz," I shall say, "I don't ever want to see you and neither does Alex." (Mind you, it's not Alex Baz wants to see, he made that clear enough.) "And, Baz, if you ring me again not only will I tell the solicitor, but I'll phone your mum." Then I'll hang up.'

'And you'll stop worrying about it, eh?'

She laughed and nodded. 'Hey, I feel much better for telling you. I'm sorry if I sounded frantic yesterday, but it's been great talking it over, getting it off my chest.'

'I'm glad. Well, Cressida' – he snapped his briefcase

shut and rose to his feet – 'I must bid you adieu.'

'Thanks for coming' – she rose also and trailed after him – 'and thanks for the wine – oh, wait while I fetch you the bottle.'

'No, no, you finish it.'

'Sure? Thanks.'

When she'd opened the door, he turned to her but did not touch her. He was meticulous about that, always careful to convey sympathy via gesture and words only: the merest touch of a hand could give rise to misunderstanding, and he was far too solicitous to inadvertently add to her troubles. 'Goodnight then, Cressida.'

'Goodnight, Richard. Shall we say seven o'clock for a week tomorrow?'

'Ah yes,' he remembered. 'On the Friday – my evening off.'

She recalled the reference. She liked the way it deftly excluded his wife.

He stepped outside, then turned and smiled at her before leaving. And she saw how light from the setting sun danced in his eyes, allowing them to communicate all those things she sensed he was too circumspect to say to her.

4

On Friday morning Mr Brightly rose as usual at half past six. He showered and shaved, put on clothes he'd selected the previous evening, then went into his study and closed the door. For fifteen minutes he read silently from the Bible, for another fifteen quietly recited the order of morning prayer. Afterwards he went into the kitchen to prepare a light breakfast of cereal, toast and tea, which he consumed while skimming various pages of the newspaper and more thoroughly perusing the financial reports. He completed his morning routine by making a fresh pot of tea and bearing it on a tray together with cup, saucer and cream jug – the refolded newspaper tucked under his arm – upstairs to his wife's bedside.

Ginny was not a sprightly riser. He set the tray on the low table between their two beds, placed the newspaper beside it, then went to the window to open the curtains. By way of encouragement he commended the day's weather. Still his wife did not stir. He returned to his own bed and folded away his pyjamas and straightened the duvet. At last, from the region of his bed's twin, came a sign of life: a little moan, a disgruntled sigh. He looked across: there seemed less of her than ever in a recumbent position and with no make-up on her face.

'Shall I pour you a cup?' he asked, bending down to kiss her forehead.

'Ugh,' she said, flinching from him.

He filled the cup anyway. 'Come on, sit up. Mrs Joiner'll be here shortly.'

'She's got her own key,' Ginny retorted, hoisting up and flopping against the velvet headboard.

'Good girl,' he said, applauding her effort. 'By the way, there's no need to bother about dinner for me this evening. I'm lunching with a client so I'll only want a snack, which I can get for myself. And I'll probably be late home: there are odds and ends to tie up before the weekend.'

'Yes, all right. Thanks, Dick. Drive carefully.'

'Goodbye darling,' he called outside his daughter's room – which opened to him immediately.

'Bye, Dad,' cried Harriet, flinging arms round his neck and kissing his cheek.

'Have a lovely day, pet.'

'And you,' she called, leaning over the banister rail to watch the shiny black shoes go swiftly downstairs, and the immaculate silvery hair and immaculately suited shoulders disappear into the hall.

In his big sleek BMW he drove at a gentle speed through lanes and byways. He preferred the country route to the office as far as it went, to meander through villages and avoid some of the rush; but north of Stratford he was obliged to take the busy dual carriageway and head east for the M40. On the motorway he chose the slowest lane, having only the distance between two junctions to travel. Within moments the sign for Warwick appeared, and he pressed down the indicator and prepared to turn off.

In the town, in one of the small streets near the castle, where the buildings are ancient and many have Georgian façades, where there are shops selling antiques and jewellery and expensive clothes, where there are old-fashioned cafés and one large old-fashioned hotel, and where accountants, solicitors, surveyors and the like have discreet offices, he parked in his allotted space, then crossed the pavement and mounted the step to a small building – formerly a merchant's house. The number 12 in brass was attached to the white-painted door, and underneath the rather smaller announcement & 12A. His name and the letters of his professional fellowship were inscribed on a brass plate fixed to the door's surround.

The door being unlocked, as it always was by this time of the morning, he turned its large brass knob and stepped inside. And his employees as ever welcomed him warmly: Dimla Khan on the reception desk smiled and said 'Good morning, Mr Brightly'; Tracy Wass looked up from her computer and said the same; Phillip Goodman, though busy on the telephone, raised a cheery hand.

'Good morning, Miss Khan. Good morning, Miss Wass. Good morning, Mr Goodman' – he made a point of greeting each in turn before looking at the mail and various other pieces of paper. He stuck to this formal mode of address down here in the number 12 part of the office out of deference to the maiden lady who was his secretary and probate clerk upstairs in number 12A, but at the same time did not object to informality between the young people themselves. Down here in number 12 it was always Trace, Phil and Dee – except when a client was present, of course, when they had the good sense to follow their employer's example.

'The rest of it's gone upstairs,' said Tracy Wass. 'Miss Orvanessy collected it.' She referred to the mail with a 12A address, which the downstairs' employees were forbidden to open.

Phillip Goodman concluded his telephone conversation and reported its nature in glowing terms. Mr Brightly heard him benignly and spoke words of approval. Then he asked: 'Did you follow up that enquiry yesterday – from a Mrs Lacey, I believe?'

Phillip, who preferred to deal with the large commissions, prevaricated. 'Yeah, well, you said you wouldn't mind handling that one, didn't you, Trace?'

'Please remember, Mr Goodman,' Mr Brightly mildly reproved him, 'no business is too insignificant. And that, as well as describing the proper attitude of this office, happens to be sound business advice.'

'Yes, Mr Brightly.'

'However, I have every confidence in the ability of Miss Wass,' he declared, beaming at her. 'Though it may turn out to be the sort of matter 12A usually deals with. Let me know how it develops.'

'Thanks, Mr Brightly. I will.'

Upstairs, he went first of all to greet his secretary. 'Good morning, Miss Orvanessy. Another beautiful day.'

'Good morning, Mr Brightly. Indeed it is.'

She was gaunt and tall and wore her greying hair in a tight bun. Her face was sallow, and its most prominent feature, a large and hairy wart, lay to the side of her nose. Every Christmas time, when the Brightlys entertained her at one of their parties, Ginny would wonder to her husband why Miss Orvanessy had never taken the trouble to have the blemish removed: it had surely ruined her marriage chances – which in any case were unlikely to be high; but a horror such as that eliminated even the faint possibility of a man's amorous attention. Then perhaps, teased her husband, Miss Orvanessy regarded the wart as a blessing. Though privately he thought he knew of one man at least whose attentions his secretary dreamed of. He was certain he knew, but the knowledge afforded him no sense of triumph, rather one of tender sympathy; and it was knowledge he was scrupulous never to betray. Thus it was as 'Miss Orvanessy' that he always addressed her for fear of encouraging her hopeless yearning. 'How's the Larchmont estate coming on, Miss Orvanessy?' he would say, or 'Dearie me, Miss Orvanessy, a horrid pile of letters I'm leaving you this afternoon!' – speaking her name courteously, only his eyes conveying the degree of affection that is due to an employee whose loyalty has been exemplary for twenty-three years. Once, he had overheard that young madam, Tracy Wass, joke to Phillip Goodman about 'Nessy' in a contemptuous tone. He'd come down on her hard.

This morning Miss Orvanessy looked worried. When

their pleasantries were concluded she reported a telephone call from a Mrs Henderson who had this morning received notice that she was hugely overdrawn at her bank, despite Mr Brightly's assurance last week of their business being concluded and all monies paid over.

Mr Brightly when he heard this tutted and sighed. What were the banks coming to these days? The mistakes they made must cost the nation a fortune. Personally he blamed computerization; no machine would ever be a match for the personal touch. Furthermore, you could go round in circles trying to pinpoint an error or a dilatory culprit. 'Don't worry, Miss Orvanessy. I'll deal with it right away myself. You can telephone Mrs Henderson if you like. Tell her the bank has evidently made a mistake and Mr Brightly is looking into it as you speak.'

'Oh, thanks, Mr Brightly,' said Miss Orvanessy, her gratitude as heartfelt as if it were her own money somewhere astray in the system. 'I'll get on to her at once.'

Stabbing out Mrs Henderson's number she felt perfectly reassured. This sort of thing had happened before; it was bound to, considering the sums of money and their manifold complications that passed through this office. But once Mr Brightly got his teeth into a problem it was righted in no time. She had utter faith in his ability. And soon her voice conveyed this faith down the line to Mrs Henderson, with evident calming effect.

Sure enough, an hour and a half later when she took his coffee into his room, 'I think we've got the Henderson matter sorted,' he told her. 'No need for you to worry any further on the matter. By the way, you know I'm lunching with a client today? Well, afterwards I may not come straight back to the office: some business has come up that I'd better go after. If anything requires my attention, just pop a note on my desk: I don't want you making yourself late on my account, Miss Orvanessy.'

'Thank you, Mr Brightly. That is kind.' Always

considerate, always the consummate gentleman; it was a privilege to work for such a man. Miss Orvanessy returned to her room and her own cup of coffee with a large lump in her throat.

When he had wined and dined his client in the nearby old-fashioned hotel – having himself partaken abstemiously – Mr Brightly got into his car and drove towards Leamington Spa. After all these years he was still never entirely sure where one town ended and the other began, but soon he passed Leamington station which decided the matter. While waiting at traffic lights he watched ladies in saris chatting and laughing, and studied the nature of the outlets bordering the street: an Indian jeweller's, a Greek takeaway, a Chinese launderette, a video shop with its windows covered in iron mesh. Beyond the junction, the neighbourhood improved; beyond the park, Victorian terraces gave way to Georgian. He drove straight past the house he would presently visit, further into town, and parked in the multi-storey. Then he set off on foot, back down the road he had just driven along and into a Georgian crescent fronted by plane trees. Many houses in the crescent had been turned into flats, though not the one whose steps he mounted.

Mrs Nanette Thompson was expecting him. He'd rung earlier in the day and told her he'd arrive between half past three and a quarter to four. It was nearly a quarter to four already, but she was still in her bedroom seated at her dressing table giving her face the final once-over. She performed this task with the aid of a free-standing mirror whose glass was magnified on one side. It was a depressing business peering up close, and got more depressing as time went by, but her eyesight was not as dependable as it once had been. She concluded her toilet with a squirt of scent behind each ear and a dab of powder into her cleavage.

The doorbell sounded as she divested herself of her dressing gown, but failed to deflect her from a leisurely choice between two particular dresses. 'I don't keep a dog and expect to bark myself,' she'd bawled to the girls only last week, when none of the lazy bitches stirred to answer the door – and only one punter in the house on the go at the time! As a result they'd had a severe telling off. She did not expect a further lapse this afternoon.

The girl who opened the door to him did not give her name (he could not recall whether he'd seen this one before), nor did she enquire after his. 'Hello,' she trilled, 'Mrs Thompson's expecting you. Would you like to wait in her sitting room? Lovely! Make yourself comfy. I'll just tell her you're here' – all delivered in the heedless sing-song of the reception girl at the barber's or one of those air stewardesses toting duty frees.

He was relieved to have been shown into her little parlour and not into the so-called reception room – as had happened on one ghastly occasion when he had found two men already waiting there, shielding their faces behind newspapers. He placed his briefcase (stamped R N B for Richard Norris Brightly) on a low table and sank into a chair beside it. Soon he heard the thump of her stressed high-heeled shoes on the stairs. A little smile came on his face.

'Ricki!' she cried, pausing in the doorway in an attitude calculated to show her silken sheathed body to advantage. She had selected the purple dress in preference to the green. Both colours looked good with her auburn hair, but the purple was slightly more sensuous, and this afternoon she was feeling frisky. 'How lovely, darling!'

He rose out of his seat, caught her embrace. 'Nanette, my dear.'

'God you look gorgeous,' she exclaimed, holding him at arm's length. 'More handsome every time I see you. It's not fair.'

'You look pretty spiffing yourself,' he returned, gallantly employing one of the archaic terms that had once been a feature of their private language.

She recognized it with pleasure. 'Ah, Ricki: weren't those the days?'

He retook his chair, pulled up his briefcase. Straight down to business she thought sadly, and plumped down on the sofa facing him.

'You know, darling,' she said, 'I'm very happy with the present arrangements. You've always done well for me. I'm very satisfied. Do I really need to make alterations?'

'The financial world is never static. To get the best out of your money it's often necessary to respond to changes. All very irritating, I know, but that's where I come in: to use my weather eye and save you the trouble.'

'Yes, I see what you mean.'

'I'm glad you're satisfied. But I really do advise you to consider a certain scheme I've devised. A scheme, I may say, that I've locked a considerable portion of my own capital into. It's been up and running for some time now − very successfully. I was looking through your file, and it suddenly occurred to me: this is just the sort of thing Nanette ought to be involved in.'

'Mm.' Her mouth twisted nervously. 'You said *locked into.*'

'That's the point, of course: the scheme has a ten-year lifespan; the money's tied in for the duration. Which is not at all unusual. It's a way of paying now for income later.' He paused, and crinkled up his eyes at her. 'You've often remarked that you don't plan to go on working for ever.'

'I certainly do not. Mm, ten years . . . I suppose that might suit me quite well. What would I have to do?'

'Produce your chequebook for a start,' he said, smiling. 'And sign this letter of authorization − as you've done before in the past. Then leave the donkey work to me. I'm sure it's in your long-term interest.'

'Well, I expect you know best. How many years have you been looking after my affairs? − no, don't tell me, I don't want to know.' She rose from her chair. On her way to the door she paused and gathered his hand. 'I trust you, Ricki. I couldn't say the same of many of the chaps who've crossed my path.' He made no comment but drew her hand to his lips. 'Shan't be a sec, my darling. I'll tell one of the girls to make us some tea. It still is tea, I take it? You won't have anything stronger?'

'Tea would be just the ticket,' he confirmed, sinking back against the velvet upholstery, wonderfully at ease.

She soon returned, and their business was swiftly concluded. And then, after a rap on the door, a girl with very long legs and a very short skirt brought in a tray. Bang on time, thought Mrs Thompson, covertly checking her watch. She'd issued her instructions before going upstairs to collect her chequebook. 'In fifteen minutes, and I don't mean ten, nor do I mean twenty, got it?' Yes, she was a bright girl this Tammy, as well as good-looking. 'Thanks, Tammy,' she said, having run her eyes over the tray to be sure all was in order – the best china, the correct number of everything, no slops.

'What do you think of that one, eh?' she asked slyly when the girl had gone out and closed the door. She kept her eyes on her pouring out.

'I thought she looked extremely young.'

'She's old enough,' Mrs Thompson said sharply, passing him the filled cup. When she spoke again she'd reverted to her sly tone. 'Don't tell me you didn't notice Tammy's attributes. She's only been with me a couple of months. A lovely girl, professional to her fingertips, and ever so popular. Some of the others have had their noses put out, lazy little . . .' But she thought better of the word on her tongue in present company. 'Come on now, Ricki, own up. Didn't Tammy catch your interest just a tiny bit?'

He sipped his tea before replying. 'My dear, if I were still open to having my interest caught – and as you know, I'm not – the girl who came in just now would not be the person to do it. For my taste she couldn't hold a candle to you. And well you know it.' He spoke the simple truth, which informed his tone.

Hearing it, Mrs Thompson was gratified. What an absolute pet of a man! If it weren't for the tea in his hands, she'd be bounding over this minute, dumping herself in his lap and giving him a smacker. She might do it yet, given a more convenient moment. 'Tea all right, darling?'

'Perfectly.'

'Remember the little times we had, Ricki? In naughty Nanette's big four-poster? Our nice little romps? They were great times, eh?'

Thirsty after his lunch, he drained his cup. 'I remember them fondly,' he frankly admitted. He was no hypocrite; he would not, in the light of present virtue, deny his past.

'Oh, Ricki,' she said softly, laying her own cup down. He saw her coming, and in the nick of time crossed his legs before she descended. 'Ricki,' she murmured, putting strong arms round his neck and allowing no course for his face but to engage with her bosom. In spite of himself he was stirred by the experience.

'No, no, Nanette,' he said, intending by this reference to a very old musical to reproach her lightly. It was not the first time during their long relationship that he'd made the allusion. She duly giggled and began nibbling his earlobe. 'No, dear, please,' he protested, struggling to grasp her forearms. 'Respect my wishes.'

'But Ricki love, deep down I *am* respecting your wishes, now amn't I? Don't get me wrong, I'm not coming on to you like you're a punter. I'd never do that; I know you're not in the market. No, I want to give you a free one, Ricki. Oo lovie, lovie, I really do.'

Certain aspects caused him to believe her – breasts jutting into him, hot breath in his ear. Yet not so long ago, when she'd decided to retire from taking an active role in the business to concentrate her energies on managing the girls, she'd confessed her relief at being done with 'that side of things' – though she had hastened to exclude his own pleasuring and even offered to resume that task, should he ever so desire. As he'd reflected at the time, she'd been pretty safe making the offer since it came some years after he'd regretfully dispensed with her services due to new-found religious conviction. Nevertheless, at the time it had seemed a compliment. And likewise now the fact that she positively desired him – for his own sake and not for any remuneration. More than a compliment, her declaration this afternoon struck him as enormously touching. He found himself wondering if it wouldn't be churlish to turn her down. A case might be made, he suspected, for a man of religious principle being duty-bound to encourage her in this novel non-mercenary impulse.

She had unslipped one of his shirt buttons and now inserted her hand. 'Like to go upstairs, Ricki?'

It was his almost overwhelming physical response that inadvertently saved him. It brought home to him the fact that his reasoning was sophistry, cunningly shaped to further desire. 'No. But . . . thank you,' he gasped. He stilled the hand inside his shirt, unwound the arm from behind his neck. 'And I won't pretend I'm not strongly tempted. Christ Himself was tempted, but found the grace to resist. As also must I.'

He might just as well have waved a crucifix in her face, she thought, finding no option but to retreat. 'Spoilsport,' she grumbled, pushing away from him, sliding silken haunches down his thighs. 'Boring old holy joe you've become.' She rose on her feet and glowered down, covering her loss of face with a show of crossness.

He hadn't intended her to lose face, only to protect his self-imposed vow of denial. He quickly got up and sought her hand with both his own. 'You do know it's with intense regret?'

'Yes, I know,' she agreed wearily. 'You went and got religion. Can't blame me, though, for mourning the waste. Never mind, I shan't embarrass you again. We're still friends?'

'My dear, *I* should be the one asking that.' He read anxiety in her upturned eyes, and thought what a hindrance it was, the confusion between affection and sex. She sought the former, he divined, but knew only how to seek it in terms of the latter. 'Excellent friends, darling Nanette, and long may we remain so,' he declared, and took her into his arms. From this close up he perceived her famous auburn hair to be grey at the roots. His hand smoothing her upper back detected a faint humping of the spine. Suddenly saddened, he searched his mind for a piece of reassurance to give. 'God loves you, you know,' he finally came up with.

Her laugh was short and mirthless. 'Does He now, really? Sent you on purpose to tell me, I suppose. Then maybe He'd like to take care of my bills.'

'You take perfectly good care of your bills yourself, with your substantial earnings – the fruit of diligence and verve, if I may say so.'

She pushed away from him. 'Yes, but this God who you say loves me doesn't approve of my methods, right? He told you to lay off, didn't He?'

'No, no, you misunderstand. My decision was for myself alone. I felt I'd no choice, that if I was called to serve God – and I felt I was – then serving Him ought to be sufficient happiness, that I shouldn't seek any other. But I wouldn't presume to speak for others.'

'Oh, go on with you! I was brought up a Catholic, so you can't kid me. Far as God's concerned my line of business is out of order.'

'You know,' he said thoughtfully, 'I wouldn't be too certain of that.' And he drew on years of private reflection concerning his own expertise to further enlarge: 'Strictures and regulations about business practices are devised by man for man's convenience. Whereas an individual's flair in a particular field is a gift from God. I happen to be of the opinion that it's up to each of us to honour that gift by using it creatively and making the most of it.'

'Oh Ricki,' she laughed, and this time merrily, 'you really are a one. But lovely with it. Here, let me give you a kiss – a chaste one, promise.'

He inclined his cheek, to which she pressed her lips.

'Chums,' she pronounced, her confidence plainly restored.

'Chums,' he agreed, his eyes holding hers the way they sometimes did, and which still, at her ripe age, had the power to bring her out in goose bumps.

Having held her gaze for a good twenty seconds, he turned away to collect the papers she had signed and stow them in his briefcase.

As soon as he was out of the crescent, Mr Brightly examined his watch. It was later than he'd hoped. He had precisely thirty-five minutes to get to Kenilworth and the home of Mrs Guisborough-West. Very keen on the cocktail hour was Mrs Guisborough-West, when she liked to have one or two friends dropping in. Over the years he had met some of these friends, half a dozen of whom had proved quite useful; this evening he hoped to make further worthwhile contacts. The only difficulty he foresaw – apart from getting there late – was the usual one of avoiding the cocktails. Mrs Guisborough-West was inclined to take another's discretion as a disparaging comment on her own indulgence: 'I won't have another thank you, Mrs Guisborough-West, as I'm driving,' did not impress her. Which was all rather tricky considering she was the sort of long-standing client he would go out of his way not to offend.

Blowing a little, he marched into the car park. He stood in the lift and reflected that the ladies, bless them, seemed always determined to press upon him things he'd sooner do without. If it wasn't Mrs Nanette Thompson's body, it was the alcoholic liquor of Mrs Guisborough-West; and now Cressida Reece, a recent recruit, had ambitions to cook him his dinner. It was a small price to pay, however, for in his long experience a lady invariably made a more satisfactory client than a man.

He was driving down the ramp of the multi-storey when Mrs Parminter came suddenly to mind. He exempted her at once from his list of ladies who were bent on coddling him in some way or other. It was true she was generous with her whisky, but that was due to her liking a glass herself. If he refused – 'No I won't tonight if you don't mind. I was obliged to drink with a client at lunch time' – she would simply accept it: 'Well just pour one for me, will you? Thank you, Mr Brightly.' (A smile, though he didn't know it, had come on his face as he pictured her – head tilted against the back of her armchair, listening and chatting.) It was this refreshing matter-of-factness of hers that made for such relaxing company. There was never a need to be on one's guard with Mrs Parminter. Of course, she was primarily a friend; had only incidentally become one of his clients, and that at her own suggestion. Given her character, it could have happened no other way.

But Mrs Parminter was an exception. Most ladies liked to be courted for their business. Which was fine by him, he was the man to do it. But it was certainly time-consuming, and not a little wearing. He would have to stay at Mrs Guisborough-West's until her guests had gone (if, as he supposed, there were guests) in order to secure her signature on various pieces of paper. Afterwards he would need to return to the office in case Miss Orvanessy had left details of a matter needing urgent attention; and also to gather up paperwork to be dealt with at home in any moments left spare from doing duty as husband and father on Saturday and the Lord's work on Sunday.

On the outskirts of Leamington, in a hurry though he was, he courteously anticipated the wish of a pedestrian to use a crossing. He pressed on the brake pedal. A hoot of annoyance came from the van behind. He and the pedestrian shared a rueful smile. Driving off, he raised a hand in graceful apology to the van driver

– which failed to mollify, for the van, making a point, promptly overtook with a screech of tyres. Mr Brightly was not in the least put out. Some people were like that, it really pained them to stop. For himself, no pressure on earth would persuade him to forgo good manners.

5

'My dear, did you read about my ex-char's windfall? One hundred thousand pounds!' shrieked Mrs Sheila Rawlins to Mrs Ginny Brightly, and in effect to everyone in the lounge at the Brown Bear.

It was Saturday lunch time. Among this circle of friends and neighbours (known generally in Chedbury as the Framley Lane set) a tradition had been established of meeting for a drink at this hour. Though it was a time other sorts of people might find inconvenient, those with housework and shopping to catch up on after a busy working week, folk such as these were not so encumbered, having sufficient leisure or paid employees to accomplish their domestic chores at other times. Meeting in the pub, they found, made a light-hearted change from all the entertaining that went on in their own homes. And the Brown Bear provided the correct ambience: old oak beams and polished oak furniture, a stock of specialist beers and an amazing variety of wines – not to mention the home-cooked food commended by Egon Ronay. The landlord, John Crick, attended personally to their requirements. Every Saturday morning at eleven thirty sharp, whatever other demands might be pressing, he took up position behind the lounge bar (sporting his trademark polka-dot bow tie) on purpose to welcome these highly valued customers. Some of the ladies liked to flirt with him. The men drew him into their banter and asked him to have one himself, they appealed to him to decide arguments and laughed uproariously at his practised drolleries. And all without exception addressed him as 'John' and did so more often than was strictly necessary. He in response stuck to Mr and Mrs.

Mr Brightly had not much liked the reference to Cressida Reece's victory, fearing the course it might take. 'Whipped out her whatsit, I believe,' he heard Jason Wright explain to Tony Colebrook.

'Her womb, darling,' said Jason's wife.

'Who did?' asked Tony, who'd been in the United States when the papers were full of the case.

'The surgeon johnny – when he wasn't supposed to. Probably got her muddled with another patient. I imagine they all look alike from a certain perspective.'

'For that sort of money he's welcome to mine,' Gloria Maskill declared. 'Fat lot of good it's ever done me. But a hundred thousand smackers I could definitely use.' Gloria, who was childless, had recently gone through an acrimonious divorce: a fact that made the others uncomfortable for when he'd lived among them Mitch Maskill was considered a good chap.

'From what I heard, Gloria, you did all right,' said Peter Boutall who was still in touch with Mitch Maskill.

Gloria smiled enigmatically and took a sip of her drink, torn between the roles of hard-done-by-wife and victorious litigant. 'Actually, I did rather wipe the grin off Mitch's face,' she admitted. Which prompted some of the men to draw Peter aside and enquire as to the nature of the sum involved.

'Of course,' Gloria confided to her female companions, 'it's a terrible temptation to splurge – get my tits fixed, book into a health farm, go somewhere exotic and pick up some gorgeous young fella.'

'Oh but you should, Gloria, you deserve it. Doesn't she, girls?'

'Listen: maybe at my age I ought to be prudent. Eh, Ginny? You don't suppose Dick'd give me a few tips?'

'Darling, of course he would; he'd be delighted. Dick?' Ginny Brightly cried to her husband. 'I just said to Gloria, you'd be very happy to advise her financially. Her settlement, you know,' she prompted him from the side of her mouth.

'Trouble is, I'm not sure I can afford you, Dick. I mean you deal in seriously big bucks, right?'

'Oh he'll always help out a pal,' said Ginny, glowing with pleasure as the eyes of all females present looked admiringly on her handsome husband. She revelled in his financial wizardry, adored it being a source of wonderment to her friends. Indeed, were it not for his enviable business reputation she was not sure whether Dick would be so well tolerated socially. Of course, his vigorous churchmanship was approved of in principle, but there had been moments – Ginny had keenly sensed them – when a ruffle of embarrassment had gone round a dinner table as Dick's presence was suddenly recalled. Of their Chedbury friends only Tony Colebrook had known Dick in his pre-conversion days. She often appealed to Tony to confirm that Dick was no party pooper (behind her husband's back, of course).

Now, like a lamb, he was complying with her expectations and promising to call on Gloria next Tuesday evening.

'Gosh,' said Gloria. 'Sure you can trust me with him, Ginny?'

'I can trust Dick,' Ginny said.

'Anyone know when the Furnivals get back from the Dordogne?' someone asked.

'Polly told Jamie the end of the month.'

'Oh yes, Polly was round the other night talking to Harriet,' Ginny Brightly recalled. 'I must say I'm looking forward to seeing Anne and Mike again. We want to quiz them about buying a property in France. Don't we, darling?'

But her husband was moving smoothly away from her. He'd obliged her enough for one morning, he considered, by agreeing to give Gloria Maskill some of his valuable time. From his own point of view he doubted whether the consultation would prove worthwhile: she'd want regular income from whatever she'd managed to wring out of Mitch, and she'd want to start getting it now; there'd be no scope for his creative skill, nothing to juggle with, no call, therefore, to admit Gloria Maskill to his select group of 12A clients. He guessed she wouldn't qualify anyway, since she was unlikely to fulfil either of his two criteria: the possession of serious wealth, or – to his own satisfaction – the presentation of a deserving case. He was also embarrassed by that silly remark of Ginny's: 'Oh he'll always help out a pal' – which she'd made in front of Betty Fielding. (The Fieldings were clients.) Didn't it imply that with regard to his fees, a client with whom he was on friendly terms might escape the full whack? No wonder Betty Fielding dealt him a look. He must remember to tackle Ginny about it. This habit she had of making glib throwaway comments could land them in serious awkwardness one of these days. He moved further along the bar to ask his old friend Tony Colebrook what he was having and learn how he had fared in the United States.

The theme occupying the ladies was still that of holiday properties abroad. Heavens she was a fool, Ginny Brightly cursed as it became clear just how many of her acquaintances were already advantaged in this respect. She'd got bogged down for ages over the choice of a conservatory, had rested on her laurels far too long as the possessor of the largest swimming pool in Framley Lane, and now they were all forging ahead of her. Even the Rawlins: a moment ago Sheila had shyly revealed that in four weeks' time negotiations would be completed for a villa on the Costa del Sol. The only consolation to be derived from this was the naffness of the location. Trust the Rawlins to get it wrong, Ginny thought.

'Four weeks,' mused Betty Fielding. 'Four weeks from now we'll be packing Minty off to Benenden. God, I hope we've done the right thing.'

There were murmurs of reassurance which were not entirely sincere: in the opinion of those who had sent their daughters to less famous schools, Benenden was flashy and its situation cruelly distant from Chedbury. The problem of trying to do the best for one's children now became the topic, and Ginny saw her chance to re-enter the race. Straining after an opening, she held on the tip of her tongue the hideous expense of Harriet's singing lessons.

Near the bar, Mr Brightly frowned into his Scotch. After a pleasant exchange with Tony Colebrook, they'd been joined by the Wrights and then by Peter Boutall. Jason Wright introduced the subject of a local protest group: women of the Eastcote estate who were agitating for the erection of traffic calming humps on a busy stretch of Stratford Road. During a recent demonstration he'd been held up in his car. 'Placards and push chairs: you never saw such a rabble! Ugly fat cows yelling "Wadda-we-want?" All on social security, you can bet your sweet life. Twenty bloody minutes I was stuck behind the wheel.'

'The unmarried mother brigade,' sniffed his wife, Nesta.

Mr Brightly turned away and rested his glass on the bar. He was familiar with the agitation of these mothers. There'd been several instances of a child's having a narrow escape. Just over a month ago a little girl was knocked down and killed. The protester-in-chief was a churchgoer. She appeared before him now in his mind's eye: stout and pasty-faced with dank ill-cut hair. He'd held the chalice to her lips. (On busy occasions such as Easter and Christmas he was often asked by the celebrant to assist at Holy Communion.)

'There was one slag in particular. Naturally, I'd put my hand on the horn – I mean what did they expect, I was just going to sit there? – hell, I'd got a meeting in Stratford in twenty minutes. Anyway, this one took exception; stuck her face right up against the wind-screen and started mouthing off. Fortunately I couldn't hear a word, having taken care to close the window. Dear Christ, they were an unpleasant-looking crew. I tell you what: sterilization'd be a boon to humanity.'

'It'd certainly save the taxpayer a bundle,' said Peter Boutall.

'Oo, careful. That doctor who took it into his head to sterilize the Reece woman lived to regret it,' Nesta Wright reminded her husband.

'Will you excuse me?'

They stepped back, shielding their drinks from Dick Brightly's abrupt passage between them. There followed an awkward silence, which Peter Boutall seized upon to open up on his favourite topic (motoring).

'T'other day I was stuck behind the wheel myself. I was making a call last Tuesday morning – no, tell a lie, it was Wednesday morning. You know that stretch of road between the Napton roundabout and the turn-off for the M40?'

Glumly the men confirmed that they did, and Nesta Wright cast about her for a more attractive topic of conversation.

In the gents, Mr Brightly washed and dried his hands. He examined his reflection in a smeary mirror and made smoothing motions with his palms against the sides of his hair. Going grey had not spoilt his looks: Ginny was right, it made him look distinguished. He could well imagine the figure he cut in the chancel, and was pleased to think that by his bearing and countenance he enhanced people's religious experience.

He went out into the corridor and turned not in the direction of the lounge bar but towards the taproom. Inside two elderly men were seated at a table: Mr Nuttal a retired greengrocer and Mr Milbank a retired farmer. Both men served as sidesmen at St Peter's. Greetings were exchanged and when they asked him to join them Mr Brightly bought a round of drinks. Taking only a minor role in the amiable conversation that followed, he promised himself he'd return very soon to the lounge. He owed it to Ginny to do so. For on Saturdays he did the things she liked in return for doing those that pleased him on a Sunday. Sometimes on Saturdays they shopped, usually they had a drink in the Bear, and in the evening they dined out with friends or entertained guests at home. Yes, in a very few minutes he'd go back to her, as was only fair.

Tony Colebrook, in the lounge, excused himself from the motoring conversation and made his way to Ginny Brightly's side. He slipped an arm round her waist. They were on very close terms. Tony and his ex-wife Carol had formed a friendly foursome with Ginny and Dick Brightly in the days when they all resided in Warwick and were members of CADS – the Castle Amateur Dramatic Society. In those days Dick Brightly had been the star, the one everyone said ought to be a professional actor. Dick's final role for CADS was at the back of Tony's mind now as he spoke to Ginny. 'Good old Dick. Do you know, it's just struck me, he really means it. He really believes in this pious stuff. I've always put it down to that last part he played for CADS – remember? – old Dick in a biretta, clutching his crucifix? Took to it like a duck to water, didn't he? See, it's always been my theory that playing that priest went to his head. The role took him over . . .'

'Where *is* Dick?' asked Ginny.

'Mm? Oh, getting a breath of fresh air I should imagine. We got caught by the Wrights . . .'

'You mean he's gone. The bastard!'

'No, no, I was speaking figuratively. Most likely he's obeying a call of nature. What happened was, Jason and Nesta started mouthing off about unmarried mothers and how there's a lot to be said for sterilization, and poor old Dick got hot under the collar – in an understated sort of way of course. But it pulled me up. Hang about, I thought: Dick's not putting it on. He's really taken this religious stuff to heart.'

'Of course he means it, you chump. He'd hardly have kept it up for ten years otherwise. Actually though, at this precise moment I could wring his neck. It's me he's avoiding, never mind the Wrights. I want us to discuss buying a property in France and he's determined we're not going to.'

'Ginny love, don't scowl. It doesn't suit you.' He squeezed her waist. 'When are you and I going to rehearse our scenes?'

She giggled. 'When Teddy wants us to, I suppose.'

'Oh, I think you and I ought to have a crack at it in private.'

She giggled again and let him nuzzle the back of her neck.

In the taproom the conversation had taken an ecclesiastical turn. 'Will you be preaching tomorrow, Mr Brightly?' enquired Mr Nuttal.

Mr Brightly answered that he would.

'Eleventh Sunday after Trinity,' pronounced Mr Milbank, to show he knew where he was in the Church calendar.

'Indeed it is,' confirmed Mr Brightly.

'Gospel according to St Luke chapter nine,' said Mr Milbank, closely watching for a sign that he'd hit on the test for tomorrow's sermon: '"Two men went up into the temple to pray: one a pharisee, and the other a publican."'

Mr Brightly nodded gravely.

'Puts me in mind of a story I heard one time when I was buying a heifer in Stratford market.'

The tale was duly repeated. Mr Brightly assumed a keen listening attitude and prepared to greet its conclusion sagely (for presumably a moral would be drawn connected with tomorrow's Gospel). But as Mr Milbank lingered among the steamy cattle stalls of Stratford market, his mind slid onto a tack of its own. Wasn't it extraordinary that by walking the few steps from the lounge to the taproom he had moved out of one sphere of his life into another? And that the scene he'd just left in the lounge would constitute his entire world if it hadn't been for God calling him. He wondered whether any other of God's servants had been summoned in such a singular manner. And whether any other actor, amateur or professional, had found himself playing a part that had enveloped him so exactly as to feel like a new skin; or speaking lines that came more naturally to the tongue than everyday language. He had researched diligently for the part (as was his practice for every role he played) and for that reason had started attending church services. Which was how he'd come to meet Canon Rawsthorne. At the time he and Ginny were having the house built on Framley Lane, so St Peter's had been an obvious point of reference. He and the canon had got on famously. Canon Rawsthorne had come to Warwick to watch his performance, and subsequently encouraged him to use his talents for the benefit of St Peter's by reading the lesson and so forth. No doubt Canon Rawsthorne was seeking to take life easier at the time, but the sincerity of his belief in his new friend and parishioner was clearly demonstrated by his suggestion that he become a lay reader. Mr Brightly sometimes thought he'd like to go a step further and offer himself for ordination; but for the moment such a course was out of the question: it was too great a sacrifice to ask of his wife, and there were the children to consider. One day when the children were off their hands, and when their level of comfort was such that even Ginny could find no room for improvement, then perhaps it would be possible.

'So there you have it,' Mr Milbank concluded.

'Aye, it makes you think,' said Mr Nuttal.

'It certainly does,' Mr Brightly agreed, rising to his feet with some reluctance. 'Well, thank you for your company, gentlemen, it was most stimulating. But I really must get back to my wife. She's in the lounge, you know. She'll think I've deserted her.'

'In the lounge, is she?' wondered Mr Nuttal. 'Aye, well then,' concluded Mr Milbank. And both shook their heads as men who had sensibly left their wives where they belonged on a Saturday dinner time, in the kitchen.

Discontent was plain on his wife's face when he

returned and looked across at her. Discontent gave her a vulnerable air; she had always been a martyr to it, it seemed to lie in wait for her, eager to spite her with news of a neighbour's new bauble or a friend's success.

'So there you are,' she said. 'Where the hell've you been?'

'I'm sorry. I bumped into two sidesmen from church.'

'Oh, church!'

'Do you think we should be getting along? If we're going out with the Rawlinses tonight that only leaves this afternoon to discuss your idea of a holiday place.'

'Oh Dick, you mean in France?'

'Wherever you like, my love.'

'Oh darling!'

He'd meant to be firm. He'd meant to take her aside and reproach her for that ill-considered remark. But instead of course he'd indulged her, just as he always indulged her. For, more than the bouts of sulking that would follow if she were thwarted, he dreaded a look that would come in her eyes: an animal look, a hint of being at bay. He knew it reflected her profound sense of insecurity. This was nothing Ginny could help; insecurity had been bred in her by a wastrel father and an embittered mother. He himself was hurt by any sign of it, and when her hunted look appeared felt desperate to send it away. Twelve or so years ago, when CADS was buzzing with rumours of an affair between Ginny and his friend Tony Colebrook, that look in Ginny's eyes had been virtually constant. He remembered those months as one dark long night: the Colebrook divorce going through; Ginny clinging like a limpet to the rock of her marriage, denying point blank any guilty involvement and fanatically determined with her displays of wifely devotion while the look in her eyes told another story. He'd said he believed her. He'd directed his heart to believe her. He'd have sworn black was white to calm the atmosphere and protect his children and no longer catch a glimpse of the fear haunting her. Then a miracle happened. The casting committee of CADS asked him to audition for the part of the priest, and playing that part changed his life. The whispers and worries and embarrassments no longer mattered, he'd been lifted above them; he'd been lifted clear of the dark long night and set on a shining plane. God had called him. The practice of a new way of life made bearing with Ginny easy, and though he no longer felt for her as formerly, his desire to protect and reassure her and grant her wishes remained strong as ever. Now, making her good-byes, her face, he saw, was the picture of happiness. How could he help but be glad? He did love being the bringer of joy.

Tony Colebrook clasped his hand. 'Good old Dick,' he said with emotion.

'Unlike Tony to get oiled at lunch time,' he commented to his wife as they went towards the car park.

'Was he?' Ginny screwed up her face. 'No, no. That was by way of an apology. All these years he's assumed you were putting it on, believe it or not. Then something happened in there to make him realize you're truly sincere — you know, about religion.'

'I wonder what that was?' The locks on the car doors sprang up, and they got inside.

Ginny fastened her seat belt. 'He said something . . . I can't remember. But I told him he was a chump. I suppose what it is: he sees you mixing with the crowd as usual . . . and let's face it they're a pretty worldly lot on the whole: so there you are one minute with your glass of Scotch, and the next you're preaching a sermon or calling on types like . . . well, the two who caught you just now. I suppose to people like Tony it's a pretty rum mixture. Anyway Dick, we'll grab a sandwich, shall we? And then I'll show you the leaflets I got from the estate agent.'

'Mm,' he said. 'Fine.' But his mind as he drove off was going over what she'd said before a sandwich came into it: in particular the word 'worldly', and her use of it to characterize the Framley Lane lifestyle as opposed, he presumed, to the spiritual world of church. He remembered the dubious expressions on the faces of Mr Nuttal and Mr Milbank at the notion of his wife's presence in the pub lounge: theirs was another sort of world. There was also the world of the council housing estate and its unmarried mothers, and the more regularized world of Symmonds Close and Cressida Reece. They were all worlds he needed to engage with from time to time as his wife's husband and a resident of Chedbury and as a businessman and the St Peter's lay reader, but it seemed to him now that he was not entirely part of any of them. Perhaps there was nowhere in the town where he did not have to damp down one area of his life in deference to another.

Then he remembered The Gables, and let out his breath. At Mrs Parminter's, thank goodness, there was never any feeling of keeping company in an environment that was only half his own.

He wondered if she'd been to the doctor's yet. He hoped she hadn't suffered a second funny turn. He wished now he'd called on her last night to see how she was. He consoled himself that he'd know one way or the other tomorrow because she always attended morning service.

6

'Let us pray,' sang out the voice of Mr Brightly, at which all those in the church able to do so got down on their knees. Mrs Parminter was one who knelt. Her knees engaged reliably with the hassock, and she sent up a quick word of thanks for having been spared the usual consequences that come to eighty-two-year-olds who take a tumble and are unable to rise or summon immediate assistance. But soon, as Mr Brightly intoned the prayer of St Chrysostom, his voice cleaving to the single note, his delivery of the words clear and unhurried as if each were a pearl he strung to its fellows with gentleness and love, Mrs Parminter was seized by a tide of emotion. Her body trembled, she gripped the prayer ledge. And was forced to acknowledge that she had indeed suffered one type of ill effect. From this she went on to deduce the precise cause of her ending up in the rose bed last Wednesday afternoon.

'It's turned him sentimental, it's made him talk drivel.' As evidence, her mother had cited the tears coursing her father's face and his attempt to take her into his arms – in full view of the nursing staff and others present in the ward. Her mother's friend Mrs Bessinger had known of similar cases: apparently a stroke would often turn a man, who in health had practised iron self-control, into a soppy whimperer. Later, making her own visit to the hospital, Mrs Parminter discovered the truth of her mother's report. Once so reticent that his style of communication was to bark through a slit at the side of his mouth, her father cried out that she was his dear little Clara, clasped her to his breast, sobbed that she was his heart's treasure. Such was the effect of a stroke. Poor, poor Father, Mrs Parminter thought now with pity; remembering that at the time she had felt only embarrassed.

At the end of the service, as she took her turn to pass through into the porch, Mr Brightly shook her hand and bade her good morning and murmured that he was pleased to see her. His remarks were more or less the same to every worshipper, but when his eyes looked into Mrs Parminter's their twinkle conveyed a private message of particular pleasure. Lacking his expressive skills she did not attempt a private reply. Outside on the path she was detained by an old friend whose daughter had brought her to church in a wheelchair, and a three-way conversation ensued, during which Mrs Parminter accepted an invitation to coffee on Tuesday morning. Afterwards she fell back to allow the wheelchair to proceed ahead of her. The congregation by now had largely dispersed; she was quite alone when Mr Brightly hurried from the porch to speak to her.

'You appear to be in fine fettle. I take it there've been no further soft landings in the garden?'

'None at all. I have been quite as normal.'

'I'm relieved to hear it. If I hadn't been so pushed on Thursday and Friday evenings I'd have called round to make sure.'

'That's very kind, but as you see there was no need. And tomorrow Dr Page is going to check me over.'

He smiled his approval of this. 'Until Wednesday then.'

'Of course,' she confirmed.

That was Mr Brightly all over, she reflected as she went towards the street. He kept his concerns to himself while others were present and only mentioned them when it was certain they would not be overheard. His sensibility was such that he did not need to be told how thoroughly she would dislike having her little accident broadcast.

In Market Square the sun glistened the pebble glass of Forrester's bow-fronted shop window. There was little traffic about; just some people being set down near the entrance to the Brown Bear preparatory to Sunday lunch. A few shoppers waited at the counter in the newsagent's. In front of the estate agent's window, tourists studied a revolving display detailing houses for sale: no doubt assessing the type of property that could be afforded in the area if their own properties were sold in London or Birmingham. How fortunate she was to live in this charming town. Fortunate to breath the relatively unpolluted air. And fortunate above all (for this was pure chance) to have acquired the friendship of Mr Brightly.

While the congregation in St Peter's knelt in prayer that Sunday morning, in a semi-detached house in Symmonds Close Cressida Reece served baked beans on toast with a poached egg on top to her son Alex. A little later, as Mrs Parminter stood chatting on the sunny church path, war broke out in the Reece household.

The day had begun calmly enough. As usual on a Sunday Cressida overslept. She rolled out of bed, drew on her dressing gown and made for her son's room – even before visiting the bathroom. She knocked on the door and went straight in. 'It's late,' she told him. 'Shall we make do with a cup of tea now and have brunch later?'

Alex, already up and in front of his computer, turned his head to look at her. And swiftly removed his gaze. She looked horrible, he thought: grimy old towelling wrap hanging loose, her nightdress showing, her hair on end, her eyes all pouchy. 'All right.'

'About ten thirty – OK?'

'Later if you like. I'm not hungry.'

'Eleven then. But no later. You can't go swimming on a full stomach.'

She left him then and went downstairs.

It came into Alex's head at that moment that he didn't

actually fancy a trip to the swimming pool this particular Sunday. His mother had fixed up these sessions. From 2 p.m. until 4 p.m. on Sundays the new Leisure Centre in Stratford reserved its pool for the use of local young disabled people. A driver came round in a minibus collecting the bathers from their homes and ferried them back afterwards. His mother had gone to a lot of trouble getting him a place on this scheme. When she'd first heard about it there was a waiting list; little hope had been offered of a place for Alex for at least a year. So she'd badgered people, enlisted the support of Dr Terence at the hospital, and the doctors and nurses at the surgery, and some lecturer she knew at the college; she'd even consulted the local MP. Sure enough, two months later the Leisure Centre's minibus pulled up in Symmonds Close.

Alex could recite off by heart the evidence she'd used to achieve this end. He'd heard her use it on the phone over and over; he'd read it time and again in half-written letters stuck in her typewriter on the dining room table. *Regular vigorous exercise of the heart and lungs is crucial for Alex – both to keep him healthy now, and to ensure he continues to develop physically.* There was nothing his mother wouldn't do for him. She was shameless, ruthless, fanatical. It was a pity she didn't bother more about herself, he thought, instead of slobbing around, letting people mess her about. People like that doctor who'd cut out her womb. If his mother had been more assertive, probably he wouldn't have cut out her womb. He'd have paid more attention, not cut her open and then gone on cutting while his mind pursued a more interesting subject. Of course Alex knew the reason for his mother going round in a dream half the time: she used up every scrap of energy pushing and shoving on his behalf. She'd breathe for him if she could, Alex thought.

It wasn't a very comfortable thought. A stopped-up sensation came in his throat. He wheeled over to the wall mirror. He studied himself as he dropped his jaw and heaved in air, working his chest up and down. He was breathing all right, but still felt constricted. Leaning closer to the glass, he felt he didn't like himself much this morning. And it could be that this feeling was justified. Maybe today he was seeing himself clearly and on other days, when he felt neutral or happy with himself, he was misguided. Maybe this was the reason he didn't fancy swimming this afternoon; he didn't want to be seen, didn't want people to feel disgusted.

Cressida visited the downstairs cloakroom while the kettle was heating. She concluded the visit by dashing water into her face and drying herself on the hand towel. When the tea was made she poured out one mugful for Alex and took it upstairs. In a minute she'd come down and pour her own.

'Here we are,' she said, resting her free hand on his shoulder as she passed him the mug.

He shrugged it off before the prickly feeling could grow that was sometimes set off by her touching him. Fortunately she didn't seem to notice. When he'd taken the mug, she used both hands to knot the loosening ties of her dressing gown.

'Drink it while it's hot,' she said.

'What if I like it cold?' he muttered.

'You say something, love?'

'Nnn.'

'Like me to give you a hand with anything?'

'N'thanks.'

'Right. So get in the bath when you've drunk your tea and sing out if you need me. Brunch about eleven.'

'Uhuh.' He'd leave it till they were eating to tell her about not going swimming.

Returning downstairs, Cressida removed the Sunday paper from the letterbox, then poured her tea and began to turn the pages. Her eyes fell, with a bit of a jolt even though she'd half expected it, on a photograph of herself on the courthouse steps. SURGERY VICTIM VOWS MONEY WILL HELP SON, ran the headline, and the report underneath made much of the not altogether pertinent fact that she had a son who was disabled. Immediately she reached for the kitchen scissors. She cut out the whole page, then screwed it up and put it in the wastebin. She'd given the same treatment to similar newspaper reports earlier in the week, anxious to keep them from Alex. Her trouble was, she thought, she would go blurting things out; she never foresaw consequences, just opened her great big gob and showed every Tom Dick and Harry what was there in her heart. Wearied by herself, because she was getting to an age when it began to look a bit late for the calm suave grown-up person she'd intended to turn into, she sighed and plonked down on the living room carpet with her mug of tea beside her and the newspaper spread out in front. Thus she read and drank and wound her hair round her fingers – until brought alert by bathroom sounds overhead. Whereupon she scrambled up and went halfway upstairs to check whether Alex had left the bathroom door open, as he was supposed to.

He hadn't. The door was shut. She ran quickly up to the landing and across to the bathroom. 'You are a bad lad,' she cried, turning the door handle.

'Get out! I'm all right.'

'But you mightn't be,' she objected, not looking in, but talking into a foot-wide gap. 'If anything happened and you called out I mightn't hear with the door closed. Use your head, Alex.'

Then she went next door into her bedroom, let the towelling robe fall, pulled her nightdress off over her head, and looked round for her underclothes.

From his seat in the bath Alex heard her go into her room. He became afraid to move. If he splashed too hard or dropped the soap, she'd imagine the seat had come unhooked or he'd lost his grip of the pulley; she'd come barging in. So he sat there, stiff and hunched. And decided it was possible he hated her.

But it was terrible of him really, even to let hate cross his mind. She was over-anxious because she loved him so much. That's what his gran said the time he confided in her. 'I used to worry my head off over your mother when she was younger,' she'd told him. 'Not a sensible thought in her head; nothing but idiotic fantasies about boys with guitars. But my goodness, she certainly stirred herself when you arrived on the scene. If ever a mother loved a son . . .' He owed his mother everything, as he'd once overheard her best friend Julie say. 'Don't tell me Alex would have done as well as he has without you fighting every inch of the way, Cressy.'

But all this love made her blind in an important respect: she failed to see that he was growing up, that he'd soon be a man. All right, so he had silly childish legs and hips. But inside his head he was powerful. He could do things she didn't begin to get the hang of. Every day he discovered more he could do on his computer. One day he'd make a pile of money out of it: you didn't need good legs to be a computer wizard. Not that it'd be any use telling his mother, she was too steamed up over her hopes and fears ever to listen properly. Or too stupid to understand. For instance, she knew the computer Uncle Jonathan had bought him was fitted with a modem; she knew Uncle Jonathan paid subscriptions for them both to be on the Internet so they could send messages to one another: she knew because he'd told her, and explained all the things it could do. Yet when he'd offered to use it for her benefit, to search out information that might help with her studies, she'd said, 'Hey, could you? That'd be brilliant, darling,' with a really soft look on her face, as if he were a little kid playing at being a space scientist and she was going along with it. She just didn't get it. But there was no end to the things she just didn't get. Like after her court case, she'd made good and sure they didn't watch the news on telly that evening. Naturally, soon as he was alone in his room he'd called up Ceefax, and there it was, everything she'd been blabbing to the reporters about her compensation award. *It's for my son. I never wanted the money for myself – except that it's justice, of course. I wanted peace of mind over my son's future. And now*

I've got it. Then followed a description, for the whole country to read, of how he'd been born handicapped and what he was like now. And the next day she'd actually removed a page from the morning paper. She was that thick! As if he couldn't find out just about anything simply by pressing the right keys.

It was time he got over to her that he wasn't a kid any more. He was fourteen and a half. He ought to have more of a say about what he wanted to do and what he didn't. Like not going swimming today. Yes, that'd be a start. He'd be firm with her, not whiny. Cool was how he'd be. 'Don't push me, Mum,' he'd tell her – like Jason said on the telly in an episode of *Home and Away*, and Jason's mum accepted, like a proper mother should whose son was nearly a man.

When two filled plates landed on the kitchen counter at which they normally ate their meals, Alex looked covertly from one to the other, comparing his portion with his mother's. While a mountain of baked beans rose from his slice of toast, its summit capped by a poached egg, her toast was sparsely covered. 'It's too much. Take some off,' he requested.

'Nonsense,' she contradicted him cheerfully. 'You'll find you need it. How many lengths have you set yourself to swim this afternoon?'

He hesitated, recognizing this as an opportunity, but held back by the pressing matter of an over-filled plate. 'I can't eat all those beans. It puts me off, a great heap like that.'

At once her expression altered. The last thing she wanted was to inhibit his appetite. She reached for his plate and spooned some of the beans back into the saucepan. 'I'll keep them warm. You might find room later.'

'Why don't you eat 'em?' he snarled.

'You don't sound very perky this morning, Alex. Didn't sleep too well?'

'Yes I did.'

'Just got out the wrong side?'

'No.'

'All right, all right.' She pulled a face at him.

He affected not to notice.

Silence settled. Cressida was unperturbed by it, having the satisfaction of seeing him eat steadily. The need to bring back the subject of swimming was engaging Alex's mind.

'That went down easily enough,' said Cressida, when he laid down his knife and fork. 'Now, how about the rest?'

'No *thanks*.'

She sighed. 'Suppose I'd better have them – waste not, want not.' But then she remembered her diet, and emptied the saucepan into the bin instead of onto her plate. He watched her, and read her mind, and felt superior. 'I nearly forgot,' she grinned. 'I'm slimming.'

'Mum, I don't think I'll . . .' He stopped, as his voice came out cracked and timid. After a moment he began again, speaking briskly: 'I'm not going swimming this afternoon.'

'What? Course you are, Alex. The minibus'll be here at half past one. Make sure you're ready for it. I suppose I'd better make a start on that essay.'

'I said I'm not going. Why don't you listen?'

In the middle of stacking used breakfast things on the draining board, she turned and confronted him. 'All right, what happened? You may as well tell me. Did someone upset you last week? Or' – her voice rose anxiously – 'did you hurt yourself? Oh Christ, I hope it wasn't horseplay, that's so dangerous in a pool; you'd think they'd be specially strict – I mean some of those kids are paraplegics. Now come on, Alex: what happened? Did someone push you under?'

'*Nothing happened*,' he yelled. 'I just can't be bothered to go swimming this afternoon, all right?'

Her jaw dropped; there was a short hard egress of breath. 'No, my lad, it's not *all right*. I haven't moved heaven and earth getting you into swimming for you to turn round and say you can't be bothered.' She paused, striving to stay calm. Inside she was feeling most uncalm, thinking of all the energy she'd sunk into convincing the authorities of Alex's needs; little dreaming she'd have to sink more into convincing *him*, into keeping him in line. It was too darn much. But there you go, she told herself, there can never be limits on what you'd do for someone you love; you just keep on till your very last gasp. 'Listen to me, love,' she cajoled. 'You need this exercise. You needs lots of regular supervised exercise. That's why nurse gives you therapy at school. But as well as that, because you're in a wheelchair most of the time, you need extra *vigorous* exercise. Dr Terence said swimming's the very best thing for your heart and lungs. You want to grow into a strong man, don't you?'

He saw the letters she had written; saw them sticking out of her typewriter and spread over the table; saw them stuffed into envelopes and arriving on desks. Shit. She was thrusting the same stuff at him, now. She just never gave up.

'Tell you what I'll do,' she beamed. 'I'll come with you. I'll ask the driver if there's room for a little extra one' – she giggled – 'I'll use my charms on him. If he won't play ball, maybe there's a bus I can get; or p'raps Mavis'd do me a special favour and run me in – she's such a good sort. Hey though, I was forgetting: I'm a woman of means. If there isn't a bus I can afford a taxi!'

His hands found the wheels of his chair. He spun away from her.

'Alex!'

He wheeled towards the stairs. She came hurrying after. Her hand reached and seized his arm.

'Get off! And get it into your head, I'm not going.'

It felt like the end of the world being threatened. A voice inside screamed the phrase she had written and uttered so often: *His swimming is crucial.* 'You jolly well are going! All the trouble I've been to, all the doctor said . . . If you think I'm going to stand by and let you ruin your health, you stupid little sod, you've another think coming!'

He heaved out of the chair and dropped onto the seat of the stair-lift. He pushed the button, then crossed his arms over his stomach as the chair moaned upwards with lumbering slowness. Lightning speed was what he desired, to shoot away from her.

She had clamped her hands to her sides to keep them from holding him back. Now she brought them up to her mouth – her foul mouth, she thought, recalling the way she'd just spoken.

'I really hate you,' he croaked as he rose, and the ugliness of his voice sounded to his ears all of a piece with the rest of him. He was glad he would not be on general view this afternoon.

She went into the sitting room and sat down heavily on the settee, where she checked her sobs long enough to mark the sounds overhead – the chair lift clicking into place at the top, its motor falling silent and the soft thud of Alex landing in the upstairs wheelchair, and the particular squeak of this chair as he propelled it into his bedroom. Finally she heard his door close. Upon which she gave in and buried her face in a cushion.

'Mum,' she wailed into the telephone, less than ten minutes later. 'Oh, Mum . . .'

'Cressida! What's happened? Is it Alex?'

'No. I mean, yes – but not like you mean. Mum, we had a blazing row, I called him . . . something awful.'

There was a short silence. 'I don't understand,' said Cressida's mother.

'He refused to go swimming. I went mad. I mean, after all that trouble I went to, he turns round and says he won't go.'

A pertinent question instantly formed in the mind of Cressida's mother. 'Which is it – that he doesn't want to go swimming this afternoon, or he wants to stop altogether?'

'What?' said Cressida. It was as if someone had blown a whistle: total silence fell in her head. 'Oh God,' she said eventually. 'See what you mean. Yeah, now you come to mention it, he said he wasn't going *this after-noon*. But it still seems wrong. I mean, it's no good if he only goes swimming when he feels like it. It needs to be regular. Dr Terence said "regular vigorous exercise".'

'Oh Cressida, do try not to be quite so . . . obsessive. You've done marvellous things for Alex, dear, but you have to understand he's not a little boy any more. I expect he feels a need to flex his muscles now and then, assert himself, show his independence.'

'But this is not a normal child, Mother. Alex has special needs.'

'Special needs don't stop him growing up, Cressida,' her mother retorted, not caring for the tone in which she'd just been addressed. 'If you don't ease up you're going to drive a wedge between you.'

'A wedge? Oh my God! You know what? I actually called him a stupid little sod.'

'A *what*?'

'Mum, I can't believe I'd do it.'

'Pull yourself together, dear.'

'I'd better go and say sorry.'

'I should leave him alone, if I were you. Just phone the swimming people and say he's a bit off colour. Then try and think of something other than Alex for a change. Now, will you be sensible?'

'I'll . . . try. Sorry, Mum.'

'Well, you've had a lot on your plate recently. I'll give you a ring during the week.'

'Yeah, thanks. Goodbye.'

'Goodbye, dear. And for goodness' sake buck up.'

Cressida wiped her nose on the back of her hand. Finding this inadequate, she went into the cloakroom and blew vigorously into lavatory paper. Then she returned to the telephone to ring up the Leisure Centre.

Alex in his room awaited events. It was hard to concentrate even on a computer game when he half expected his mother any minute, bursting in to work on him again having thought of a new argument. She might even phone Gran and get her to talk to him.

Then his back started to play up. A penalty of his body being out of proportion, with the upper torso much more developed than lower down, was a jarring pain that would strike his legs and the small of his back. He'd been taught exercises to alleviate this and stimulate the growth of muscles supporting the spine. He lay down on his bed, stomach first, and attempted part of the exercise routine. Eventually the pain eased off. He saw by his watch it was ten past one. If his mother was planning another attack she'd have to be quick. He hauled himself up and leaned his arms on the window sill above his bed, and watched through the muslin curtains the bend in the close round which the minibus arrived every Sunday. Dreading its appearance, telling himself that she wouldn't be so daft as to assume he'd change his mind and meekly appear soon as the doorbell rang, yet unable quite to believe in a mother who'd quit over a thing she passionately believed to be 'crucial' to his well-being, he waited out the fateful time. By twenty to two he knew she had made the necessary phone call. He knew he'd won. It was total victory.

No sooner had he congratulated himself than a wave of pain filled his lower back. His grip on the window sill faltered, his legs gave way; he twisted down on to the bed and lay cursing himself for having hung for ages in a position that was asking for trouble. Swimming, he recalled, was specially good for this crampy sort of pain; after a Sunday session in the pool he could be free of it for a couple of days or more. But at least he'd established a point. It was worth some discomfort, achieving that. He repeated this thought many times to himself.

Just after two o'clock, by which time Alex would understand she had no further intention of pressing him on the subject, Cressida made him a mug of tea and carried it upstairs. She knocked on his door and waited – not her usual habit – for permission to enter.

'Come in,' he called.

'Cup of tea, love?' she asked, going in. 'I've just made a pot . . . Oh' – her eyes found him on the bed – 'you OK?'

'Just doing my exercises.' He sat up, reached for the mug. 'Thanks.'

'Um, I'm really sorry, Alex, for, you know, slagging you off this morning. I'd give anything to take it back.'

''S all right.'

She hesitated: simultaneously reached out to touch him briefly and turned away. To her surprise her hand was caught. Just in time, he gripped her departing fingers, squeezed them one upon another. 'I love you, Mum,' he quickly mumbled.

'Love you too,' she said, and, because the moment felt too fragile to prolong, continued in the direction of the door. 'I'll probably go swimming next Sunday,' she heard as she reached it.

'Well,' she said, turning before leaving the room to wrinkle her face at him in a friendly fashion, 'see how you feel when the time comes.'

7

'I'd like you to pop into the Angela Symmonds for one or two tests,' Dr Page told Mrs Parminter on Monday morning. Having concluded his examination, he returned to his desk to consult his computer screen.

Mrs Parminter re-clothed herself hurriedly, mindful of other patients in the waiting room with appointments as overdue as had been her own. His remark put her into a fluster. She hated to have things sprung on her, and a visit to the cottage hospital she had not foreseen. What she had foreseen was a decent stab at diagnosis. 'But what is your opinion, Dr Page?' she demanded, sitting on the chair by the side of his desk.

He had started to tap on the computer keyboard, and this he continued to do as he replied: 'It could be one of a couple of things. These tests I have in mind might help us decide.'

'But in your judgement, what would you say is the likely cause?'

His fingers fell still, but he gazed at the screen for a few further seconds before turning on her a jolly look. 'It wouldn't surprise me if you'd simply fainted. You say you were bending down over a lengthy task in the garden. Although you don't remember doing so, very likely you stood up suddenly. The blood rushing from your head . . .'

'Yes, yes,' cut in Mrs Parminter. 'But I suppose an alternative possibility is a mild stroke.'

His jolly look vanished and he regarded her thoughtfully. 'That is a possibility. Which is why I'd like you to pop into the Angela . . .'

'But if it were such a thing what would you recommend?'

He turned again to the computer. 'You're not allergic to aspirin, are you?'

'Allergic? You mean does taking an aspirin upset me? No, not at all.'

'Well, as a matter of fact the very best thing might be to take half an aspirin night and morning.'

This came as a surprise to Mrs Parminter. 'Really? Ordinary aspirin?'

'Oh yes. Evidence suggests that the humble aspirin has wider benefits than we've ever supposed.'

Once she was used to the idea Mrs Parminter felt drawn to it. Its simplicity appealed to her. 'Well, an aspirin a day can't do any harm – I might as well get on with it. As for tests at the cottage hospital: it seems a shame to take up their time when there are so many people with troubling complaints.'

He smiled knowingly, as if he'd discovered her weakness. 'I realize it isn't everyone's cup of tea visiting a hospital, but they're a very friendly lot at the Angela Symmonds. Many of our senior patients go there regularly – get their feet attended to and so on, and those other bothersome tasks that are tricky to do for oneself as the years go by.'

'I'm quite capable of cutting my own toenails, thank you,' said Mrs Parminter, sitting tall. 'I've always been an active woman.' She decided to conclude the interview: she had kept her word to Mr Brightly, she had secured a practical piece of advice. 'Thank you for the aspirin suggestion. Most interesting. Most helpful.' Saying this, she rose to her feet and turned to the door.

Deciding that further mention of the Angela Symmonds Memorial Hospital would prove unfruitful, Dr Page merely urged her to contact him if a similar event occurred. Which she promised to do, and whereupon they wished one another good morning.

On her arrival home from the surgery, Mrs Parminter made herself a cup of coffee and carried it into the sitting room together with the morning's post which she had not previously had time to open. She sat with the envelopes in her lap and sipped her drink. Eventually she set the cup down on a little side table and opened the uppermost envelope. It contained a newsletter from a charity she supported, the charity devoted to promoting research into the disease that had prematurely deprived her of her husband. She studied and considered it in every detail. Her conclusion in the end was the one she invariably drew: that any progress made was confined to relieving symptoms; that a cure was no nearer at hand. The second item of correspondence did not detain her beyond its opening sentence, which asserted that her name had been entered into a draw and she was in line for a major prize. Tut-tutting – for she imagined such a letter in the hands of an impressionable and hard-up person – she tore it in two and set it aside. The final envelope bore the name and address of her bank. She was able therefore to correctly anticipate its contents: a sheet of paper on which cheques drawn and orders carried out were itemized. In a moment she would rouse herself. She would collect her cheque stubs and shop receipts from the bureau, she would take these and the bank statement to the table where she would sit in businesslike fashion comparing one with another until convinced of the accuracy of the bank's accounting. Some frightful cases of banking error were reported in the newspaper from time to time and she had resolved never to allow her own affairs to be thus incommoded. Meanwhile she reached for her cup. As she finished her coffee, her eyes rested on the sum of credit at the end of the balance sheet.

It was a large sum, one that got steadily larger as the months slipped by. Every now and then she gave instructions to transfer a portion of it from her current to her capital account. In this way the highest rate of interest on offer from the bank accrued from as much of her money as could be set aside. Even so she was aware that she was not doing as well as she might. A conversation with Mr Brightly had brought this home to her. In fact, after prolonged and careful consideration, she had asked Mr Brightly to invest a portion of her capital: and this he had done. So at least as far as this amount was concerned she could be consoled that she was doing better than bank rate. The rest must stay as it was, as her late husband had arranged. The charity might lose as a result, but sentiment would not permit her to alter her husband's arrangements to any greater extent.

Her feeling was that it was John's money, that she was in charge of it due to an accident of fate. Though as a matter of historical record, a significant portion of their joint wealth came from her inheritance. The money she received on her mother's death had enabled the purchase of a very grand house in Edgbaston, two of whose rooms were turned into consulting and waiting rooms to serve a growing band of private patients. But John's money had been striven for; hers had merely arrived. Perhaps it was this that informed her feeling that the money was morally his: she remembered too well how a life had been dedicated to long hours of arduous work; and if she had ever forgotten, letters arriving from the Royal College of Orthopaedic Surgeons with details of the pension under which she benefited would soon have reminded her. And perhaps it was strengthened by the unfairness of John's not living to enjoy much of the retirement he'd earned. The feeling that it was really his money had led to her decision to bequeath everything to the charity funding research into his illness, rather than to her comfortably-off nephew.

Mrs Parminter well remembered the evening when the idea dawned that it would be nice if the charity were to gain some little extra benefit as a direct result of her stewardship. It would be nice to mark the years of her widowhood in this way, so that they would have been lived positively not passively. The conversation with Mr Brightly had prompted this idea, a conversation that she herself had initiated with a request for information on the workings of the business world. He had obliged her with the most vivid explanation. Never before had she understood that businesses and industry depend on the decisions of ordinary people to invest. She saw what a poor look-out there would be for the national economy if everyone with savings ventured no further than the conventional institutions. And a cartoon picture loomed in her mind of the sort that often appeared in the *Daily Telegraph*: the poor little country creased in the middle from a dead weight being attached to it; and a label on the weight with the inscription *Parminter*.

At the time she had merely thanked Mr Brightly for elucidating what she had always considered a dry subject. But she'd continued to think. She thought about his clients and felt them to be uncommonly favoured: it had been plain from the light in his eyes when he referred to them that Mr Brightly put the same passionate energy into the charge of their money as he put into the charge of souls. She had thought of her capital sum, and recalled that this had been added to as a result of the difference between the selling price of the grand house in Edgbaston and purchase price of The Gables in Chedbury. This addition, it occurred to her, could in all conscience be regarded as hers. Finally, she'd become attracted to the idea of making good sense of the years of her widowhood. If she were to entrust a sum to Mr Brightly to invest, then these years would stand in their own right: the extra gained by such an investment would be a sign of this.

'I wonder, Mr Brightly, if you would consider taking me on as a client,' she had surprised him by saying on the next of his evenings off.

He had looked at her in astonishment, taken aback, she understood, by the months that had elapsed since their one and only conversation on the topic.

'Most certainly,' he had said when he was recovered. 'If that is your wish, I'd be delighted.'

'In a modest way, you understand. A matter of forty thousand pounds to be precise.' (For that was the difference between the sum realized by the sale of the Edgbaston house and that given for The Gables.)

He had found her precision amusing. But when his laughter died he'd declared that he had just the scheme for her – presuming it was capital gain she was after and not income.

'Exactly so,' she'd confirmed. 'I've been thinking over what you said, and I can see it makes sense to do as well as I can for my legatee.'

Very soon afterwards she'd signed the relevant papers. From that time to this he had given her progress reports. It was a boost to her to know she had ventured independently into a world she and John had understood little. And it was heartening to be linked tangibly to Mr Brightly, to be a member of the favoured group of clients . . .

Her eyelids had drooped and now closed. A balance sheet floated by, swooped, swirled, zoomed up close, then turned into blackness. A pair of strong male hands came from the blackness, cupping something precious that she couldn't quite see. They were Mr Brightly's hands, of course, for there were his shirt cuffs with the oval links. And his hands, of course, must be holding treasure. Very likely it was her treasure . . . But before she could be sure, the image was replaced by an enormous bedspread, which in turn was revealed to be covering the lower portion of her father's body. Her father was sitting up in bed looking at her. 'Your mother claims I've turned sentimental,' he barked from the corner of his stiff mouth. 'Pah. Rubbish. I've always had feelings, but I locked 'em away.' Then his arms in their pyjama sleeves thrust towards her. She backed off. 'Locked 'em away,' his voice continued, pursuing her as she retreated.

Agitation brought her awake. What? Why? 'Bother!' she said aloud, as her eyes focused on the bank statement and she recalled she had yet to check it. The chore would now have to wait until this afternoon, for at two o'clock Mrs O'Connor would arrive to clean the upper half of the house, and it was first necessary to do some tidying up.

Mrs O'Connor arrived promptly, and after the usual pleasantries took herself upstairs together with dusters and vacuum cleaner. Mrs Parminter settled at last to the task of checking her bank statement.

'There's a cup of tea for you, Mrs O'Connor,' she called up the stairwell when she had satisfied herself that the bank had correctly tabulated her outgoings and when Mrs O'Connor had been plying her duster for over an hour.

Mrs O'Connor came downstairs and rinsed her hands under the kitchen tap. Seated at the kitchen table, Mrs Parminter poured out. She had already placed a plate of chocolate digestives on the table, a biscuit Mrs O'Connor was partial to.

'Well, we've done it,' Mrs O'Connor announced, sitting herself down. 'Gone and booked that cruise I told you about, paid our deposits. We sail from Southampton on July the tenth next year, arrive back four weeks later.'

'How wonderful,' said Mrs Parminter, who had never taken a cruise in her life and had no regrets on this score.

'Yes. I said to Patrick, it'll be the holiday of a lifetime. Now dear, how're you going to manage? Will I mention it to our Gail that you could do with a hand?'

Mrs Parminter made a non-committal sound. She hardly liked to declare she could make do for four weeks, for fear of Mrs O'Connor's taking her duties at The Gables less seriously in future. On the other hand it seemed churlish to raise difficulties in face of the holiday of a lifetime. In any case, July of next year was so very distant that Mrs Parminter could not rouse herself to think seriously of it.

'Tell you what,' said Mrs O'Connor. 'Will I tell her you'd be obliged by a good going over, say at the end of the second week? I dare say you could flick a duster round yourself the rest of the time.'

'That would be most kind.'

'It's settled then.'

Mrs Parminter had no doubt that the matter had been settled to Mrs O'Connor's satisfaction before the subject was raised. With Mrs O'Connor it was a constant struggle for the upper hand. She thought of the many domestic servants she had employed during her lifetime, never before with any ambiguity as to who was in charge. While Mrs O'Connor described details of her cruise, Mrs Parminter's mind flew back to former times. When she was first married they had employed a live-in cook, a Mrs Fenn, of whom she had become fond and come to address with affection as Fenny. She remembered the tears that had been shed when Fenny departed. Tears they had shed together, for the parting was imposed on them by Mrs Fenn's being called to work in a munitions factory. At the same time and by the same means she had also lost her charwoman. And then had begun her own war work – which was the way she had liked to regard her forced plunge into cooking and washing and cleaning. She'd dressed for the part in a pair of John's old trousers and an old jumper, and had wrapped her hair in a scarf tied turban fashion with a knot on top. Looking back, the sense of sacrifice and importance she'd derived from tackling household chores seemed quite ridiculous. But it must have been tiring, she supposed, the tall Edwardian house in Solihull to clean, the meals to cook for a husband and child, their clothes to wash, patients to soothe, the clerical work she'd been landed with when John lost his secretary to the war effort, and the make do and mend that went on.

Mrs O'Connor set down her cup.

Mrs Parminter braced herself. The predictability of their exchanges was sometimes almost more than she could bear. 'Another cup, Mrs O'Connor.'

'Oo, not for me, dear, no. One cup is my rule.'

Gently, Mrs Parminter sighed.

'That reminds me,' Mrs O'Connor cried when she was halfway to the door. She adopted an expression she considered suitable for the issuing of mild rebukes. 'I see you've forgotten to call the plumber again. The upstairs lav still doesn't flush properly.'

'No I haven't,' Mrs Parminter told her, lying with spirit. 'Mr Edwards is very booked up at the moment. He'll come as soon as he can.'

'You want to get in Gerry Weeks. He made a great job of our Gail's central heating.'

'Thank you, Mrs O'Connor, but I prefer to wait for Mr Edwards.'

'Mm. Well I'd better get on.'

Mrs Parminter washed the used china and put it away, and hoped she would remember to phone Mr Edwards before Mrs O'Connor's next visit on Thursday. Why was it excusable to let things slip one's mind at forty years of age, but reprehensible at eighty? People would deny this was so, but Mrs Parminter knew better. She collected her newspaper and went to read it in the garden.

The paper told her of wicked things happening in Bosnia, hopeless things happening in the Sudan, irritating things happening at home. After a while she closed her eyes on these things, and began to drift into a different garden, the garden she had known in the early years of her marriage in wartime Solihull. She was sitting with a cup of chicory-based coffee beside her, snatching a few minutes' respite from her morning labours. Some planes roared by overhead; her hand rose to shade her eyes as she strained to count them. The newspaper at her side had small square maps on the front page with arrows purporting to describe war manoeuvres. Gradually she became aware of someone's presence. Robert was standing about three feet away from her, in short grey trousers which ended just above his knees, a Viyella check shirt and Startrite sandals. He held to his body a plane modelled from balsa wood. Speaking solemnly, while regarding her from under his eyebrows, he said: 'I like you with hair best.'

Her hands flew up. She found she was still wearing the turban. Quickly her fingers untied it and set her crimped hair free. 'There. Is that better?'

He nodded.

'Then don't I deserve a kiss?'

Dropping the plane, he hurled himself against her and buried his face in her neck. Her arms went tightly round him, she could feel . . .

But no, she couldn't feel any small body. Her arms were empty. She opened her eyes wide and took in her Chedbury garden. In which she was utterly alone.

The phone rang in Cressida's house late that evening. She feared hearing Baz's voice and answered cautiously. 'Yes?'

'Hi Cressy, it's me,' said her friend. 'Did you phone at the weekend?'

'Oh, Julie. Yeah.'

'I guessed it was you saying "Um", then changing your mind.'

'Well I hate speaking into those answering machines. You say something wrong then you're stuck with it.'

'We went to Paul's folks for the weekend; came back late last night. Everything OK? No more trouble from Baz, I hope?'

'No, and I'm not too bothered any more. I reckon I know how to handle him.'

'Right. How's Alex?'

'A bit off, as a matter of fact. We had a blazing row.'

'You didn't!'

'Did. He refused to go swimming. No special reason, just didn't feel like it.'

'The little monkey. After all the trouble you've been to.'

'I know,' said Cressida, much cheered by her friend's response.

'Honestly, kids; they're all the same. Remember how Chloë pestered for a violin, and we paid out all that lolly? Well, she's jacked it in. She's got a new best friend who does ballet dancing – so you can guess the rest.'

Cressida groaned in sympathy. 'Alex did concede, after we'd made it up, that he'd probably go swimming next Sunday.'

'Oh brilliant. What're you expected to do – faint with gratitude?'

It was always a tonic talking to Julie, thought Cressida, laughing.

'How're you diddlin' apart from Alex? I trust you've been celebrating your winnings properly. Been out with anyone?'

'Er, not *out*. But I've got someone coming for a meal on Friday.'

'Really? You mean you're cooking for him already? Things must be advanced. Why haven't I heard about this?'

'Because it's not the usual . . . I mean, I've known him quite a while, but sort of impersonally. Then last time he was round I detected a shift. I mean, I fancy him like mad, but I wasn't sure he'd be interested. In fact I'd made up my mind he wasn't likely to be. But, as I say, last time there were signs . . . Anyway, he said yes to dinner pretty promptly, so there you are.'

'So long as it's not your money he's after – only kidding. What's he like? What does he do?'

'He's a lawyer,' came the reply, Cressida having decided for some reason against mentioning his financial interests. 'And he's amazingly tall and incredibly handsome. He's what you might call the distinguished type.'

'Hell, Cressy, you'll have to pull your socks up.'

'Don't be rotten. But the real knee-trembler is the way

he looks at you – his eyes go all twinkly and they bore right in . . .'

'Oo, stop it! Is Alex all right with him?'

'Yes. I mean, don't get me wrong, Julie, this guy is incredibly proper. If it wasn't for the way he has of looking at me . . .'

'But you're aiming to loosen him up, right?'

Cressida sighed. 'I most certainly am.'

'So what will you give him to eat?'

'That's what I was going to ask you last night. You're the expert. What d'you suggest?'

They discussed food and menus, and Julie advised Cressida to keep things simple, not to be all strung up over the cooking and be too exhausted for more important matters. Cressida agreed with this. By the time she replaced the receiver she was feeling, not so much that a good time lay ahead, but that a good time had just been enjoyed.

A little while later the thought occurred that she might have overstated the evidence for Richard being interested in her. But she excused herself on the grounds that every person requires a dream – it was a well-known fact. And sometimes even far-fetched fancies come blissfully true.

8

When Mrs Gloria Maskill opened her front door to him on Tuesday, a surprised expression leapt to the face of Mr Brightly. He felt the expression arrive and made a calculated decision to leave it there. 'I see that I've called at an inconvenient moment,' he said, eyeing in a pointed way her flimsy scarlet wrap that was held together by a half-knotted sash. 'Forgive me, but I thought I was to call on my way home from the office. Around six o'clock,' he added, exposing his watch. 'That was my understanding of the arrangement. However, another time perhaps . . .'

A white arm shot from its satiny scarlet sleeve, and a white hand with scarlet fingernails seized his forearm. 'Don't give me that pompous vicar stuff, Dick,' snarled Gloria, yanking him over the threshold. 'I had a bath, and was too idle to get dressed afterwards. I don't plan to seduce you, so you can stop looking sniffy.'

'I'm relieved to hear it,' he said.

She had released him and was leading him into a large sitting room full of enormous and very low settees, long low tables, and squat lamps. On reaching the room's centre she turned. 'Drink?' she asked, jerking her head to one side and causing her long dark hair to swing over and the scarlet wrap to expose an even wider expanse of curvy white flesh.

'No thank you. I like to keep a clear head for business.'

'Very commendable. Coffee, then? Tea?'

'A cup of tea would be welcome.'

101

She moved off towards a second doorway. 'Fruit tea? Herb? Indian? China?'

'Indian please.'

'Shan't be a sec,' she called as she disappeared. 'Make yourself comfy.'

Not planning to seduce him, eh? Irritated and bored, he sank into the only single armchair in the room, thereby ignoring the pointed signal of papers arrayed over a low table directly in front of a sumptuous settee. Gloria Maskill was a type of woman he strongly disliked. Oh yes, she was beautiful: that is, if he were shown her photograph and those of other people during one of those idiotic games they had on television and asked to select the correct label for each portrait, *beautiful* would be the label he would search for to place beneath Mrs Maskill's likeness. She had one of those magazine faces which in every particular approximated to beauty. But to his mind she was not attractive; there was nothing about her to excite the imagination or arouse feelings of tenderness, and her assumption that were she so minded he would be hard put to resist her was an insult. He felt annoyed all over again with his wife for landing him in this tedious position. He had better things to do than play silly games with a vain and idle woman – for little or no profit, if his hunch as to the state of her finances and her current ambitions didn't prove wide of the mark.

'Oh,' she said, re-entering the room with a tea tray. 'What are you doing over there? I've laid everything out on that table. Well, we can drink our tea first, I suppose. Milk and sugar?'

He got up at once, having no wish to prolong matters, and went to sit on the settee behind the paper-strewn table. 'Just milk, thank you. I wasn't sure I had your permission to see your papers.'

'Isn't that what you've come for?' She brought his cup over to the settee, her bright red mouth twisting sardonically.

He took the cup and thanked her, and waited apprehensively as she went to collect her own tea then came behind the table to sit beside him. She crossed her legs, and a bare white knee protruded; and possibly a portion of bare white thigh, but with his eyes fastened on the papers before him he couldn't be sure.

'Now you'll have to explain,' he said. 'Where do we start?' He'd give her until half past six and not a moment beyond, he promised himself.

Mrs Gloria Maskill, it eventually transpired, was not as silly as she appeared. The facts of her divorce settlement as she related them caused him no surprise – the capital sum, the expected income, her ex-husband's retention of a fifty per cent interest in this house. But then she mentioned a nest egg, and intimations came to Mr Brightly of an evening that might not go to waste after all. 'I'm assuming,' she said, 'that sharing confidences with one's financial adviser is like sharing them with a priest? I mean, the same rules apply, you'll treat our tête-à-tête like the confessional?' It was no moment, he decided, to put her straight on the limitations of a lay reader's role. 'Absolutely,' he confirmed. So she relaxed and expanded. The nest egg was the bulk of an inheritance that had come to her long before Mitch Maskill entered her life. She had therefore never felt the need to share with him knowledge of its existence. It had been her own little secret – and must so remain if her settlement was to go unchallenged.

He made understanding and encouraging noises.

She stretched out an arm and brought forth a building society book. 'I was young and hadn't a clue when I came into the money. So I bunged it in here. Sometimes I thought vaguely about stocks and shares and so on, but when Mitch came on the scene it seemed like too much hassle.'

'Do you mind if I jot down a few figures?' he asked, taking a notebook from his breast pocket.

'Go ahead.'

'Mm,' he murmured as he scribbled. 'Uhum. Ah, yes.'

'So you see, darling, why I jumped at the chance

103

when Ginny volunteered your expertise. It's well known that you're an absolute wiz: Betty Fielding can't praise you enough. Though, of course, mine is only a modest nest egg.'

'All the more reason to nurture it carefully.' By now he was feeling cheerful indeed, having calculated that it would remain a nest egg for the foreseeable future, her other assets being more than adequate to sustain a middle-aged woman in pampered luxury. He closed the notebook and put it away. 'As a matter of fact I believe I know of the very scheme.'

'You do?'

'Indeed. Let me look into it, and I'll get back to you in a day or so. Yes, looking to the long term, I believe we can be very creative with such a useful little sum.'

'Oh that is great news,' cried Gloria, her eyes shining. 'I could kick myself for leaving it so long.'

'No need to do that. You've plenty of time.'

'Well, I'm relieved to have got off my backside at last. I've often said to myself: Christ, Gloria, you ought to do something about that dosh Aunt Miriam left you. And now I have. I can sit back and feel virtuous knowing brilliant Dick Brightly's got it all in hand.'

He smiled, and allowed his eyes to meet hers, now that he was feeling well disposed towards her.

She took this for a signal that they had passed onto a more intimate plane, and settled back, lolling her head against the upholstery, and regarded him from under her lowered lashes. 'Tell me, Dick,' she invited huskily, 'how did such a sensual man come to take up religion? And don't try denying you're sensual. You have the most suggestive eyes I ever beheld. Want to know something? When a woman's dealt a look like the one I'm getting from you right now, it does something to her. She melts, Dick. Melts.'

'What a tease you are, Gloria. Heavens, is that the time? I promised Ginny I wouldn't be late. She's rehearsing tonight.'

As he struggled to rise from the low and squashy

104

settee, he saw her pouty lips jut sulkily. 'I'm so glad you think I may be able to help you,' he said, by way of reminding her that a few seconds since she'd been very contented. 'I'll call by next week – on Monday if that's convenient.'

'Okey-doh,' she said philosophically. 'Yes, Monday'll be fine.' She walked ahead of him and opened the front door. 'Thanks a million, Dick. I'm truly grateful.'

'A pleasure,' he told her, smiling but avoiding eye contact. And against his former expectations, returned to his car a happy man.

'I've something to show you,' said Mrs Parminter. Mr Brightly was over at the sideboard pouring out measures of whisky. She reached into a box on a low table beside her chair. 'I was turning out a chest on the landing earlier, when I came across some old photographs.'

The sound of these words was very stark to her. 'What a fib, Clara Millicent!' a nannying voice in her head would admonish whenever, as a child, she departed from the strict truth. She had long ago learned to suppress this voice but it had had its effect, and therefore she was vividly aware that *came across some old photographs* ill accorded with her obsessive search for them.

Since Monday afternoon when she was visited by an image of her young son as she dozed in the garden, she had hunted high and low. She longed to hold such an image before her eyes, to dwell on it. She knew there were some photographs somewhere but not, she discovered, in any of the obvious places – a drawer of her bureau or John's old desk or her bedside cabinet. When she rested from her searches, or lay down to sleep, her mind pursued the problem. And when she rose up the search resumed: through a trunk in the attic, through a chest of drawers that had once been Robert's, through John's old briefcase, through a tallboy in one of the spare bedrooms. Then this morning she hit on the idea of the chest, and there inside beneath folded blankets had discovered an old Basildon Bond box secured by rubber bands which proved to contain the snaps she was after. Over the landing carpet she spread them out. Robert at about four years of age stood in the sun and squinted back at her, or frowningly posed with an over-large cricket bat, or laughed uproariously during a tug-of-war over a slipper with a Dalmatian puppy. Some of the snaps she'd thought of showing to Mr Brightly, and when she replaced the photographs in the box she'd left those on top. Now as he brought over her drink, she handed him the ones she'd selected.

'Robert as a youngster,' she told him. 'They are surprisingly sharp, considering they were taken with our old box Brownie.'

He settled down to examine them. The child's face was new to him. Robert as a student was the Robert he was familiar with, for the photograph which hung on the wall above Mrs Parminter's bureau was taken when Robert was at medical school. Now he studied a chubby child in knickerbockers and Fair Isle jumper, with low-swept hair and wide-open eyes. 'Quite a serious little chap,' he commented. 'Aha, but not here – he looks very merry in this one.'

She nodded: 'The one with the dog. Yes, but on the whole he was a serious child. He'd come out with the funniest things. I remember once I was sitting in the garden taking a breather from the housework, when I looked up from the paper and found I was being examined. There he stood – with such a solemn expression. Then: "I like you with hair best," he said – as if on a whim I'd snatched off my hair and set it aside. Yet I'd only wrapped a scarf round my head to save it from the dust. A funny turn of phrase. So . . . uncertain he looked.'

'But you know, children can be seriously upset by a change in the appearance of someone they love. I remember Harriet squealing with horror . . . Ginny was in a play at the time and had to wear some complicated make-up. She was practising putting it on at home one day when Harriet came in from her nursery school. She called hello to her mother – who turned and—'

'Oh dear, yes! And now I come to think of it, I hadn't long been covering my hair in that way: I'd only recently lost my cleaner to the war effort. So it still looked quite strange to Robert, I suppose. Poor little fellow! And to think I imagined it was his quaint way of saying a turban didn't suit me. I ripped it off at once, of course, but . . .'

Her voice trembled and died. He looked up sharply and saw a spasm briefly take her face. Suddenly he was less sanguine about her. He'd been delighted when he arrived this evening to learn she had been given a clean bill of health: apparently the doctor attributed her fall to giddiness brought on by bending down too long. But now Mr Brightly doubted whether he'd heard the whole story. He had nothing specific to go on, but somehow she struck him as less robust. He lowered his eyes again to the photographs.

'Oh I say, isn't this you?' He rose and took one of the snaps to her for confirmation.

Looking at it, she felt cross. She saw what had happened: the image of Robert in the foreground had so claimed her attention that she'd been distracted from noting her own in a deckchair behind him. 'Yes it is,' she admitted grudgingly.

He took the photograph nearer the light. In those days she had not worn spectacles. Her eyes were clear and large under straight dark brows. 'Robert took after you,' he said eventually.

'Yes, most people thought so. But I saw a lot of John in him.'

He returned to his seat and began to look through the photographs again, making further comments. It seemed strange to be talking of a child who, if he'd lived, would be his senior by four or five years. She sipped her whisky and told him a little of what her life had been like during the war years. When she asked him to refill their glasses, he handed the photographs back to her. 'Thank you for showing me.'

She placed them in the box and waited to receive her drink. 'Now, tell me the news,' she demanded. 'What has been happening? Did you know, by the way, that the O'Connors are booked to go on a cruise next year?'

Cressida, in a plain black dress of thin velvety material, looked beautiful tonight. Mr Brightly told her so. Then, as Cressida blushed and Alex ran quick eyes over his mother, he thought his opinion ought to have been kept to himself. He was not normally given to imprudent and personal remarks. The truth was he had been caught off guard. It was Alex in his wheelchair who had pulled open the front door. Cressida was discovered standing in the centre of the sitting room with a bag of nuts in one hand and a wooden dish in the other. 'Oh dear, there's always *some*thing I go and forget,' were her first words – which he scarcely heard, stunned as he was by the impact of a svelte blonde with her hair piled elegantly on top of her head. He was particularly uneasy as to Alex's reaction. What did that thoughtful appraisal mean?

If their guest only knew, Alex was gratified. The remark confirmed his own view – if in overstated form. He'd remarked earlier that she looked nice when she came into his room changed and ready for the evening ahead. 'You look nice, Mum,' he'd told her. Though really the niceness he saw was only relative: he liked her best wearing her pretty blue dress, with her hair newly washed and flowing out, and hardly any make-up. But his feeling was, that the way she had got herself up for a guest this evening was a whole lot better than the way she got herself up for other guests on other evenings. Specially for a gang of students who sometimes came round, people she was friendly with at college – a couple of women and three or four men, all several years younger than she was. The way she'd looked that last time they were here made his blood run cold – the tiny skirt stretched round her bottom and thighs, the baggy top. Mortified he'd been, and had shut himself up in his room and refused admittance to Dave, who had come specially (his mother claimed) to view Alex's computer. (Dave was a student of information technology.) So Alex had wondered and half dreaded how she'd appear tonight. He'd known she wouldn't be content with the blue dress, not if the fuss she'd made over the right wine and the right food and the house being clean were anything to go by: no, it was obvious she'd go to unusual lengths over her appearance too. So when she came into his room earlier he'd felt relieved and grateful; and when Mr Brightly expressed approval just now, a second look at his mother revealed a commendable effect that he'd missed straight off: that she actually looked properly grown-up. His respect for her soared. Crumbs, she might even end up getting a sensible sort of man to marry her, a man with something about him, like Mr Brightly here (though a younger and single version, of course) – instead of some layabout gink of a student, as he'd lately begun to fear.

Cressida's delight at Mr Brightly's compliment had been instantly spoiled by misgivings over her son's scrutiny. But then their guest produced a present for Alex, and Alex's evident satisfaction with this allowed her again to breathe easily. She placed a dish of nuts on the coffee table and bent down to retrieve a few she'd spilled. As she did so she noted the unrestricting nature of her dress – a crushed velour sheath from Marks and Spencer's. The one thing she hadn't liked about this dress was its label, showing size 16; but the zip on a size 14 refused to close round her (a bitter blow after a week's solid self-denial), and the slightly larger dress did have a gratifying slimming effect. So she took the size 16 home, carefully snipped off its offensive label, then checked once more how the dress looked on. Before her wardrobe mirror, moving this way and that, she saw that her body's ability to shift independently of its silky covering was a very sexy phenomenon. Whatever the label stated, she felt she was a size smaller in principle.

'Will you have a glass of wine, Richard?' she asked as she straightened up from her nut-gathering. When he said he would, she went into the kitchen to open the bottle of Chablis that had been such a trouble to purchase. The self-service grocery in Chedbury didn't stock Chablis, so she'd had to go specially to Stratford – not having the confidence to offer him any wine other than the type he'd brought her last week and presumably found acceptable. She filled two wine glasses, and one tumbler with orange juice for Alex. It hit her afresh, as she put the drinks on the tray, the remark he'd made when he arrived: 'Why Cressida, you look beautiful this evening!' And the way he'd stared . . . God, he must really fancy her! A thrill squeezed her stomach. She steadied herself with a deep breath. Alex had already been made alert, she recalled; they must be careful not to give anything away in front of him. But it was great that Richard and Alex were hitting it off. How clever of Richard to bring Alex a computer magazine. The evening could not have been given a better start.

'Let you and me wash up, Alex. Cressida has earned a rest.'

Cressida protested. So Alex and Richard decided it would be all right if she stored away the washed china and cutlery.

Cressida returned to the dining room to remove the table mats. There was no doubting the meal's success – despite her having dumped a slice of chocolate mousse onto the tablecloth instead of Richard's plate. Rather than feeling embarrassed and clumsy, she like the others had collapsed laughing. Richard had been the first to recover. He'd insisted on scooping up that same slice for himself and then serving her and Alex – which was perhaps just as well, with the hostess reduced to a helpless jelly and tears spurting out of her eyes. It had been clear from the start that Alex was enjoying himself. Prior to Richard's decree about the washing up, he'd offered to show Richard the computer game he was in the process of inventing. Alex did not issue invitations to just anybody. She returned to the kitchen and stood in the doorway admiring the sight of Richard with his hands in the sink and his shirt sleeves rolled up and her dingy apron covering his front, and Alex reaching from his wheelchair for washed and drained china to polish. Oh, it was a brilliant evening! Grinning and humming to herself, she gathered up plates and bowls and bore them off. How cosy she felt; everything so natural and friendly. And how different was this son of hers tonight to the sulky child who'd wheeled himself to the chair lift as soon as her friends from college arrived one evening a couple of months ago, and later refused to let one of them into his bedroom to see his computer. It had really hurt the way Alex had shown her up. Not to mention his snarling comments afterwards. All right, so maybe they're not my ideal friends, she'd wanted to shout back, but at least they're fun and they're company – things I've been sadly deprived of, stuck in with you all these years, you ungrateful little toad. Don't you understand it's been bloody lonely? It was the truth and a fair defence; though of course she hadn't told him anything of the sort, she'd have sooner died. But why was she raking over that grief now? Wasn't it just lovely basking in Richard's company with an approving and responsive Alex? A treat was what it was. Bliss.

When Alex and Richard went upstairs to try out the computer game, Cressida followed and sat herself down on Alex's bed. Finding scant interest in what was happening on screen, she turned her mind to the subject of Mrs Brightly. So busy with her own life that she neglected her husband, was Cressida's hunch. She'd had a chance to examine Mrs Brightly on two occasions: once, laughing with a crowd of friends on the vicarage lawn at the church fête, and the other time at the Christmas bazaar, again surrounded by cronies. Mrs Brightly had not cast a look in the direction of Cressida and Alex – which was quite unusual, because most of those gracious types liked to bestow a kindly smile as Cressida pushed Alex by in his wheelchair. Mrs Brightly, thought Cressida, looked the sort of woman who would make her nervous. It was amazing when you came to think of it, that such a person could be married to a man who produced the exact opposite effect. With Richard you couldn't help but relax and start feeling good about yourself. Nevertheless, married they were. And since Richard was also religious there was not too much hope for Cressida in the conventional sense. So pooh to convention! This was a man, she felt, who lacked a woman who was properly appreciative. And here was she, Cressida Reece, positively bursting with appreciation, and with lashings and lashings of love to give, soon as he gave her the signal.

'Alex, old chap, I think you're tired,' Mr Brightly said quietly. For the boy had gone very pale.

Behind them, Cressida jumped to her feet. 'Gosh yes, it's after ten! He's usually zonked out by half nine at the latest. Aren't you, Alex?'

Alex sheepishly agreed that he was.

'Bedtime,' Mr Brightly pronounced. 'Thank you, Alex, for showing me that. I don't know – all this mental stimulation and such good company and a lovely meal – I haven't enjoyed myself so well in a long time.'

'I'll show you another of my games some time, if you like,' Alex offered. 'I had this brilliant idea last week: it'll take me ages to work out, but it could be a winner.'

'I'd like to see it very much. We've a young genius on our hands, I do believe,' Mr Brightly told Cressida.

'I'll be back in a tick, love,' she promised her son.

'It's OK, Mum, I can manage.'

Mr Brightly and Cressida went down to the sitting room.

'He wearies so suddenly,' said Cressida. 'Collapses like a pricked balloon. I should've kept my eye on the time.'

'My fault, I fear.'

'Gosh no, not at all. Sit down – please.'

'Just for five minutes. It's getting late for me, too.'

'Alex really adored showing you his game. Which was why he didn't notice he was getting tired. Never mind' – she made a visible attempt to stop fretting – 'after a good night's sleep he'll be good as new.'

He smiled across at her. Hours ago her hair had begun to unravel, to trail hank by hank down her neck and back. During dinner she'd become mildly tipsy, he suspected; or maybe it was just that she was thoroughly enjoying herself – she was a very jolly girl. She'd laughed so much at one point that tears had run, which she'd unconsciously rubbed at and given her eyes muddy mascara wings. But disarray hadn't marred her charm. Rosy from the wine, she was a big, beautiful, jolly young woman.

But now she'd become less jolly. Her anxiety for her son was plain to see, and it tugged at his heart. He recalled the time he'd watched her in the rain attempting to shield her disabled son, and the desire this had sprung in him to render her assistance, to make a difference to her life. And he recalled also the method by which he planned to effect this assistance. 'I suppose you haven't yet had time to study those papers I left with you?'

'Oh, yes I have. It was really interesting. Mind you, I've got a few queries, there were one or two things I wasn't quite clear on. Do you think we could go over them another evening?'

'Of course.' He reached into the breast pocket of his jacket for a diary.

'As soon as you like,' she offered. 'Or if you're all tied up we could save it till next Friday.'

He looked at her quizzically.

'Your evening off,' she reminded him.

113

'Ah – of course.' He put the diary away, not able to recall repeating to Cressida the jocular term he employed to amuse Mrs Parminter, but concluding that obviously he had. 'Friday it shall be,' he agreed.

'Great. And I'll go over the papers again. I'll make notes,' she promised.

In the tiny hallway he could think of no more appropriate leave-taking than to kiss her hand. This he did, after expressing his thanks for a lovely evening and a splendid meal. Then, addressing her steady gaze, he smiled and bade her goodnight.

'Goodnight,' she whispered, as he stepped outside.

When he reached the pavement he heard her door softly close.

9

In the weeks following the signing of papers concerning the deployment of her nest egg, Mrs Gloria Maskill, while careful to keep the sum involved close to her chest, made very free with Mr Brightly's role in the matter. More than satisfied she was, she declared. Her mind was completely at peace. It was the most terrific good fortune, she told her friends, to have landed the services of Dick Brightly. The so-called financial advisers who usually called at a house were never truly independent: it always turned out they were plugging some outfit or other. But with Dick it was different. A bit of this, a bit of that, and constant judicious shifting about, was Dick's recipe for success: a process that was far too time-consuming for the ordinary punter to manage, who in any case would lack the requisite skill. But lucky little Gloria could leave it to Dick. Piece of cake, darlings, she said.

After her recent divorce, it was balm to her soul to be in a position to boast, to rub it in that she'd secured an advantage. Particularly in front of Deirdre Houseman. For with Deirdre Houseman, various friends had let it be known, Mitch Maskill had found solace that first time their marriage came under strain. (Actually it was never clear there'd been more than tea and sympathy between them. Hell, Deirdre was a clerk with a haulage firm before her husband made his pile. Bit of a scrubber, really. Mitch would've had to be desperate. But it had been galling enough just hearing the rumours.) So she invited several of the girls round, made sure of Deirdre's

115

attention, and let it be known how very pleased she was with life, post divorce; how solid her future now looked. Because, no doubt about it, Dick knew his onions. One had only to observe his and Ginny's style of living to appreciate that. Of course, she sighed, squinting at the enamel on her fingernails, Dick made it clear he didn't take on just any old client. God no; he was incredibly choosy. So would they all please keep stumm about this? Actually, it was being close chums with darling Ginny that had swung it in her case, Dick had implied. 'Though he did have that twinkle in his eye at the time. And I can't help feeling – because he did take *infinite* pains with the *tiniest* detail – I can't help feeling he's got a bit of a soft spot for yours truly. He'd go to the stake denying it, of course – you know what he is. But the look I was getting . . . Mm, it did rather give him away. And he's such a dish – don't you think? – as well as a veritable genius with the necessary. But girls, this is strictly off the record, yeah? Because I'd hate him and Ginny to be embarrassed by people pestering for his services. I'd feel just awful.'

'Dick, darling,' said Mrs Ginny Brightly to her husband, while hooking a finger through the top buttonhole of his jacket, 'Dick, darling . . .'

'Yes, my sweet?' said Mr Brightly.

'I want to ask you a favour.'

'Oh?' He unhooked the finger and put her hand to his lips – thereby demonstrating no offence was intended when he allowed it to fall. But he still couldn't step away from her, for now she laid her head on his chest. 'What is it, Ginny?'

'You know I told you how thrilled Gloria is with your work on her business affairs? Well, she's been swanking about it. It was mentioned last night at rehearsal. People were joking that they were jealous and said they wished you'd look after *their* money. Betty Fielding didn't say a word of course, just stood there looking smug. I felt so proud, Dick. Is that silly? I felt all aglow. Because it's nice having a husband people admire. Anyway, Nesta was there last night – she's wardrobe mistress for the production: did I say? – and afterwards I drove her home. Well, in the strictest confidence she told me about this money she came into a couple of years ago. Jason told her to stick it in Something Or Other Consolidated, but it's not performing all that well and really she suspects Jason hasn't a clue. So she wondered, darling, if as *the* most *enormous* favour . . .'

'No,' said Mr Brightly, firmly setting his wife aside and wishing he had done so a minute sooner.

'What d'you mean "No"? You haven't heard what I'm asking yet.'

'I can guess.'

'You know I hate it when you cut me off. It's horrible. Rude.'

'I don't mean to be rude. But it was plain you were going to ask me to take Nesta on as a client, and as I've no intention of doing so, I thought I'd save us a pointless discussion.'

'Of all the meanies! Why won't you? What've you got against poor old Nesta?'

Mr Brightly, who had never been keen on Nesta Wright or her husband, recalled an occasion several weeks ago in the Brown Bear; an occasion when he'd been obliged to endure the Wrights holding forth on the subject of unmarried mothers. But there seemed little point in mentioning this now to Ginny; she was not, he judged, in a receptive mood. 'Would you excuse me? I've a briefcase full of documents to deal with before tomorrow morning.' He turned from her and went through the hall, heading for the study.

'That's right,' she yelled, 'clear off. Never mind that you've placed your wife in an impossible position with one of her closest friends.' She waited to see if her words would have an effect. They did not. 'You do realize,' she yelled, speeding after him, 'that I'm supposed to be spending tomorrow afternoon with Nesta having my costume fitted? How do you imagine I'm going to feel?'

'Ginny, *please*. Simply tell Nesta that you did pass on her request, but regretfully I had to decline, my time being fully committed to the needs of existing clients. And Ginny, if any of your other friends make a similar request, please convey the same message. I'm quite capable of finding business for myself, thank you; and most definitely prefer to do so.' He drew up a chair and opened his briefcase. Then a further point occurred to him which seemed worth making: 'You know, I'm not entirely sure that it's an awfully good thing, conducting business relationships with friends and neighbours. They're bound to swap notes and gossip, then these petty jealousies start up.'

'Why?' she gasped. 'Why ever not? Everyone does it. Jason sold everyone their houses, for heaven's sake. Peter supplies the BMWs, and Dougal's our doctor. You ought to be pleased they hold you in high regard; you ought to be flattered. Huh – I know what it is. If ever I get a kick out of something, you have to spoil it – never mind that the things *you* get a kick out of, like church, I'm very understanding about, putting up with boring sermons and dreary people. I happen to get a kick out of my husband being sought after, but can you be obliging about that? Oh no. Well, let me tell you, it's worse than just spoiled. It's a hideous embarrassment. Because I told Nesta you'd be pleased to help her.'

He shook his head. 'Oh Ginny, Ginny.'

'Well why wouldn't I tell her? You've been chirpy as anything dealing with Gloria's business.'

'You landed me with Gloria that Saturday in the pub. I only agreed to save your face. But I warned you not to make a habit of it.'

'All right, so I won't make a habit of it. Just do it this once. Just Nesta, Dick. Please, for me?'

'No. I'm sorry, but there it is.'

'Bastard!' she screamed. 'Mean, selfish, pompous bastard!' And turned and ran from the room flinging the door shut behind her.

*   *   *

In the morning he set a cup of tea beside her, then went to open the curtains. A cry of anguish caused him to pause. 'Would you rather I left them closed?'

'My head, oh my head!'

Unsure as to her requirements he compromised by parting the curtains only a yard or so. 'It's too bad you've a headache,' he said, returning to her bedside.

Her clenched fist held the edge of the duvet to her cheek. 'I've had the most terrible night. I shan't get up. Couldn't face it anyway.'

'But it's your costume fitting this afternoon.'

'I'm amazed you mention it. That's what started my head up, of course – the thought of disappointing Nesta. Well I can't do it. I shan't go.'

He remained there for a moment or two, his eyes exploring the wallpaper pattern. 'Is there anything I can do for you before I go?'

'How can you', she sobbed, 'be so . . . heartless?'

Last week Harriet had returned to school. Today was not Mrs Joiner's day for cleaning. Once he had gone, Ginny would be alone in the house. But what could he do, with a busy office awaiting him? Besides, this sort of episode had occurred before: it was undoubtedly a strategic headache.

'I do hope you'll be better soon,' he murmured, and went off to work.

'A distinct whiff of autumn in the air this morning,' Mr Brightly observed to Miss Orvanessy, who was approaching his desk bearing a fat file of documents.

'Is there, Mr Brightly?' As if autumn were lurking in one of its corners, she glanced nervously round the room.

'I opened the car window, as is my habit – it's good to get a blow of fresh country air first thing – and yes, I definitely caught it: that faintly acrid mustiness. Rather difficult to describe, but I dare say you know what I mean.'

Miss Orvanessy shivered. 'I do indeed.'

'Do I detect in your tone a lack of keenness for the season of mists and mellow fruitfulness, Miss Orvanessy?'

'Mist I can put up with, but I do intensely dislike fog, Mr Brightly. No, I can't say it's my favourite time of year.'

Mr Brightly leaned back in his chair to allow space for the file to be placed in front of him. Miss Orvanessy spread it open on the desk, then stepped backwards. At which he dealt her a smile not only of thanks but of kindly understanding, remembering that not everyone can sail to work in large-car comfort, the smog filtered out and pleasant music playing: he visualized Miss Orvanessy, a scarf drawn over her mouth, picking her way through the fog-shrouded back streets of Warwick with their uneven pavements and terraced housing, and fume-belching buses and cars passing.

Bringing his eyes to focus on the file, he said, 'I believe you wished to draw my attention to something.'

'Yes, Mr Brightly. The date here. Can it be right?'

He felt a need for time to consider the point. All his working life he had been grateful for an ability to leap from one subject to the next with unbroken concentration, but this morning it had temporarily deserted him. 'Um, let me see. What date is this?'

'The date for probate, Mr Brightly.'

'Surely probate was granted a couple of weeks ago. I thought the Marchmont estate . . .'

'Marriot, Mr Brightly. This is the Marriot file.'

'Dear, oh me.' He leaned his chin on his hand. 'I do beg your pardon. Um, leave it with me a while.'

'Are you . . . ? Is anything wrong, Mr Brightly?'

'Not at all. Everything's fine,' he began. Then stopped. For to tell unnecessary lies was a poor habit to get into; furthermore, to call everything fine when he had recently taken leave of a wife with a roaring headache was callous to say the least. 'As a matter of fact, Mrs Brightly was not feeling too clever when I left her this morning.'

'Oh, I'm very sad to hear that. No wonder you're worried and a little distracted.'

'It was only a headache. And she has a dozen friends who would be there in five minutes were she to call them up.'

'But you can't rest easy,' declared Miss Orvanessy, 'because that is your nature. You are always concerned by another's troubles. Shall I go and brew you some coffee?'

'That would be most kind.'

She left him, and he endeavoured to fix his attention on the Marriot file. But a picture of Ginny rose in his mind — her small form in the bed, the cover gathered up in her little fist. Miss Orvanessy's commendation was still fresh in his ears: that he had let it pass seemed to make him a hypocrite, for rather than feeling concerned this morning, he'd been glad to escape. And last evening he feared he'd been brusque with Ginny. She loved to have something to show off to her friends — a part in a play, a lovely thing for the house, a clever husband — but this was hardly a serious sin, it didn't harm anyone; really it was quite an innocent failing. He imagined how obdurate he must have seemed to her last night, and overbearing. Then he reached for the telephone.

'Virginia Brightly,' came the rushed light answer.

'It's me, darling. How are you?'

'Oh, *you*,' she said crossly.

'Look, get up and get ready for your fitting with Nesta. You can tell her I'll see her about those investments one evening next week. I'll call and make an appointment when I've had a chance to check my diary.'

'Oh Dick, do you mean it? Yes you do, you do,' she hastily amended. 'Thank you so much, you angel man . . .'

'But Ginny, I really do have a very stiff workload at the present time. So please, no-one else. You don't want a collapsed husband on your hands?'

'Never! Dick, I promise, if you'll just be nice this once

to Nesta, the others can whistle for your help far as I'm concerned. I love you, Dick.'

'All right, dear. Now I must get on. Have a pleasant afternoon.'

He replaced the receiver just as Miss Orvanessy returned. 'I've telephoned Mrs Brightly,' he reported. 'I think she's recovering.'

'Oh, that's wonderful news,' Miss Orvanessy cried, and then pressed her lips together and inclined her head as she reverently put a cup of coffee before him.

The Brightlys passed a pleasant evening. For once neither the Chedbury Players nor the Chedbury Singers required the attendance of Mrs Brightly, and Mr Brightly did not retire to his study after dinner to open his briefcase or consider a text for Sunday's sermon. (Though he'd certainly assumed he *would* be spending some time in this manner: it was after all his customary method of passing an evening at home.) They ate their lamb chops and out-of-season new potatoes and Spanish broccoli, and Ginny Brightly regaled her husband with a detailed and amusing account of her costume fitting. This contained several references to the joy of Nesta Wright on learning of the financial advice she would shortly receive. Which led Mr Brightly to suspect that his wife was still not perfectly easy as to his co-operation. When he'd telephoned her to relent this morning, she'd snatched up her victory and made off with it to Nesta, and now, with these frequent references, meant to demonstrate there was no escape route open to him, he could not go back on his word. Evidently, his obduracy last evening had dented her confidence. He felt badly about this. He'd handled her ineptly, he considered. Though he remained clear in his mind that as a rule it was neither wise nor comfortable to derive business from people who enjoyed ready access to him, and that though an exception could be made it should be a rare occurrence, he ought, he knew, to have taken time to explain this to

Ginny; he ought to have discovered a method of gaining her compliance without leaving her bruised and resentful. Unfortunately, fatigue and pressing work had led him to take a short cut. He ate his individual treacle pudding (purchased by his wife in Marks and Spencer's) and resolved to put her completely at ease. For what was done was done; next time – though he hoped there would not be a next time – he would handle matters differently. Dabbing his mouth on his napkin he rose to his feet. 'Thank you darling, that was excellent. I'll ring Nesta now, while it's fresh in my mind.'

Ginny's excitement at this bounced her onto her feet. 'Oh good. Yes darling, do! You talk to Nesta and I'll stack the dishwasher, then we can have a drink and take it easy. You never know, there might be something amusing on the box.'

Five minutes later he joined her in the sitting room. 'It's all fixed,' he reported. 'I've promised to call round there on Tuesday. Mind you, she wants me to arrive before half past five if possible, and finish our discussion before Jason gets home: she says Jason has a habit of asking irrelevant questions. I shall have my work cut out, but I promised to do my best.'

'Thank you for being such a sweetie, darling. Now what will you have to drink?'

'Um . . . Oh very well, a small whisky.'

He put the television on, seeing they were destined to remain with one another, and settled in an armchair to watch the nine o'clock news. Ginny brought him a tumbler, then collected her own drink and took it to the sofa. She stretched out full length and said, 'Cheers darling.' For a while she watched the television, then – a news item about a bloodbath in Chechnya failing to divert – reached to the coffee table for *Homes and Gardens*.

After the news and weather forecast, a comedy show came on. Mr Brightly found himself captivated by the two female stars of the show, and he frequently laughed out loud. His wife found the material disagreeable. 'I can't stand to look at that fat one,' she complained. 'And I don't think they're at all funny.'

'It's a skit on *Casablanca*. They're Bogart and Bergman.'

'So what?' she asked. 'Give me the real thing.' Noisily, she flipped over the magazine's pages.

Mr Brightly turned the volume up one notch. 'Ha, ha, ha,' he laughed. 'That's very clever. They're awfully good, you know.'

Ginny closed up *Homes and Gardens*. She smacked it down on the coffee table's glass top. With an expression of long sufferance she turned her face to the screen. 'Thank goodness for that,' she said when the credits rolled.

A film now began. Unaccustomed to solid viewing, Mr Brightly fell into a doze.

His wife was enjoying the film in an abstracted way; it engaged her eyes pleasantly while her mind ran over a few things. Dick had been very good about Nesta, she thought. But there were other friends of hers who also were avid to secure his advice. There was something about this fact that was utterly thrilling, and she spent a few minutes puzzling as to what it could be. At last it came to her: it was possessing something (her husband) that everybody else wanted a piece of. Like a great big cake. She ran her tongue over her lips and imagined doling out this cake at very sparse intervals and in tiny portions. Her friends pleaded and wheedled and drooled, and manoeuvred to be next in line. Gloria Maskill had already been served; now it was the turn of Nesta Wright. Who else would she favour? Perhaps Maria Edgely, who was in Ginny's good books for being so warm and generous over Ginny getting the best part in the play. Perhaps Deirdre Houseman who had expressed her longing in the most flattering terms. But Deirdre was the teeniest bit common; obliging Deirdre hardly seemed worth the battle with Dick.

Dick's eyes were closed, she noticed. She regarded him tenderly and also speculatively. 'Don't fall asleep over the telly, darling. It's terribly bad for the back.' She rose and stretched. 'Mm-ahh,' she yawned. 'I think I'll go up. Not such an engrossing film, really. Don't be too long,' she advised, landing in passing a kiss on his forehead.

Moments before his wife's kiss descended, Mr Brightly had dropped right off. Coming awake, he took note of her departure and endeavoured for the next twenty or so minutes to make sense of a film that had largely passed him by. Then he gave it up and shut down the television. He turned off all the downstairs lights and went upstairs. In his dressing room he hung away his suit, disposed of soiled garments and laid out clean ones for the morning. He took a brief wash in the bathroom, reserving the greater portion of his body for cleansing during his morning shower, then slipped on a bathrobe and stole towards the bedroom, prepared to lay hands on and get into his pyjamas in the darkness if his wife had already extinguished her lamp, as he considered likely.

In fact she was sitting up in bed wearing a sheer black nightdress. He considered the significance of this as he groped under his pillow and then, with his back to her, shed the bathrobe and put on pyjamas.

'I'm wearing my naughty nightie, darling,' she gently pointed out.

He felt awkward and embarrassed, for normally, say forty-nine times out of fifty, she wore prim little cotton numbers that were, so she informed him, far more comfortable. 'What dear?' he asked, turning, playing for time.

'My nightie,' she said, lifting back the duvet and showing him a greater portion of it. 'Like to jump in beside Ginny? Fancy an ickle cuddle?'

Just for a moment he hesitated. Then, 'I won't, if you don't mind. Thank you all the same,' he said, and climbed into his own bed.

'Tired, dearest?' she asked, after a short silence.

''Fraid so. Suffering from work overload, as I believe I told you.'

'Poor old Dick. 'Nother time then, pet.' She reached over and switched off the lamp.

Lying on his back in the dark, Mr Brightly heard again the comfortable tone of her voice and reflected that her disappointment had not been great. He knew he'd been correct in his immediate assumption: she considered it prudent to reinforce his compliance in the matter of assistance to Nesta Wright – as if his compliance were a down-payment and she now proposed to come up with the goods. It was not the first time Ginny had sought to seal a bargain with sex. Years ago he'd concluded that if it were necessary to buy the commodity he might as well purchase from a true professional. He turned onto his side, irritated to discover that in spite of retaining his self-respect he had not altogether remained immune. Her offer had induced a reaction.

He searched his mind for some calming topic to dwell on. Tomorrow was Friday, he reminded himself. In his lunch hour he would visit again that computer shop in Castle Street. He would pick the brains of the helpful assistant there. Then in the evening he would take an inexpensive something or other to young Alex Reece. The lad's pleasure at receiving this zoomed larger and larger, entered every corner of Mr Brightly's mind and drew him in peace to sleep.

10

Kept from her sleep by lust, Cressida Reece tossed in
bed and imagined herself caught up and tangled in an
episode of frantic passion. 'Richard, Richard,' she cried
out loud. Then shot bolt upright and strained her ears.
Had Alex heard her cry out? It horrified her to think he
might. Sweating, she cast back the bedclothes, and then,
because if Alex were stirring she would be unable to
hear with her heart thumping so loudly, got out of bed,
carefully opened her bedroom door and peered along
the landing. Under her son's bedroom door there was
no line of light. Not the faintest sound came.

Deciding there was little point in returning to bed, she
unhooked her old wrap from behind her door, groped
over the bedroom floor for the socks she had worn a few
hours earlier, and with these items of clothing pulled
on, squeezed past Alex's chair lift and crept downstairs.
In the kitchen she made a mug of tea. She sipped from
it and put it down, walked about, took it up and sipped
again, and finally went into the sitting room. Here, she
parted the curtains a foot or more and stood between
them, cupping the mug with her hands and staring out
into the close.

There was no suggestion of light at any of the
windows of the houses opposite. Feeble moonlight
shone on the roof tiles. A street lamp lit a portion of
pavement, road and grass. She pictured her slumbering
neighbours. She pictured herself, wakeful, alone. It
seemed probable that every other soul in Chedbury lay
snugly asleep. Her heart ached with the loneliness of

her position – which was not new to her, for many times in the small hours she had stood at this same window deliberately forcing herself to keep alert because Alex was poorly. She had looked into the close for reassurance, imagining how easy it would be to rouse her neighbours and beg to be driven at all speed with Alex to hospital. It had never come to that. There were no dramas to recall; only herself keeping watch, her anxiety for Alex, and her silent battle with isolation.

Well, it was a different kettle of fish tonight, she told herself briskly. She had not shunned sleep on Alex's behalf. Her eyes looked to the bend in the close round which tomorrow evening she hoped to see Richard come striding. But what if she didn't? How would she bear it?

Tomorrow evening she had set up in her mind as a test. Every Friday, since he'd first made that quip about Fridays being his evenings off, he had come without fail. But – and this had to be faced – never without some specific purpose. First came the Friday when she'd invited him to supper. Next the Friday when he'd promised to explain the investment plan. The following Friday she'd allowed him to arrive in the belief that she was ready to sign up to this plan, and had then been obliged to explain that as yet there was no money to invest, time still remained for the Health Authority to lodge an appeal. A few days later she learned there would be no appeal; her money was safe; and when Friday came, in response to her eager phone call, Richard duly returned for her signature. A bare two days after that, the joy of this last visit fading, she'd become eaten by suspense, wondering whether the Friday ahead would again bring Richard. By the Wednesday she could bear it no longer. She'd rung him up – finally catching him in around 10 p.m. – to report that Alex was now ready to demonstrate his latest invented computer game. Richard had answered that of course he would view the game on Friday. She'd heard a note of surprise in his voice and had pondered over the meaning of this for hours, wondering if it signified he'd intended coming anyway, and if so, whether she'd spoiled things by betraying lack of confidence. Then of course it had been necessary to work on Alex, to pretend it was Richard who had phoned her with a request to view the computer game.

This had not been easy to do. For one thing, Alex was a knowing child these days. For another, their relationship had subtly altered: she was all of a sudden anxious for her son's good opinion, wary in case he should criticize her. She'd resolved never again to involve Alex in her schemes.

So now, tomorrow, another Friday loomed. During the past week, with her longing and uncertainty growing, excuses for phoning Richard in order to make certain of a visit had constantly jumped into her mind. She'd thought of phoning to say Baz was pestering her again and she needed to talk about it. She'd thought of asking Richard to bring her some commodity from Warwick that could not be obtained in Chedbury. She'd thought she might claim to be considering driving lessons and ask if he'd mind advising her on the purchase of a car. It had taken more will power than she'd known she possessed in order to resist these thoughts, and specially last evening with only twenty-four hours to go. Yet she'd succeeded. Biting her lips, tugging her hair, she'd held out. She'd gambled on an unspoken arrangement between them that might only exist in her own head.

Now her efforts seemed irrelevant. She knew only too well the sort of state she'd be in, viewing this bend in the close sixteen or seventeen hours ahead – guts churning with hope, stale and tired from anticipation. And her vigil would end in either happiness or grief. There could be no halfway house.

Suddenly, angrily, she closed the curtains. She would not stand at this window watching for him tomorrow, however tempted. Instead, well before the time she expected him, she'd start on some sensible task, the kind of task that would prevent her going anywhere near the sitting room window. It came to her then that she would do some baking. She pictured it: her hands deep in dough, flour up to her elbows, milk on the stove nearing the boil, an eggy mixture in danger of curdling, an oven heating. It wouldn't matter to Richard if he arrived and discovered her in the midst of all this; he'd simply stand and talk to her, watching and appreciatively sniffing. She felt better, now, with a plan to carry her through the worst of the waiting. She focused on it, making a list of the tools she would set out tomorrow. Scales, bowls, tins, greaseproof; knives, spoons, spatula, whisk: she ticked each item off as she trod the stairs. While discarding her wrap and socks, she was breaking eggs into a bowl. Climbing into bed and pulling the covers up to her chin, Gas mark 5, she thought.

Cressida's baking was well advanced. The smell of it brought Alex into the kitchen. 'Have we got company this weekend?'

His mother said they had not.

'So why're you making all this stuff?'

'I felt in the mood,' she shrugged.

'Oh,' said Alex. 'Cool.'

The doorbell rang as Cressida was lining an enamel plate with rolled-out pastry. 'Damn,' she cried as a knife slipped from her hands.

'I'll get it,' Alex offered. 'It's Friday, so it's bound to be Richard.'

And so it was. Cressida, putting her head round the door frame, saw him step over the threshold. 'Alex,' he cried gladly. And then: 'My goodness, that's a most inviting smell.'

'Mum's cooking. It's typical: she doesn't go near an oven for weeks, then she goes mad.'

'Hi, Richard,' called Cressida. 'You've caught me at it. I've nearly finished.'

'You don't mind if I watch?' He entered the kitchen and was immediately struck by her high colour. He supposed this must be due to the heat of the oven, since nothing had occurred to precipitate one of her ready blushes: all he had done so far was arrive. She was smiling at him brilliantly, lifting with floury fingers a trailing hank of hair.

'Cressida, you look charming.' – he simply couldn't repress the remark. 'Doesn't she, Alex?' he continued, inviting her son to share his amusement at her smeared face and streaked apron and the phenomenal amount of surrounding clutter.

'Chocolate buns are almost ready. We'll have one when they're cool.'

'We'll hardly stop at one,' said Alex.

Casting his eyes over the heaped work surfaces, Mr Brightly lighted on the bowl that had been used for the chocolate mixture. 'Aha! I don't suppose I might . . .'

'Oh aye,' Alex objected. 'I was going to scrape that.'

'All right,' said Cressida. 'One of you can have the mixing spoon and the other the bowl.'

'I bags the bowl.'

She found a clean spoon for the bowl and passed these to her son, then offered her friend the chocolate-covered spoon. As he took it and put it to his mouth, their eyes fastened. A thud happened in Cressida's stomach. She seized a tin of golden syrup, levered off the lid, and started to fill the pastry case. Then the buzzer went on the oven. She took a cloth and removed the buns and tipped them onto a wire cooling rack; then turned up the heat and slid in the treacle tart.

Having removed all the goodness from bowl and spoon, Alex and Mr Brightly abandoned these utensils. Then Mr Brightly produced the latest issue of the computer magazine he had bought during his lunch hour. Alex gave a cheer of pleasure and wheeled off with it to the sitting room.

'I wonder if they're cool enough?' pondered Cressida, prodding one of the buns.

'Shame to allow them to become *too* cool,' Mr Brightly countered, anxious for this rare treat.

'Yeah, they're better warm. You can put them on a plate and take them in. I'll make some tea.'

They ate their buns and drank their tea and talked. Sometimes Alex put in a word but mostly was absorbed by the magazine. Then, 'Hey Mum, listen to this,' he cried. 'There's stuff in here about those new facilities Uncle Jonathan was on about. Remember me telling you?' And he began to read aloud from the article, stopping now and then to exclaim or comment. Considerately, he leaned over the side of his wheelchair towards their visitor, thus allowing the text to be shared.

Cressida duly listened, but heard nothing of *Hot Java* or *Netscape*. Her ears fastened on his enthusiasm, her mind on the natural way he had included her. 'Hey Mum,' he had cried, despite her inability to get to grips with the subject. It was lovely, that.

Then Richard glanced across at her and smiled.

This is real family life, she marvelled to herself; and in defiance of her diet, reached for a second bun.

Mr Brightly, smiling at Cressida, was remarking to himself that she was the picture of happiness.

A moment ago, the strange almost raucous voice of the boy at his side had brought him up sharply against the fact of his deformity. (Since he had come to know Alex, the deformity had retreated in importance, it no longer seemed the boy's primary characteristic.) Alex continued to read and expound, and to slightly unsettle Mr Brightly's ears. Mr Brightly rested his eyes on the boy's head and pictured his mother shielding it as she pushed him through the rain. He wondered why this image should haunt him as it did. He looked across at her and caught her eye. They exchanged smiles.

She is the picture of happiness, he said to himself. And all because of a magazine I bought for her son, and the pleasure it's giving.

He found himself immensely moved. And it was suddenly clear to him why, in this unsmart domestic setting, he felt relaxed and contented – relaxed and contented in the way he felt also at Mrs Parminter's: it was because happiness of a simple or unselfish kind was not to be had in his own home setting. In Framley Lane discontent was the mainspring of life. It lay behind the luxurious furnishings and wonderful extensions, it shaped the features of his wife and of their friends; it shaped Ginny's hopes and ambitions and regulated the love she offered to her husband and children. One would hardly expect to relax in such a setting. Was this why Giles, their son, so seldom came home? Why Harriet in the school holidays kept largely to her room? Why Ginny was out most evenings of the week and hated to see blank weekends on the kitchen calendar? Why he himself retired to his study? And why a rare evening in each other's company ended in falling asleep in front of the television? He could not deny his own part in all this. He'd stoked the discontent pretty thoroughly himself over the years: susceptible to Ginny's hunted look, physically upset by her frantic insecurity, he'd striven to supply every last thing she desired; and had discovered he could never supply enough, that there was no limit to the things that must be acquired or experienced. It was so good, therefore, so renewing, to know that in a small way he was attempting to reverse this process by diverting some of the fruits of his talent away from Brightly consumption (and that of certain others who were also too sated with wealth to be properly appreciative) towards more deserving and laudable causes.

A buzzer interrupted this train of thought. Cressida leapt to her feet. 'The treacle tart; I'd completely forgotten it,' she cried, rushing to the kitchen.

Alex turned sideways and grinned. 'You know she's on a diet?'

'I didn't,' Mr Brightly replied. 'But I expect she's made the tart for you.'

'She may have intended it for me, but I bet she ends up eating half of it. To begin with she'll be strong. Then she'll decide a tiny little piece won't matter. Then she'll say, "Come on, Alex, let's finish it off."'

'I can't see that your mother needs to diet.'

'No? Well, maybe she is looking slimmer.'

When Cressida returned, Alex examined her critically, then relaxed his face and started a yawn.

'Don't let yourself get over-tired, love,' she warned.

'No. OK. Maybe I'll go up.'

'Want a hand?'

'No, 's all right. Thanks for the magazine, Richard. It's really useful.' He tucked it down the side of his chair, said, 'Goodnight,' and wheeled away.

'I'll look in later,' his mother called.

'Now,' said Mr Brightly when Alex had disappeared, 'let me help you wash up all those pots and pans.'

'Gosh, no. It can wait till later.'

'Well then: how's college this term?'

'Not bad.' She began to talk about her new topic of study led by a tutor who hadn't taught her before. Then a thud sounded overhead. 'Excuse me a sec,' she said, and a moment later he heard her feet on the stairs and her voice crying, 'You all right, Alex?'

Mr Brightly listened and waited. No cries for help summoned him above. Two minutes later she was back, patting her chest in relief. 'It's OK. Panic's over. Alex chucked a book on the bed and missed, that's all.' She flopped down on the settee.

'You can see how it is though, Richard? Alex insists he can be left. He can manage fine, he says. But it kills me if I ever have to go out and leave him here on his own. I don't mind if he's at school or with a responsible adult. But leaving him here . . . I mean, say if he toppled out of his chair – which he swears is impossible – but say something like that did happen. He'd be virtually helpless; it'd be incredibly difficult for him to get up on his own. He could be trapped in some dangerous situation' – her eyes widened as she conjured examples: 'the boiler might blow up and the whole house catch fire; or a pipe might burst. Or it could be something not dangerous exactly, but really unpleasant – like the electricity cutting out and Alex stuck halfway upstairs in the chair lift.'

'Yes, I do see,' he agreed. 'I see that you'd have some anxiety at the back of your mind. But perhaps that should be set against Alex's natural desire for independence.'

'I know,' she sighed. She thought for a moment, then flung backwards in her seat and ran her hand through her hair, grinning at him. 'We're always talking about me, do you notice? I'm sick of me. Go on, Richard, take me out of myself; tell me something about you for a change.'

'Hmm.' After a little consideration, he crossed his legs and clasped a knee and embarked on the story of how, as an amateur actor, he was asked to play the part of a priest; and of the uncanny familiarity of those words in his mouth; of how the priest's convictions became his convictions and fired him to live a different sort of life. But he took his time getting to the point. He found himself spending rather longer than was necessary painting the scene, describing the friendliness of CADS members, the great times they had had, the productions that had been roaring successes and those that had been flops (though omitting any mention of the black time he himself had undergone due to the rumours about Ginny and Tony Colebrook). He dallied because he was wondering why on earth he'd chosen this story to tell. Why should it seem appropriate to confide an incident of great personal importance to this yellow-haired girl whom he'd only recently come to know? Particularly as he'd confided it to no-one else. Not that it was a secret exactly. People had observed the change that had occurred in him and had made the connection. Members of CADS had claimed to be knocked out by his performance, and then, when the play was behind him and it became obvious that the part wasn't, naturally enough they'd started pulling his leg. Ginny had made a very successful joke of it at a party, he remembered. 'I'm relying on you, darlings,' she'd cried, falling onto her knees in front of members of the production committee. 'For God's sake, find me the antidote. Find a play with a big fat *villainous* part in it for Dick. Evil as you like, darlings.' A lot of fun had been had with that. Tony Colebrook, he was sure, had brought the tale with him to the Chedbury Players. In fact he gathered Tony had referred to the incident just a few Saturdays ago in the Brown Bear. To be fair to Ginny, considering she hadn't a trace of a religious impulse in her entire make-up, she'd been remarkably good about it. In the early days of their move to Framley Lane she'd worried lest the time he was spending on church business should halt the rise in their living standards, and he'd redoubled his efforts in order to demonstrate the opposite. No, it couldn't be denied that the outer effects of what had happened to him were common knowledge. It was what had taken place inside him that remained a mystery, a secret of his soul. Yet here he was describing it. Quite easily as it happened.

Her eyes never moved from his face. As he got to the meat of his story they seemed to grow larger. They were eyes, he was sure, that frankly mirrored feelings; if she felt inclined to giggle or be embarrassed or hold reservations, he would see it. But she was rapt, serious, willing to be transported. He told her it all.

Afterwards there was silence between them. Her eyes continued to observe him – and, he would swear, continued to grow. Then her lips rounded and her breath whistled out. 'That is . . . amazing. The man who wrote that play: he really spoke to you.'

'Well, actually it was God who spoke to me. The play was His vehicle.'

'Could be,' she acknowledged, nodding slowly. 'Or, could be' – and her awed tone made clear that the suggestion she was about to put forward was the one she favoured – 'could be you were put in touch with your true self when you spoke those lines. Like it was *your* voice, *your* words – only because of the way you'd been brought up and how your life turned out, you were never in a position to speak them before. Do you see? Phew!'

'I do believe the voice of the New Age is speaking here,' he said with a smile.

'No, it's *me* speaking. It's my personal idea. And actually, I think it's pretty sound. Don't get me wrong. I'm not saying God didn't have a hand in it. He could've seen how you were turning out – speaking the wrong lines and doing things that weren't really you, and being spiritually unsatisfied. And He could've thought: Hey, I know – I'll make it so Richard gets that part in the play . . .'

She saw he was smiling broadly. 'So what's wrong with that?'

'Nothing,' he said. 'Nothing at all. I'm just appreciating the way you're working round to take care of both our interpretations. And do you know, I find I'm very drawn to yours.'

'You're laughing at me.'

'No, I'm not. I'm delighting in you.'

Her cheeks flamed. She looked down at her hands. And an instinct told him to change the subject.

Funnily enough, he remarked, he didn't miss acting at all; he heard quite enough about amateur dramatics these days from his wife, Ginny, who, as Cressida might know, was soon to appear in a forthcoming production by the Chedbury Players. And incidentally, if Cressida and Alex would care to be present at one of the performances, there'd be no trouble about tickets, no trouble at all; they could leave the tickets to him. Cressida, however, gave no sign about tickets one way or the other. Rather than, 'Thanks, that'll be great,' which was what he expected to hear, nothing came from her other than a tiny smothered hiccup. He peered at her. From under her lowered lashes came two fat tears, one from each eye. They slid slowly over her cheeks. That hiccup was no hiccup, he deduced. Chances were it was a sob.

She shuddered violently; gasped, 'Sorry, Richard,' and ran from the room.

He discovered her in the kitchen hanging on to the sink. Squeaks and gasps came from her, and a sound like a door grating. It was quite clear she was crying her heart out. 'Cressida, my dear, whatever is it? Did I upset you? Is it Alex? Please, please tell me.'

She felt powerless to say anything but the simple truth. 'I love you, Richard. I know I shouldn't, but I do. I love you . . .' But here her voice faltered: she turned and threw her arms round his neck and clung to him tightly, whispering over and over, 'Love you so much.'

The impact of this on Mr Brightly was like a massive and instantaneous blood transfusion. Blood thundered through every vessel of his body while his legs trembled under the onslaught. He tipped his head back, lifting his face from the lure of her hair. He closed his eyes, and in his heated mind his wife raised her bedclothes to show him her diaphanous nightgown and Mrs Nanette Thompson squealed in his ear that she wanted to give him one free of charge. Both offers had tempted him, but not, oh Lord, like this. His arms, whose spontaneous rise he had checked, remained rigidly mid-air. The awkwardness of their position at last came through to him, but not whether to move them up or down, only that they mimicked Christ stiffly extending his wounded hands to his disciples, as depicted in stained glass in St Peter's Chedbury. The thought proved mercifully calming, allowing him to exhale and his limbs to relax. 'Shh,' he soothed, 'sh-hhh. Come on, Cressida, let's go and sit down.'

He got her into the sitting room, pushed her gently onto the settee where she had been sitting previously, but did not immediately sit down himself. For a while it was as much as he could do to breathe in and out and take small directionless steps over her carpet and savour his relief that he'd succeeded in keeping his hands off her. It was Cressida flinging forward to lay her head on her knees, and her muffled cry, 'Oh God,' that made him understand there was work to be done, this was no time for self-congratulation. Cressida's feelings, which were undoubtedly bruised, required urgent attention.

He went over to the settee and sat beside her, since it would be distancing and cold of him to sit elsewhere, and he manoeuvred for one of her hands.

Some time elapsed before he could speak. Words sprang with facility to the tip of his tongue, but his mind, leaping ahead to her reaction, forestalled them. It would be truthful and kind, for instance, to confess he loved her too, but once the word love was out he knew very well she would pounce on it. She would use it to dispute his other strong feelings: that a love affair with an older married man would be against her best interests; that by embarking on such an affair he would betray the very vulnerability that had brought him to visit her in the first place. It was going to be necessary, he realized, to stick to selfish objections. And so, asking her not to imagine that he didn't feel anything for her, he went on to remind her of the confidences he'd given some minutes ago. She had taken him seriously then, for which he'd been thankful; she'd understood how precious and important it was to him, that turning point in his life. If she would think on a little further, she would surely understand the impossibility of his taking a step in an opposite direction. And the fact was he was married. Given his convictions, he was bound to stay loyal . . . But here he faltered. Somehow it seemed ridiculous to say 'loyal to Ginny', who was not, he was certain, loyal to him. He began the sentence again, and this time concluded 'loyal to my marriage.'

There, he'd said it. He was not entirely satisfied, but hoped it had been enough. 'Please don't be sad, Cressida,' he added.

'Sad?' she said, lifting her head. 'I'm not sad, I'm mad. Mad as hell with myself. I've gone and done it again; just like I always do. Opened my great big mouth and ruined everything.'

'No, no . . .'

'Yes, yes,' she shouted, snatching away her hand. 'After the way I've acted tonight you won't want to know any more. It's true, you'll see. If you ever need to speak to me about something, like the investments, you'll get on the phone, or you'll drop by after work saying you've only got five minutes and will I please sign these documents. But you won't come round. We won't see you on Friday nights any more. 'Cos I've been embarrassing. I've blown it.'

'Cressida, what are you talking about? I'm not at all embarrassed. And of course I shan't stop coming. You and Alex are my dear friends. For as long as I'm welcome, I'll be here.'

'No you won't,' she said flatly, her tone dull, as if weighted down by a jaded knowledge of human nature. 'And I'll tell you for why. Maybe you're not feeling embarrassed right now, but just wait till tomorrow morning. It'll all come back – how I threw myself at you; and you'll remember stuff you've read in the papers and seen on the telly, about people who develop an obsession for someone and make a nuisance of themselves – you know – keep ringing up and writing letters and making trouble. And you'll think: Hey, that could be me; maybe it'd be better to steer clear of Cressida Reece for a while. Then soon you'll be thinking: I'm well out of that.'

Now he was not only astonished but shocked as well. 'It wouldn't occur to me to think anything of the sort in a hundred years,' he protested. 'Really you know, I'm quite annoyed with you, Cressida. You've slandered me and you've slandered yourself. What a lot of nonsense. It's your nature to protect, not to harm.'

Now it was Cressida who was astonished. She turned her face to him.

'Well,' he demanded, 'am I right?'

'Um,' she said, feeling dazed, 'yeah. Yeah, I s'pose you are.' But it was not so much that he was spot on about her character that astounded her, as his faith in it, which was evidently stronger than any instincts of self protection. How many blokes, she wondered, presented with the picture she'd painted of an obsessional nuisance, wouldn't feel well warned off? Not many, she'd bet. She shook her head at him. 'Know something? You're amazing, Richard.'

'And so are you. And lovely and funny and honest . . . and tired. You're tired out, aren't you? Look: why don't I get us a drink?'

She laughed weakly. 'I could murder a cup of tea, now you mention it. I'm dry as dust.'

'Don't move, stay there. I'll make it.'

'All right, then,' she said, and at last sank back against the settee's cushions.

Cressida closed the front door and leaned her back against it. She was jiggered, wrecked. He had tipped up her chin and looked into her eyes. 'Till Friday then, Cressida,' he'd promised.

'Till Friday, Richard,' she'd answered. And she'd known, and knew still, he would keep his word. Sighing, she heaved away from the door and went through the hall.

The mess in the kitchen seemed to have expanded while her back was turned: grown extra tall, extra wide, more intricately jumbled. She raised a hand and switched off the light. She switched the lights off in the hall and the sitting room, then lumbered upstairs. After the briefest of visits to the bathroom, she flicked off all the remaining lights, and in the dark of her bedroom pulled off her clothes letting each item lie as it fell. At last, gratefully, she climbed into bed.

She lay on her back, weighed down by her limbs. One of those hefty sculpted Greek goddesses – but with all her bits intact – washed up from the sea and half sunk in the sand, was how she imagined herself. Would she ever rise again? she wondered, and thought it was maybe just as well she and Richard hadn't made out. She wouldn't have been much use. She hadn't realized how utterly worn out she'd got. All that worrying over whether or not he'd turn up tonight had done it, she supposed. That on top of everything else. Maybe she'd feel differently in the morning, but right now she couldn't feel regretful about his turning her down. Because in one way he hadn't. Of course, there was no evidence of this, she had nothing to show off or talk about. There was a limit to the importance you could invest in speaking about a friend. 'My friend Richard says . . . When Richard and I did so and so,' she heard herself say over coffee at college. And it was going to be dodgy talking to Julie on the phone: which was entirely her own fault; she shouldn't have raised her friend's expectations. Maybe she could say she and Richard had decided to let things cool for a while, giving the impression this was mainly her own decision. Maybe this would satisfy Julie and stop her questions. One thing: the week ahead should be relatively carefree. She wouldn't be worrying herself sick wondering if Richard would show up on Friday. It was awesome how surely she knew she could rely on his word. Awesome, too, the faith he'd shown in her. Yeah, that had been really something.

She turned onto her side and drew up her knees, and – as if she'd switched off one last light – went instantly out.

11

When Mr Brightly received a telephone call from Mrs
Nanette Thompson stating an urgent need for a friendly
chat he was visited by the idea – very briefly it was true,
for he soon scooted it – that this was God's doing: God
had observed his virtue, his manly self-control, and
God had decided a measure of encouragement was now
in order, in the form of a small reward.

During the drive from Warwick to Leamington Spa he
raised his eyebrows, laughed and shook his head at
himself. But the fact was that for the past few weeks,
ever since Cressida's avowal of love for him, Mr
Brightly had walked the streets of Chedbury with an
extra spring to his stride; he had knocked on the doors
of parishioners and preached them sermons and shaken
their hands with a sense of enhanced validity. For only
he and his Maker knew the cost of keeping his hands off
Cressida Reece – though he was undoubtedly helped to
do so by the complexity of his feelings towards her. Lust
was easily surmounted by tenderness, he found, and
physical longing by imaginative curiosity. His thoughts
continually returned to her. He wondered about her life.
How did it feel, he pondered, to be focused on someone,
as she was on her son, who outpaced her in intellect yet
was physically dependent? Her frequent protest that
she was doing her best seemed to provide a hint. 'I *am*
doing my best, Alex,' she would respond to her son's
complaint or criticism. Mr Brightly had heard her say
something of the sort on several occasions. And once
when her mother telephoned, he'd heard her again.

'Mum, I *am* doing my best, you know.' He was not blind to her weaknesses. She was sloppy in her habits, inclined to leave chores for a later time; she was easily swayed by a more forceful personality, and would usually accept in any clash of opinion or attitude that hers was the one in need of modification. (He noticed, for instance, that she made no attempt to change the course of their relationship from the one he had laid down. She did not see it as a challenge that he declined to make love to her, as many women would.) But she had strengths, too, and these had deeply impressed him. As evidence there was the pile of campaigning letters she'd written over the years, and the accounts from both Cressida and Alex of the obstacles put in their way and how Cressida had battled to overcome them. The play of weakness on strength, or of strength on weakness, fascinated him: he wondered which way round it was. Did the fierceness of her mother love allow her to act forcefully despite a naturally indolent nature? Or did the continual struggle on her son's behalf drain her of energy and make her listless in her own support?

So much consideration did Mr Brightly give these and other aspects of Cressida that he could only conclude he was obsessed. Sometimes, picturing her, he went further. I adore her, he thought. I could take her to bed with all the ease in the world. I could see myself moving in: it would be no trouble at all saying goodbye to Ginny and Framley Lane. Yes, I could see myself settling down nicely to a modest, decent, loving life with Cressida and Alex.

It was the lightest of pipedreams. He well knew that. It was an instance of the escape-to-simplicity fantasy that comforted many a middle-aged man with a burdensome job and over-sophisticated habits. But it was not outrageous in the sense that to enact it would go against his character; he really could see himself fitting into the role, and that a more modest style of living would chime well with his religious principles. It was the unbreak-

144

able nature of his responsibilities that made it a fantasy; responsibilities to his wife and children, to his employees and clients, responsibilities to the business itself, whose set-up was highly complicated – deliberately so; no-one save Richard Brightly understood the half of it; he could only retire by wrapping it up.

On arrival in Leamington, Mr Brightly drove up the ramps of the multi-storey car park, carefully slotted into a space, then went to the machine to collect a ticket. He laid the ticket on the dashboard, made the car secure, and took the lift to the street. At a brisk pace, passing shops and cafés and banks and building society offices, he made for the direction of the park and Mrs Thompson's residence.

There was vigour in his stride. His bearing was erect yet easy. He took note of these things from his advancing reflection in a plate glass window. It struck him that the man he saw reflected was a man in his prime, a man at the height of his powers.

And yet a man, he reflected, who consistently denied himself the natural physical outlets. Feeling as he did about Cressida Reece, now more than ever he could not countenance any of Ginny's offerings. And Ginny did still offer. He always knew when she was about to do so. First would come her speculative frown (precipitated no doubt by her recollection that the bill for correct husbandly behaviour towards her friend Nesta Wright was still outstanding), then a kiss discharged onto his cheek or forehead, and finally her recommendation that he should not sit up too long. And sure enough he would arrive in the bedroom to discover tonight it was the turn of the sheer black nightdress.

He rounded a corner, and the crescent containing Mrs Nanette Thompson's house came into view. Simultaneously in his mind, Mrs Nanette Thompson herself materialized in her shiny purple dress and high-heeled sandals. He remembered his last visit. He remembered having his face thrust into her bosom, and how her perfume filled his nostrils and her voice came in his ear: 'I want to give you a free one, Ricki. Oo lovie, lovie, I really do.' Could it not be said that something had inspired her to make this uncharacteristically generous gesture? Who was to say God hadn't? And the thought leapt to Mr Brightly (who was at that moment vulnerable to such thoughts due to a degree of involuntary arousal) that maybe this was all of a piece: Mrs Thompson was to have her chance to practise generosity, and for a brief half-hour the ban he had imposed on physical gratification was to be temporarily lifted. God was a merciful God, it should not be forgotten. And wasn't there a school of thought that held constant suppression of the sexual urge to be an unhealthy procedure? This would be particularly so, he shouldn't be surprised, for a man in his prime at the height of his powers.

He took Mrs Thompson's four front steps in two clean bounds and firmly depressed her bell button.

For a split second the consequences of this action proceeded normally: a ringing sounded within, and Mr Brightly pleasantly but formally composed his features. However, the door was not opened to him cheerily by one of Mrs Thompson's girls. A rumbling started up, as of speed being gathered, and the door was hurled upon, furiously banged and thumped – evidently by an enraged beast to judge from its cry. Now shouts rang out, threats and curses. Mr Brightly, who unconsciously had taken several small steps backwards, hovered hesitatingly as the door opened to allow a twelve-inch gap.

'Come in,' cried Mrs Nanette Thompson from further down the hall. 'Quickly, for Chrissake.'

Unsure whether he wished to comply, Mr Brightly went forward. A girl whose face was vaguely familiar opened the door just wide enough to admit him, and when he had stepped over the threshold closed it behind.

Several feet away Mrs Thompson was clinging to a Dobermann pinscher. '*Nice* man,' she purred to it. '*Friend*.' The dog's growl of disbelief rippled through the length of his sleek black body. 'Oh Ricki,' cried Mrs Thompson, 'am I glad to see you! Show him into the parlour, Aimée, while I lock up this effing hound. Move, blast you. Come!'

Mr Brightly had seen quite enough of Mrs Thompson to know that the picture had changed since his last visit. Love was not in her mind. Whatever else occupied her – led her to wrestle with a dog and exclaim wildly – love did not. Abstractedly he took the seat he was shown. 'Of course,' he murmured when Aimée said she'd better go and check that Mrs Thompson was OK and Bruno settled. He was about to express surprise over the establishment's acquisition of a dog when he decided against causing any delay. Mrs Thompson would soon enlighten him. He certainly trusted she would soon enlighten him. For this visit was occurring, he felt it opportune to remind himself, smack bang in the middle of business hours. He had perhaps hurried here precipitately. And then a worse thought formed from the uneasy haze at the back of his mind: that what lay behind her urgent summons was likely to prove disagreeable. For instance, a problem with money.

'Nanette, my dear.' He grasped her forearms and kissed her cheek, but frowned rather than smiled, the possibility of a problem with money persuading him to temper his affection with sternness. 'Whatever are you doing with that demented dog? Not the right sort of pet for you at all. I should have thought a nice little Peke – or better still a Persian cat. Yes, get a cat. That dog will frighten off your visitors.'

'Darling, shut up and listen.' Mrs Thompson pushed him back into his chair and sat in one opposite. 'Thanks for coming so quickly, I really appreciate it. The thing is, I need you to help me out. Honestly, you'd hardly credit the trouble I've had. You remember that girl, Tammy? She brought in the tea last time you were here; you know: the time you told me about the new investment plan and got me to sign those papers?'

Mr Brightly chose not to commit himself.

'Yes you do, Ricki: attractive young piece, something about her? Well a right snake in the grass she turned out. And there was me thinking I'd found someone at last with manageress potential – brains as well as the usual talents.' Mrs Thompson gave a bitter laugh. 'She's got brains all right, evil little tart. And plenty of cheek into the bargain. One morning I go into my kitchen, and there she is, cool as you like, sat at the table with a fella I'd never set eyes on in my life before. "Can I introduce you to Leroy, Mrs Thompson?" she says, like we were having a ladies' coffee morning. "Leroy's me boyfriend." That was cardinal rule number one broken. No boyfriends in or near this house,' Mrs Thompson explained. 'Never, under any circumstances. For reasons which I'm sure I don't need to spell out.'

Mr Brightly looked wise, and Mrs Thompson resumed her story.

'Before I could say a word – never mind tick her off for breaking the no boyfriend rule – *he* takes over. Starts talking about the business and how it'd be possible to triple the takings by putting in specialist equipment. Aye, aye, I thought; never mind boyfriend, this is her pimp – and an ambitious pimp, too, I pretty soon discovered. He wanted to know if I'd be interested in a partnership, because with his contacts and expertise we could expand in a really big way, attract a wider clientele. Miss Tammy sat there listening and grinning. I could see what they were planning; they thought I was ripe to be taken over. Of course, I told him nothing doing, the business was fine as it was, and anyway what had it to do with him, and would he please depart? He said he could see I needed time to think it over, but he'd be back for my answer in a couple of days. And while he said it, he very deliberately cracked his knuckles.'

Mr Brightly sucked in his breath.

'Don't worry, I didn't argue. I kept my mouth tight shut and nodded to Tammy to show him out. *Then* I let fly. And Tammy . . . Well, talk about a transformation . . . I'm no prude, Ricki. I've heard plenty of language in my time, but there are some expressions that should never cross the lips of a female, in my opinion. That may be an unfashionable view, but it's the way I feel.'

Looking grave, Mr Brightly nodded.

'Of course, the upshot was I had to get rid of her. And there was only one way to do that.'

'You paid her?' asked Mr Brightly, finding his voice.

'I did. Paid her a great deal. The girl has an inflated idea of her own worth. Though of course in paying her to go away I was doing likewise to the pimp Leroy.'

'Uh-hm,' coughed Mr Brightly. 'Forgive me, but I fear you may have been ill advised. They are unlikely to be satisfied however great the sum you parted with. I am very much afraid further is likely to be heard from them.'

'So what was I supposed to do, eh? Go to the police? Demand protection from the Boys in Blue? I don't think so, Ricki. And what do you suppose would be the outcome of employing a guard or a bouncer? Any bloke of that sort would be bound to acquire the self-same ambitions; it's a perennial hazard in this game. No, there was only one sane course open to me, and that was to get Tammy out of the way with enough loot to buy me a breathing space, and then spend a fortune making the place secure. You'd be amazed the stuff that's been put in here: I'm not talking just locks and bolts and spy-holes, but real high-tech equipment. The only feature I'm not too sure of is that b. dog. It's supposed to take its tip from me as to who's a friend and who's a foe, but it seems hell bent on savaging anything that arrives in trousers. Could be tricky, that, when we re-open for business.'

'Ah. So, er, business operations are temporarily suspended?'

'Well of course they are, Ricki. I had no option, with work going on all over the place. I've put it about that I'm taking a holiday and having the house decorated meanwhile. You have to be so careful what you tell the punters, it's the easiest thing in the world to upset them;

the last thing you want is punters thinking they might run into a spot of bother. So for the look of the thing the decorators are starting tomorrow morning. Anyway, Ricki, do you get my drift? This bit of trouble has led me into considerable unforeseen expense.'

Mr Brightly cleared his throat. 'Unfortunately,' he began. But she cut him off.

'Don't give me *unfortunately*, Ricki. I know all about *unfortunately*. I've had *unfortunately* up to me armpits. What I want to hear is what you can do to help me out. You've got well over a hundred grand of mine tied up in this and that, and I need some of it back. Of course it may turn out I don't actually need as much as I think; once business gets under way the situation will ease. But I've got bills to pay. I need to have something where I can get at it, Ricki. I need it *pro tem.*'

Mr Brightly gave no immediate answer. His dismay at being confronted with such a request was compounded by his unease at meeting a new side to Mrs Thompson. Her manner to him before today had always been soft, almost wooing; or, if the subject between them was to do with his expertise, deferential and trusting. Today she was brisk, frank, sharp. She even looked different. He had never before seen her wearing so little make-up and dressed so plainly. The thought briefly diverted him that her clothes – twinset and tweed skirt and businesslike shoes – comprised the sort of outfit Her Majesty was sometimes recorded in during her off-duty moments.

'Now don't let me down, Ricki,' coaxed Mrs Thompson. 'Not in my hour of need. I only want a portion of what's rightfully mine.'

'But Nanette, my dear, I am not your banker,' he protested. 'I am merely your financial adviser.' He spoke mildly and cautiously, for his total lack of experience in dealing with the woman Mrs Thompson presented today was suddenly borne in on him: he was as good as dealing with a stranger. 'It happens that you accepted certain advice of mine, and that I proceeded to invest your money as you wished, and declared that you so wished by appending your signature to a legal and binding document. It was always clear that these were measures for the *long term*. I have never handled any monies of yours intended as liquid assets. That is not my province.'

'Fucking hell,' cried Mrs Thompson, losing all restraint, 'what sort of language is that? You sound like a lawyer. All right, all right, I *know* you're a lawyer' – she put up the flat of her hand to prevent interruption – 'there's no need to talk like one. I asked you to come here as a friend – to talk like a friend and help me out as a friend. 'Cos that's what you swore we were: *excellent friends* you said, as we sat here in this very room not three months since. Or were we only excellent friends 'cos you were getting what you wanted out of me, Ricki – my moniker on your bits of paper? And this time it's got to be all legal and proper because it's me that wants something from you, eh? Is that it?'

Mr Brightly told himself that he must immediately say something to calm her down. Matters were deteriorating swiftly. Scarcely a vestige remained in this reckless creature of the Mrs Thompson he knew and was fond of. 'Nanette, Nanette, Nanette,' he soothed, hoping by repeating her name to reinstate her. 'If you will only give me a few quiet moments to think, I'm sure we can arrive at a solution. The problem has been rather sprung on me, you know. Just a few quiet moments?' He brought out a notebook and pen; and the wild look cleared from Mrs Thompson's face.

'I'm sorry, Ricki,' she wailed, 'I truly am. I don't usually sound off. It's not me at all. But I'm upset, Ricki. I've been scared witless.'

'Shh,' he reminded her, with a kindly smile.

'Sorry. I'll get us some coffee.'

'Yes, that would be a help.' He began to jot down figures. And without another word, Mrs Thompson left the room.

Alone with his pen and notebook, Mr Brightly blew

out his cheeks. He stared at the figures he had written down, made a few calculations and wrote some more, then sighed and returned notebook and pen to his pocket. He composed his features pleasantly in order to inspire confidence in her when she returned, and waited, hands resting lightly on knees, for his coffee.

'I think I've resolved our problem,' he announced the moment the door opened.

'You have? That's wonderful. You are the cleverest, most brilliant man, Ricki,' she simpered, setting a tray down on a low table. She brought him a cup and a sugar bowl. 'Tell me then, darling. I'm all ears.'

Mr Brightly stirred sugar into his coffee and launched into his proposal.

He could make a sum available to her, he explained. Would she be happy with twenty thousand pounds? Mrs Thompson thought she would, but hoped a loan was not being proposed; she could get one of those from the bank and pay through the nose for the privilege, which, given her assets, she didn't see why she should. Not a loan, confirmed Mr Brightly. More of an accounting exercise. Since, strictly speaking, her assets were not able to be got at until ten or so years had elapsed, she would be advanced twenty thousand pounds, and the 'advancee' (so to speak) would take that sum plus accumulated profits at the end of the investment term. The effect from the point of view of Mrs Thompson would be that of withdrawing for present use twenty thousand pounds from her investment portfolio. Furthermore, said Mr Brightly, who had felt rather stung by her assumption that he intended to employ usury as a means to assist her, he did not intend to charge her one penny for drawing up the relevant documents – which would be a complicated exercise and take him the best part of a day to complete.

'Oh now, there's no need for that, Ricki. I'm not seeking charity.'

He inclined his head, conveying an end to the discussion. Then, with his head bowed and his eyes on the

152

carpet and her effusion of delight pouring into his ears, it came to him that though her signature would be required on the various documents, he could not countenance returning to this house for that purpose. Not yet. Not so soon after his foolish walk here this morning orchestrated by lustful hope and blasphemous justification. It would sicken him to retrace those steps. Shrivelling at the very thought, he suggested to her smoothly that she should call at his office in Warwick tomorrow afternoon at four o'clock, by which time he would have ready the necessary paperwork. 'Would you be so kind, my dear, to save me that extra time? I may not be in the office myself, but my assistant, Miss Urvanessy, will have everything to hand. She will show you where you must sign, and she will hand you your cheque.'

'No trouble at all, Ricki. Delighted. Remind me again of the address.'

Rising to his feet, he gave her his card.

'Thank you, darling. You are so, so good to me. Mm, let me give you a kiss.' She stood on tiptoe, and he proffered a cheek.

'You do understand, Nanette, this is a special favour. One I couldn't bring off every day of the week.'

'Of course I do, Don't worry my sweet, twenty thousand smackers will more than save my bacon. I'm canny with money, you know. I'm a pretty shrewd businesswoman, as I think you've remarked yourself.'

'Indeed.'

She clung to his arm as he moved towards the door. 'But do come again soon. You know your Nanette adores to see you. You're still the handsomest man who ever calls.'

Mr Brightly was bracing himself against the reappearance of the Dobermann pinscher. But his exit was orderly, if unusually swift: once at the front door, Mrs Thompson was eager to have it opened and closed with all possible speed. Her manner made him recall the source of her troubles, and he cast anxious eyes up and down and across the road; but no-one, neither pedestrian nor passing motorist, approximated to his memory of Tammy or idea of Leroy.

'Would it be all right if I left now, Mr Brightly? Is there anything further you require?'

Mr Brightly sighed and propped his chin on his hand. And Miss Orvanessy came out of the doorway into the middle of the room.

'Is anything the matter, Mr Brightly?'

'No, no. You get along.'

'I will if you don't mind. The weather's beginning to close in.' Miss Orvanessy surveyed the papers strewn about, and the stacked files. 'But before I go I'll just' – she stepped forward and daringly removed his drained coffee cup – 'take this and rinse it out.'

'Now don't go making yourself late, Miss Orvanessy.'

With the cup held before her, she left the room.

Mr Brightly rose from his desk and went across to the window. He gazed downwards – at the veiled lighted shopfront on the corner, at the fog swirling round a street lamp. He moved away and went briskly into the corridor.

'Miss Orvanessy, let me give you a lift. It won't take me two minutes to pack up my papers. I think I'll finish my work at home.'

Halted in the act of winding a scarf round her neck, Miss Orvanessy appeared shocked. 'Oh, no,' she cried, 'it would be right out of your way. I couldn't possibly . . .'

'Just spare me two minutes?' he asked, knowing she could never bring herself to refuse a request.

'This is very kind of you indeed,' Miss Orvanessy said as they drove away from the vicinity of the castle towards a meaner area. It was the third time she had uttered thanks.

'How is your mother these days?' Mr Brightly asked.

'She's not too bad, thank you, for her advanced years. She has a visit twice a week from a Meals on Wheels lady, and we have a very kind neighbour who pops in on other days. How I should manage without this assistance I can't imagine. Though when Mother is having one of her off days I find I have just enough time in the lunch hour to get home and reassure myself that all is well.'

This information startled Mr Brightly. He couldn't recall when Miss Orvanessy last took a day off on account of domestic difficulty or sickness, or indeed if she ever had. 'If there is ever anything I can do to make things easier . . . I mean to say: if it came to the point where your mother required help on a regular basis, do please tell me. I couldn't possibly manage without you in the office. You are irreplaceable, Miss Orvanessy, there aren't two ways about it. Without you, our work in 12A would go to pot.'

She didn't answer at first, and when she did her voice was thick and stuttering. 'Oh . . . that is so very . . . thoughtful. You're kindness itself. You always have been . . . Mr Brightly.'

To allow her time to recover he sought in his mind for a businesslike topic, and in his haste selected the one that had been occupying him all afternoon.

'Tomorrow a rather difficult client . . . No, no; it's unfair of me to label her difficult; the poor lady has had a very bad time of it lately. Just merely do not be put off by her manner, Miss Orvanessy, when this client, Mrs Thompson, comes into the office to sign some papers. She is scheduled to arrive at about four o'clock. Unfortunately, I may not be around just then, but it's a simple enough matter. I'll mark the places where she must sign, and when she has done so I'd like you to hand her an envelope. I'll put everything in your hands in the morning, of course. I just thought I'd mention it now.'

'That will be no problem at all, Mr Brightly.'

'It's a left turn we take at the junction, I believe?'

'Yes, left at the junction, then first on the right and three doors down.'

Mr Brightly drew up outside a small terraced house, then got out of the car and went round it to lend an arm to his passenger.

'Thank you, thank you,' she began again.

'A pleasure. I hope you pass a pleasant evening. My regards to your mother.'

With which he climbed back into the driving seat, closed the car door and with the merest hum from the engine drove smoothly on through the foggy streets.

On the motorway Mr Brightly employed front and rear fog lights and drove at twenty miles an hour in the nearside lane. He decided to continue his journey through Stratford-upon-Avon rather than via the bypass to the country lanes; it seemed sensible to keep to areas of street-lighting as far as possible. But once he arrived in the town he began to regret this decision; it was clogged with traffic and home-bound pedestrians. At last he arrived at the bridge and joined the cars queuing to cross over it.

For a man of optimistic outlook, his spirits were inordinately low. This was due to a wasted day, he supposed, to moving money about unproductively: moving money about and causing ripples which led to the necessity to move more money still. And the sum involved being rather small made the amount of time consumed doubly irksome. However, at least he had settled on the route of this moving about. There only remained to draw up the documents and then get Ginny to write her signature on those applying to R and V Holdings and R N B Associates – of which companies she was a bored and uninterested co-director (R and V standing for Richard and Virginia, R N B for Richard Norris Brightly). But somehow even the thought of the work nearing completion could not lift his spirits, and on an impulse, on reaching the end of the bridge, he indicated that he wished to turn right; he flashed his headlights at the line of slow oncoming traffic until he was granted a space, then swung over the road and parked on the forecourt of the Swan's Nest Hotel.

He got out of the car, pulled up his coat collar and walked by the side of the hotel along the river bank. After a few moments he stopped. He gazed through the seething fog to the lighted theatre on the far side of the river which seemed to loom and sway like an ocean liner. Then something caught his eye nearer by and lower down: small, white, gliding. A wraith, he said to himself, though knowing it was almost certainly a swan. It glided away and became merely an impact in his own eyes. Then, as he blinked into the fog trying to gauge the point at which true sight became after sight, a gigantic happiness filled him. It arrived on the wing of sudden understanding. Chastity, he saw, was a gift. A special way of loving. And it was a positive way, not negative. Possessing chastity he could love Cressida Reece as hard as he liked, without harm to her or to anyone else, or any scandal to God. Next time he was plagued by longing he would welcome the discomfort. He would relish it as chastity in action.

It was a re-energized Mr Brightly who returned to the car – tall and striding, his coat collar framing his handsome silvery head.

He drove back into the traffic and after a few yards took the right-hand fork. There was now little doubt in his mind as to the true cause of his earlier despondency. This was not after all the irksome chores undertaken on behalf of Mrs Thompson, but acute self-dissatisfaction. On the exposure of some tawdry wishful thinking he had been taken by a thorough personal dislike. His own poor opinion, he now understood, was the one thing he couldn't put up with. Well, here was a solution: if he could hang on to this view of chastity as an active force, he would be spared further experience of the one thing he couldn't put up with – at least in the area of physical urges. Fortunately there were other virtues which, if diligently fastened to, could keep one's sense of self-worth intact. For this, he recognized, was the very heart of his nature: not the world's judgement of Richard Norris Brightly (the

157

world's judgement was often blunt and crude) but Richard Norris Brightly's.

With his optimism at full throttle, he brought the speed of the BMW down to a virtual crawl in deference to arriving at the Chedbury boundary.

12

In the spring, Cressida looked back over the winter past and told herself it was the cosiest ever. Richard had come virtually every Friday. She and Alex had rubbed along together well, despite the odd flare-up of irritation and anxiety (usually Alex's irritation at her anxiety). When her friend Julie had stayed with them she'd commented on this improved relationship: Alex was far less twitchy and much more relaxed, she'd said. Cressida considered the improvement was thanks to Richard. It was remarkable how he brought out the best in them, as if, as soon as he entered the house, all the dross fell away exposing the bedrock reality: that she and Alex were a mum and a son who truly loved one another. The good effect could last for days.

She'd explained to Julie that she thought it was Richard's doing. This had been a big mistake, because Julie had immediately assumed 'the affair' was on again and had wanted to know when she was going to meet this Mr Wonderful. She'd also enquired how Richard rated in bed. Fantastic, Cressida had bluffed, rolling her eyes. Then she'd looked away and said she didn't really want to talk about Richard in those terms, since she was madly in love with him. Of course, Julie had smelled a rat, and eventually Cressida had confessed he was married: which was why, she'd explained, Julie wouldn't be meeting him this visit: because of his position in life he had to be very discreet. Julie had looked alarmed. 'Christ, Cressida, I hope you're not getting yourself into another mess over a bloke.' 'Look, I love

159

him, right?' Cressida had snapped. Which had fortunately shut her friend up on the subject.

Of course, there'd come a Friday when Richard couldn't make it, due to his wife's requiring his presence (yet again) at the play. But he'd made it up to them by popping round for an hour late on the Saturday afternoon, gathering strength, he'd said, for the final performance and the cast's party afterwards (which was an experience he'd been dreading, poor lamb). Once or twice over the winter he'd actually telephoned – to ask whether Alex had got over a cold, or how she'd got on in an exam at college. And the time she got an A grade for an essay (her first A grade ever) he'd sent her a bouquet via Interflora with a card attached saying WELL DONE! Richard had helped her choose a car, and then, between her driving lessons with the Chedbury School of Motoring, had sat beside her while she drove out on practice runs. This he had done despite the rather obvious curtain twitching that accompanied their progress in and out of the close. 'My conscience is perfectly clear,' he'd smilingly answered when she'd mentioned the heavy hint dropped by Mavis Hutton. (Cressida hadn't wanted to mention the hint; she'd dreaded Richard being frightened off by it; but in the end had done so, feeling it was only fair to him.) 'It's an act of faith to remain unaffected by adverse comment,' he'd told her. Richard often said that – that something or other was an act of faith. He'd said it when urging her to buy a car before passing her test. Cressida had wanted to do it the other way about, she'd wanted to be good and sure. She was always terrified of eating into Alex's money (as she regarded her compensation award) unless it was certain Alex would benefit. But Richard and the act of faith had been vindicated; she'd passed the test at her first attempt. Alex had been overjoyed. And life had markedly improved. It was wonderful not having to push Alex places, and better still not being the butt of his grumpiness at being propelled round the streets like a baby.

Yes, the difference Richard made was truly staggering. She did sometimes yearn for a little bit more (a damn good seeing to, to be brutally honest), but that was just greedy. Richard having scruples meant sex just wasn't on the cards. And she accepted it, she really did. She'd even turned over in her mind whether to encourage a guy at college who'd made it clear he fancied her, and who might have been good for a quickie. But in the end she couldn't be bothered. She'd have felt guilty with Richard afterwards. Though, as she'd told herself at the time, feeling guilty was plum stupid, because presumably Richard did it regularly with his wife.

But she'd resolved not to think of Richard's wife. Specially not to envy her. She was more than grateful for what she had. What she had was a miracle.

'I don't care for our new vicar, I'm afraid.'

The first time Mrs Parminter confided this in her direct way to Mr Brightly, his reaction had been the predictable one. His eyebrows went up; he twinkled his eyes at her. 'Oh?' he said. 'Now why is that?' – making her at once feel abashed that she had rushed to judgement; for after all, she had shaken hands with the man and exchanged a few words on two occasions only: the first was after the service of induction when the Reverend Michael Nunn was installed as vicar of Chedbury, the second was after morning service a fortnight or so later. (Mrs Parminter was not quite so regular in her church attendance these days.)

When Mrs Parminter said again to Mr Brightly, 'I don't care for our new vicar, I'm afraid,' it was three months later. Even before the remark was out she knew she had made it before, exactly the same words in exactly the same order. But she could not halt her tongue, which had become increasingly devoted to giving accounts of her thoughts and to endlessly repeating those accounts. I have become one of those repetitive old people who must continue a tale to the bitter end come what may, a dismayed Mrs Parminter had frequent cause to remark to herself.

In answering her, however, Mr Brightly did not fall into the same trap. He did not smile and ask, 'Now why is that?' as Mrs Parminter recalled had been his response on the earlier occasion. In fact, his response this time rather surprised her, being somewhat out of character. He jumped to his feet and walked about, and eventually ended up by the window where he stood swaying on his heels and looking into the garden with his hands thrust deep into his pockets. Then, 'He is a new broom,' he said (more to himself than to her, Mrs Parminter thought). 'Yes, our Mr Nunn is certainly that. Evidently, no detail of the way we've been running our affairs at St Peter's these past ten years can safely be spared his vigorous attention. The Church Building Fund, for example, to which I've devoted my time and expertise . . . Ah, dear me. It's always a problem explaining complex financial arrangements to those who lack a feel for the subject. One can only hope . . .'

But the hope remained a mystery, since Mr Brightly interrupted himself to remark on the glorious June weather and how delightful to see the early roses full out.

Mrs Parminter remembered this and every other thing that was said and done that evening. She remembered because she went over it so often. And because afterwards he no longer came to visit her.

When she failed to see him at church on the Sunday following that Wednesday evening, she thought nothing of it. The new vicar, almost from the start, had seemed to take against his lay reader. Mr Brightly with his usual good humour had denied that dislike came into it, patiently explaining to Mrs Parminter that most lay readers were peripatetic, taking their assistance to parishes where it was urgently needed – parishes currently lacking a priest due to illness or an interregnum. Only a few lay readers were permanently attached to a particular parish, he said, and this was generally to assist an elderly or ailing incumbent, as had been the case with Canon Rawsthorne. The Reverend Michael Nunn was young and fit and dynamic. He was progressive in his outlook, liking to encourage ordinary members of his congregation to lead acts of worship and take a share of the pastoral duties. For all these reasons, the attachment of a lay reader to the Chedbury parish was clearly superfluous. This and only this, Mr Brightly had insisted, inspired the decision of Mr Nunn to direct Mr Brightly's services towards the peripatetic pool of lay readers. So it had caused Mrs Parminter no surprise at all when Mr Brightly had been absent from St Peter's that Sunday morning, for she presumed he'd been sent to conduct a service in some other parish. (In her heart, however, it was one of the things Mrs Parminter held against the new vicar, this cutting out of her friend – his beautiful voice, his distinguished bearing – from her Sunday worship.)

But naturally she expected to see him arrive at her house on the following Wednesday evening, since he had not mentioned to her beforehand any inability to do so. Something has cropped up, she said to herself when he failed to come. She felt no particular alarm, and anticipated a telephone call or that he would drop in during the next few days, giving an explanation. When a second Wednesday came and went with no sight of him or word, then she did become anxious. It was so unlike him. In her mind she went over that last evening with him again, repeated every word, pictured every gesture; and decided his manner at times had not only been uncharacteristic, but also edgy, perhaps even nervous. It's something to do with this new vicar, she said to herself, this Mr Nunn. I don't care for him, I'm afraid.

'Where's Richard tonight?' asked Alex, wheeling into the dining room doorway.

Cressida, who was typing up an essay and had lost count of time, looked at her watch.

'Gosh, isn't it late? I expect he was held up at work.'

It was a natural thing for her to think because he'd been held up at work and had arrived late on the previous Friday evening. She remembered how tired he had looked, and that at one point in the evening while she was making coffee he had unexpectedly sunk his head on her shoulder. 'Richard?' she had enquired with an uncertain laugh. At which he'd moved away. 'It's nothing, Cressida. Except that I'm under rather a strain at work. And am a little tired.' Then he'd made a joke. She remembered the fact of the joke and herself smiling at it, but not the joke's nature, because she hadn't been attending properly. She'd been busy kicking herself for letting an opportunity slip. Fancy questioning his action with that silly laugh, she'd scolded herself, instead of soothing him with kisses and drawing him closer. It was typical of her that she'd let surprise get in the way.

So recalling what had occurred on the previous Friday, she felt comfortably certain that he'd be along later. 'He'll be along later,' she said to Alex, as she resumed typing her essay.

'Shall I put the kettle on, then, and put out the mugs?' Alex called, wheeling away into the kitchen.

'Yeah, why not?'

They had thought so little of it at the time, Cressida marvelled. But looking back, she saw that Alex saying 'Where's Richard tonight?' had marked the moment when her life became poised on the brink of a big black hole.

The next day, Saturday, she'd kept fairly close to the phone. And very close indeed all Sunday. Before leaving for college on Monday morning she'd written a note for the Interflora man: *Please leave package at number 16.*

Yes, she had actually expected flowers, she recalled.

On the Tuesday afternoon she'd left college early. At home found no letter awaiting her, nor any note from

Mavis Hutton saying she'd taken delivery of a bouquet. So Cressida had gone to the telephone. She stood by it for some time, looking at it and chewing a strand of her hair, debating with herself. Then she snatched the receiver up and dialled Richard's number at work.

'He's away on business,' a Miss Orvanessy informed her. 'I'm afraid I can't say any more just now.'

Each word spoken by Miss Orvanessy had been separate from every other. She'd sounded like a nervy robot, thought Cressida. Then she recalled Richard telling her something about this assistant of his, this Miss Orvanessy: something to do with a disfiguring blemish which Richard thought was the cause of her jumpiness with strangers and her humble gratitude for any kindness. For a while Cressida comforted herself with the belief that her manner over the phone was Miss Orvanessy's customary one, the manner anyone burdened by a hideous facial disfigurement might employ, and that Miss Orvanessy had no special reason to sound nervous that afternoon. Cressida held her peace until Friday morning, when she thought it reasonable to ring Miss Orvanessy again, to enquire whether Mr Brightly had returned from his business trip and if so, could she speak to him? 'Hi, Richard, I was worried about you,' was the way she thought she'd begin, and that she'd work around to, 'Can we expect you tonight?' But this depended on her nerve holding up. Though surely it shouldn't be such a hard thing to ask, she reasoned with herself. This was Richard, remember? Good, kind, considerate Richard, who'd admitted to having feelings for her, who demonstrated by his dependability that he cared for her, and in whose twinkling eyes she often detected much, much more.

A man's voice answered her call. 'Yes?' he said brusquely.

'Oh. Um, Mr Brightly please. I'd like to speak to him.'

'Richard Norris Brightly?'

'Well, um, yeah. Or Miss Orvanessy, if Mr Brightly's not in.'

'Who's speaking please?'

'What?'

'Your name, caller?'

Cressida held her lips together against the mouthpiece while she considered whether she should or should not speak her name. Seconds seemed to stretch into minutes. Eventually, still undecided, she replaced the receiver.

'Hello, Ginny.'

'Dick! You bastard! Where've you been? What did you think you were playing at, going off without a word for *three whole days*? I've been worried sick. I didn't know what to think . . .'

'I'm in Coventry, Ginny. With the police . . .'

'People have been ringing up at all hours. Perfect strangers wanting to know if they could speak to you. One chap even came to the house, and I didn't much care for his manner. How do you think I felt? Police, did you say? Why? What's happened?'

'They've arrested me, Ginny.'

'Oh, that's just ridiculous. I'm sorry, I don't care what they allege, but they've got the wrong man. Tell them, Dick. Make it clear you're not like Jason Wright – claiming you don't drink and drive when everyone knows . . . Oh, but make them understand we're not the sort of people who go knocking the police – we were right behind them that time Jason got booked. But they have to see this isn't the same. It's God's own truth you don't drink and drive, and hundreds of people will stand up and swear to it. Tell them, Dick. Better still, put *me* on. I'll put 'em in the picture – don't I often say you'd be perfect at the wheel of a hearse?'

'This isn't a driving matter, Ginny.'

'Uh? But I thought . . . Aren't you on your way home? I thought you'd been stopped, or been in an accident or something . . .'

'I didn't say that. I've hardly said anything . . .'

'Exactly. I'm glad you admit it at last. It's really horrible of you, Dick, the way you keep me in the dark. It's humiliating when people ring up and say "Where's Dick?" and I have to say "I'm sorry I don't know" and they practically accuse me of concealing your whereabouts. It's a horrible position for a wife to be put in.'

'I'm sorry, Ginny.'

'Easy to say that now.'

'As a matter of fact, Ginny, it isn't. I'm only allowed this one short call. Just to let you know I'm all right.'

'You mean they haven't finished with you? But this is harassment! Get on to Roger . . . Oh God, I've just thought: Dick, you haven't forgotten the party tomorrow? You haven't forgotten we're expecting upwards of forty guests? You'd better not have forgotten. You'd better be home in very good time . . .'

'Actually, Ginny, I should cancel the party.'

'*What*? You can't mean it.'

'I'm really very sorry, Ginny . . .'

'You swine! You unspeakable rotter! Right. It's one thing to be put in an awkward position with strangers, but I will not be humiliated in front of our friends. I won't stand for it, d'you hear? Of course we're giving the party. And I warn you, Dick, let me down and I'll . . . I'll . . . I'll bloody well sue for divorce. So think about it. Do whatever you have to, but *be* here!'

'Goodbye, Ginny.'

'What? Dick? *Dick* . . .'

Ginny Brightly went quickly to the sofa. She plopped down, squeezed her palms together between her knees, hunched forward. She tried to halt the whirligig going on in her head: the rapid series of pictures, the jumble of her thoughts, all concerning the fiasco her party was destined to become due to her husband's perverse and unaccountable behaviour, and the scorn her friends would hide behind smiles, and the gossipy speculation that would keep them going for weeks or even years: 'Do you remember that party at the Brightlys' when Dick didn't even bother to show up? Poor Ginny was mortified.' These words ran into other words to do with betrayal and Dick's habit of never telling her things . . . Then at last, as the brakes took hold, she dragged to the forefront of her mind one or two words that seemed to merit contemplation. Police, she thought. Coventry. Arrested: but not for a motoring offence.

Soon her obvious course of action was plain and it propelled her back to the telephone. Whatever was up, she knew Tony would stand by her, for Tony always did. And Tony being a man would know what to do.

Tony Colebrook was roused from watching a televised football match, and consequently did not answer the phone with his usual pleasantness. He snapped his telephone number into the mouthpiece, and his finger snapped down the TV volume with the remote control then hovered to reverse the process.

Ginny felt hurt. After all that had occurred, after staring into the nightmare of a wrecked party and social humiliation, she didn't need Tony to be short with her. 'It's *me*, darling. *Ginny*. Something horrible has happened. Really horrible.'

At once he turned off the TV and gave himself to the task of coaxing out her story. The news that Dick might not return to Chedbury tonight quickened his interest. 'Look, I'll try and discover exactly what's afoot, then drive over, shall I? We can digest this together, whatever it is.'

'Oh yes, Tony. Please do that. I don't know where precisely in Coventry they've got him . . .'

'Leave it to me. I'll find out. But it may take me some time. So try and relax, darling, eh? Soak in a nice warm bath. Have a drink.'

'All right. But you'll let me know the minute you find out anything?'

'Of course I will, darling; I'll fly to your side. Don't I always?'

'Mm-mm. Hugs and kisses, Tony.'

'Hugs and kisses, Ginny.'

* * *

At twenty minutes to midnight Tony Colebrook pulled off the road and took up his mobile phone. Even before he cleared his throat, he heard Ginny's urgent cry, 'Tony?' 'Yes, it's me,' he told her. 'I've just left Coventry. Be with you soon, angel.' This by no means satisfied her, but he begged to be allowed to complete the journey. 'The moment I arrive you'll hear every word I managed to glean. Hang on a little longer, there's a good girl.'

Driving off, he reflected that it was not the word to speak over the phone. It was not a word easily said to her face – if at the same time he was to keep his own face straight. He'd had to duck his head and bring out a handkerchief when the word came out during the guarded discussion in the police station: perhaps because he was tired or over-stimulated: or perhaps because the unexpectedness of the word had lent it freshness, so that he seemed to hear it for the first time with its sound taking precedence over its meaning. Em-bezz-le-ment, he repeated now out loud, and laughed and punched the steering wheel. To Tony's mind, the quaint archaic ring of those four syllables attached more properly to the activities of witches, or furry burrowing creatures, than to the upright, smooth-talking men of substance – solicitors and accountants and civil servants and executives – who customarily drew the word to their doings. Those were your actual *embezzlers*. The chaps, like Dick, who *embezzled*. Tony was hard put to judge which version of the word was most hilarious.

He concentrated his mind on the subject of tonight's inquiry. On 'my holy friend' as he often referred to him at parties. 'My holy friend Dick Brightly tells me . . .' He could hear, now, the wry note in his voice. For hadn't he always suspected Dick of putting it on? Mind you, he'd never suspected the extent of his putting it on. Or the motive behind it.

He'd assumed that Dick had become so addicted to

169

playing that part in CADS that he'd hit on the device of becoming a lay reader in order to continue playing it. (How many people, wondered Tony, had ever even heard of lay readers?) Never had the idea occurred to Tony that Dick's act of holiness was carefully constructed: its purpose to build a personal fortune by means of conning old ladies and retired gents and the amateurs who preside over church organizations. What a brilliant scam. And how ironic that a proper priest should be the means of its all crashing down. Apparently, a new vicar had come to Chedbury, young and inquisitive, and had taken a dislike to the rich man of finance whom he had found there in place as the Chedbury lay reader. Questions had been asked. Advice had been taken on how agreements, entered into before this new cleric's time, might be scrutinized and dissolved.

Arriving at a roundabout where Chedbury was shown on the signs, Tony turned his mind to Ginny Brightly. He sobered up at once. Ginny and he went back a long way. They were old mates, long-time confidants. Periodically they were lovers.

When Carol, Tony's former wife, had discovered evidence of an illicit weekend, she had instituted divorce proceedings. And then, at the first mention of the word *divorce*, he and Ginny had ceased to be lovers. This was Ginny's decision. Indeed, for the couple of years leading to the decree absolute and for one or two subsequent years, Ginny had affected to believe that they never had been lovers, properly speaking. He had never met anyone so fanatically determined to maintain her grasp of the golden goose. Not that he blamed her. As a provider of the good life Dick clearly outstripped him by miles. But Ginny had continued to rely on Tony's friendship, and eventually, when all seemed safe, to permit an occasional amorous fling. Their friendship (officially Tony's friendship was with both Brightlys) had brought Tony to mix with the well-off Chedbury set and had led him

170

to swap membership in CADS for membership of the Chedbury Players. It had worked out well. On the whole it had suited him that Ginny remained with Dick. The intermittent nature of their affair gave generous scope for other loves – or other lays, he corrected himself, remembering that no-one had managed to take the place in his heart reserved for that minx-with-an-eye-to-the-main-chance, Ginny.

So how would it pan out now? he wondered. More to the point, how would he like it to pan out? But before he could do justice to this question, the corner with Framley Lane arrived, and he changed down two gears and took it neatly.

Tony spoke the word to her. Ginny repeated it twice. Then, thinking that her face and tone conveyed poor comprehension, Tony enlarged, both as to the legal meaning of the word so far as he understood it, and how this might apply to her husband's activities. Ginny prowled about the room making what Tony considered to be off the point remarks. He grew irritated. He had done all this running about for her, had spent a disagreeable time in a police station endeavouring to squeeze information out of grudging mouths, had spoken on the phone to a charmless individual named Roger who had been at school with Dick and was now acting for him, and by whom, incidentally, he, Tony, had been severely patronized: he had done all this and she hadn't so much as offered him a drink.

'Roger doesn't like me,' Ginny mused in response to Tony's unfavourable comment. 'So he was bound to be cool when you said it was me you were enquiring for. The reason he doesn't like me is because his wife doesn't. She's the most frumpy gallumping woman you can imagine: a bishop's daughter, which she seems to imagine makes her top-drawer.'

Tony lost patience. 'You might give a fellow a drink. I've spent the last five hours running errands for you.'

'Oh,' she said, turning and looking at him: almost,

Tony thought, as if asking for a drink were to claim undue notice. But she went nevertheless to the drinks cabinet and mixed his favourite tipple, gin and tonic. And evidently while she was doing so, thought things over. For, 'I suppose it's bound to come out,' she said as she brought him his drink. 'There's no help for it, is there, with a court case coming up?'

There was a faraway look in her eyes. He suspected that her grasp of the situation was still far from complete. But before he could address himself to this, the gin going down reminded his stomach of more substantial neglect. 'Sorry to put you to bother, but I discover I'm ravenous. It's been ages since my last mouthful.'

'Mm?' She had just this minute sat down, but now rose: though not as it turned out to go into the kitchen. Instead, she wandered over to the Pembroke table and peered down at a family photograph. 'I'll probably go for a divorce,' she reflected. 'Yes, I think that'd be best. Don't you, Tony? Maybe on the grounds of mental cruelty, because I have suffered, you know. Oh yes, things have been quite ghastly lately. Dick's been most odd. Do you know he made me resign as director of two of his companies? – not that it made a ha'penny worth of difference to me, there was nothing for me to *do* as a director, other than sign papers which were all double Dutch. But the way he did it – standing over me, you know? Literally forcing me to sign.'

'I expect, seeing this coming, he was trying to protect you,' Tony suggested. 'Look, could I possibly fix myself a sandwich?'

'When everyone hears it was mental cruelty, they'll feel sorry for me. Oh, I suppose some people'll be mean, there's always someone ready to be beastly, but my true friends will understand. They'll see that it can hardly be my fault if Dick decides to go off his head. Because that's what I think is at the root of all this. Just think, Tony. All that ridiculous religious affectation and churchgoing Dick went in for: wasn't it part and parcel

172

of the way he's gone off the rails in business? It was unbalanced. We just didn't see it because he appeared so rational and in control. But we were hoodwinked, Tony. Everyone was.'

'All I know for certain right now, my angel, is I'm bloody starving.' He made purposely for the kitchen. 'What've you got in the fridge?'

This at last got through to Ginny. She ran after him. 'Be careful, Tony. The fridge is bulging, but mostly with stuff for the party.'

'What party's that, Ginny, for Pete's sake?' he cried, wrenching open the fridge door. He removed a plate and lifted its cover.

'Here, let me. There's beef or chicken . . .'

'Chicken, I think, at this time of night.'

She took the plate from him and then stood there, apparently weighing it. 'Oh yes, I see what you mean. I hadn't thought . . . But yes, I suppose we will have to cancel the party. Actually, I was thinking earlier that you and I could go ahead with it, without Dick. But of course, you're right, it wouldn't do. You will phone everyone up for me, darling? First thing tomorrow. Explain that with Dick going off his head like this, I've simply no option.'

'Where's the bread?' Tony took the plate from her. 'Come on, Ginny: *bread*.'

Casting round, Ginny spotted the bread bin. She moved towards it, gathering butter dish and a knife on the way, and proceeded to cut and butter slices, and hammer home her request. 'You will do the phoning round for me, darling? I couldn't face it, myself. You can explain what a horrible time I've been having . . .'

'Yes, yes,' he agreed, watching her hands, willing them to make haste.

'I really and truly believe the way Dick's gone on lately was latent madness coming out. Enough slices, darling?'

'It'll do for starters. Got some mayonnaise?'

She went to the fridge and reached for a jar and

returned with it to the bread board. Hungry though he was, he registered that she was moving in a dream-like fashion. She doesn't really get it, he told himself. But at least – with her busy hands and her upward glances and her beseeching smile – she now appreciated the fact of his presence and that he had needs as well as uses. 'One thing we can be certain about in all this,' he suggested casually: 'poor old Dick won't be snuggling down tonight in his own little beddy byes. It's just you and me, angel.'

Her silence implied that she was considering this fact from all the angles. As indeed she was. What a beast, expecting me to come across on top of all this, she was telling herself. However, Tony's assistance right now was indispensable, it would pay her to keep him sweet. 'You'd better put your car away in the garage,' she said. 'Otherwise in the morning it might be noticed on the forecourt. People will think.'

'What'll they think?'

'That we spent the night together, silly. There'll be gossip.'

'Dear God . . . You don't think it's possible your neighbours will have something other to talk about during the next few weeks?' At her blank stare, he started to laugh; he laughed so hard he felt unsteady and had to seize the table edge.

'What's so funny? Tony!' she screamed, starting to shake. 'Tell me why you're laughing!'

He shook his head and wiped his eyes. Her indignant expression provoked an itch in him to slap her. Instead, he brought her down to earth with words. 'It's just occurred to me,' he said: 'I'm jolly glad I wasn't persuaded to let old Dick invest any of *my* hard-earned cash. Unlike some of our friends.'

Still clasping the knife, Ginny sat down. Her face took on a naked appearance. It put Tony in mind of how she'd looked one evening a year ago as she stepped out of a hotel shower. (He and Ginny were enjoying a few stolen days together at the time.) The nakedness of her face had been due not just to dampness from the shower, but to an absence of the emotions it had reflected for much of the day: the pouting annoyance when they were checking in and she suspected the couple ahead of them were given a superior room; the greedy intensity during a shopping expedition; the sulky envy at afternoon tea ('*Chanel*,' she'd hissed as a good-looking woman was escorted to a seat; 'that gorgeous suit is *Chanel*'). Emerging from her pre-dinner shower, her face had been bare of these and all other expressions, until he caught her up and began kissing her breasts, when it reflected pleasure.

But now, on her blank face, he observed the arrival of horror. He felt tenderness and remorse. 'Ginny, my love . . .'

Her jaw dropped. Panting through an open mouth, she was slowly explaining a thing to herself: *Dick stole from our friends*. She saw her friends form up: not, as before, to clamour for her husband's financial advice, but to clamour for vengeance, to exact restitution. They formed up outside her house, they broke down the door and ripped down her curtains and tore up her rugs, hauled up pieces of furniture, ransacked drawers, made off with her special clothes, her best jewels . . .

Her panting became sob-laden. He went to her and released the knife from her hand. 'It's all right,' he soothed. 'Easy, Ginny; easy now.'

Her arms went round his neck. 'Help me, Tony,' she pleaded. 'Help me salvage what I can from this mess. Help me get away.'

'In the morning we'll have clearer heads,' he promised. 'We'll be better able to think things out.'

'But you will help? I can't manage alone. Promise you'll help me, Tony, promise, promise.'

'I promise, darling,' he said. And keeping one arm around her, he reached out with the other and topped a layer of bread and chicken with one of bread and mayonnaise to form a halfway decent sandwich.

*   *   *

As dawn broke, and light glimmered faintly behind the curtains, and chuntering started up among the starlings that Ginny Brightly waged war against every spring, sending handymen up ladders to plug nest holes under the eaves; and as the night-duty sergeant from Chedbury police station drove home along Framley Lane, Ginny Brightly came awake. She opened her eyes and recalled where she was lying: not in her single bed in the master bedroom, but in the spare room's king-size bed with Tony. And she went on to recall other matters, all the words she had recently exchanged and the thoughts that had entered her brain. Her mind was disciplined this morning; it did not buzz and spin with these recollections but went from one to the next in orderly sequence. She thought of Dick's failure to return home the other evening. Of his continued absence and Miss Orvanessy's incomprehensible explanation. Of strangers telephoning and the man who had come to the door. Of Dick calling her at long last from a police station in Coventry. And then she thought of Tony's discoveries and how full of false starts her understanding of these had been: it had seemed to take her half a lifetime to gather the full picture. At this point her children came into her mind, as they had not come last night, and she thought dispassionately of each in turn, foreseeing that they would continue in the pattern their different natures had already established. Giles, her son, would continue to achieve success – the first class degree he was forecast to take and then a first class job. Her daughter Harriet, on the other hand, was now presented with a first class excuse to abandon the path her mother had struggled to keep her to; she would leave the school she loathed and pursue her pathetic little ambition to become a nursery nurse. Well, bully for Harriet, the outright winner in all this, Ginny exclaimed bitterly to herself, for her father with his misdemeanours had presented her with the perfect opportunity to do as she wished. Then her flash of bitterness dissipated, as Ginny went cold. Her mind, continuing its trawl, came to the moment when it thudded into her brain that Dick had not only mistreated the funds of faceless strangers, but of people who were known to her, their friends and neighbours. And she remembered the way she had imagined these friends and neighbours forming up to seize her precious things. She had known in that moment it would be necessary to leave her house. She had known that her best hope lay in extracting its maximum value.

Now, light glowed strongly behind the spare room curtains, and the starlings called with piercing insistence, and vehicles passed frequently along Framley Lane. And Ginny Brightly discovered she was still stuck with the same course, the new day presented no better option. But this morning that option struck her as dismal. For her faculties were sufficiently refreshed by sleep to arrive at the heart of the matter, and she faced the fact that the most precious thing in her life, her leading position in the exclusive Chedbury set, could not be taken with her when she left. It was about to be destroyed. Very soon the regard and respect and affectionate envy people felt for her, which she had worked hard to achieve, would be replaced by something quite opposite.

13

Cressida, at the wheel of her Vauxhall Astra, pulled a tissue from a box lying on the passenger seat and vigorously blew her nose. She then scrunched the tissue up and pressed it into the wodge of older balled-up tissues and screwed paper wrappers and car parking tickets with which the compartment under the dashboard was stuffed. Through the windscreen she observed a junction looming and a sign which mentioned Chedbury, and she indicated left and changed down. All these actions were performed automatically. Her mind was on none of them, but on the past half-hour at college from where she was now fleeing. From start to finish her mind roamed the length of that tutorial. Wasn't it just typical of her, she lamented, to have been so embarrassing? Typical to have gone and cried?

As the car bore her steadily towards Chedbury, she acknowledged that while she would wish very heartily not to have cried it was inevitable for her to have done so. It was simply not in her to utter the words 'I've got a personal problem' without then bursting into tears. And she'd had to offer something. She'd been obliged to give some explanation for a scrappy and often incoherent essay that had earned C- instead of her customary B+. In the end she'd blurted out the truth. And then . . . Poor sod, she wailed to herself, thinking of the tutor whose enquiry had started her off, and who was really just a baby, being several years her junior and male to boot. She recalled his appalled expression and his edging a little away from her and his stuttering words. 'What a bitch of an afternoon,' she imagined him telling a wife or girl friend. 'I had this mature female student with a personal problem crying all over me. Not a pretty sight.'

Oh stuff him, cried Cressida, telling herself no harm had been done, that maybe a glimpse of the messy side of life would help him grow up.

Her defiant feeling was still uppermost when she arrived in Chedbury. Consequently, instead of continuing along Stratford Road towards Symmonds Close, she swung into Market Square and niftily stole a scarce parking space from under the nose of a driver who'd spent the past five minutes patiently waiting for one. Affecting obliviousness, Cressida reached for her purse and jumped out of the car. She crossed the pavement and entered the newsagent's, and in the belly of the shop came to a halt. Her eyes ran over the shelves on which boxes of chocolates stood on their sides. Her hand, creeping towards the modest half-pound box she had envisaged as appropriate consolation for her present distress, suddenly shot upwards to the shelf above and drew down the full pound. The box had a satisfying weightiness. It begged to be stripped of its slippery cellophane. Hastily, before contrary thoughts could surface, she bore it to the counter and opened her purse.

The assistant took Cressida's five-pound note and pressed open the till. Then a woman she had served earlier and with whom she was on friendly terms leaned across with a further item of news to convey. Sighing with impatience, Cressida shuffled her feet and gazed down at the newspapers piled on the counter: copies of the local weekly newspaper, fresh in that very afternoon. Cressida's eyes ran over the headline: CHEDBURY MAN CHARGED WITH . . . and remained hooked by the final word, FRAUD.

'I'll take this newspaper, too,' she called, interrupting the shop assistant's friend.

'I'll see you tonight, Eileen,' the assistant said. 'Sorry

about that,' she told Cressida, passing over the change.

With her heart chugging like a tanker going up hill, Cressida hurried through the shop, stuffing as she went her purse into her pocket and tucking the paper bag containing the chocolates under an arm. On the pavement outside she came to a halt and unfolded the newspaper. Information seemed to judder to her, piecemeal: Solicitor Richard Brightly. Financial adviser. Family man. Wife and two children. Luxurious house in Framley Lane Chedbury. Well known in Warwickshire. Prominent churchman. Charged with defrauding his clients, many of whom are local people. 'I may be ruined,' claims Kenilworth widow, Mrs Guisborough-West. 'I put my trust in Mr Brightly and now it appears he has cleaned me out.'

The bag of chocolates fell to the pavement as Cressida wrung the very life out of the newspaper. She beat it against her breast and screamed.

'Hush dear, is something the matter?' asked a woman – the first onlooker brave enough to step up to Cressida and become part of the spectacle.

Her example encouraged others.

'Is she ill?'

'Do you think she's in shock?'

'Can you tell us what's upsetting you, love?'

'Ee's-ay'n-ah-un's-oney!' screamed Cressida, meaning He's taken my son's money, but unable to get her mouth round the syllables.

'She is ill,' said the first woman decisively.

'Should we call an ambulance?'

'Perhaps the surgery. Who's your doctor, love? Do you live round here?'

'Are you poorly, dear? I'll go and get her a glass of water.'

'Oh-oh-oh,' wailed Cressida, meaning No, no, no. She buried her face in the twisted newspaper.

'That's the *Chronicle*,' said a man, peering closely.

'That's right,' said the woman called Eileen. 'I was

180

talking to Anne in t' shop when this lady was buying it. Eh, I say: you kn 1e news that's plastered all over the *Chronicle* this week?'

'No?' someone prompted.

'That man, Mr Brightly, who was big in the church. He's been' – she lowered her voice, but compensated with exaggerated lip movements – '*diddling folk.*'

'Oh, my lord! You don't suppose this lady . . .'

They looked at Cressida, who had quietened somewhat. 'Are you feeling better, dear?' asked the woman who'd been the first to come to her aid. 'Would you like us to find somewhere nice and quiet where you can sit down for a bit?'

'Here we are,' cried the woman who had run for a glass of water into Parkes the butcher's where she was known. 'Take a sip of water, love.'

But Cressida pushed the glass aside. Shudderingly and lengthily she expelled air. Then, 'Excuse me,' she said, 'but has anyone seen my car keys?'

They searched the ground about their feet. A man came up with the bag containing the chocolates. 'There's this,' he said. 'Is it yours, love? Did you drop it?'

Cressida patted her pockets, then brought out her keys. 'It's all right, I've got them.' She thrust through the throng towards her car.

'She's never going to drive, the state she's in.'

'Maybe we ought to stop her.'

'It's a bit awkward . . . Just a minute, love . . . No, it's no good, she's belting up.'

'Miss, are you sure you didn't drop this?' The holder of the bag peeped inside. 'It's a box of chocolates,' he reported.

'Then they are hers,' cried the woman called Eileen, seizing them from him. 'I saw her buying them. Wait,' she cried, running forward to rap on the Astra's window. But Cressida was intent on backing out of the parking space and kept her head averted.

Helplessly, they watched the car zoom backwards

into the centre of the square, pause for a fraction of a moment, then accelerate away.

A discussion then broke out concerning an appropriate conclusion to the chocolate problem. It was felt that when the lady recovered from her upset she might well return to the newsagent's in search of her purchase. 'I'll take them in to Anne,' Eileen offered. 'She can set 'em aside.'

'You know,' said the woman who had run into the butcher's and whose hand still clasped the glass of water, 'I'm sure I've seen her about the town. But not in a car – on foot, I'd say – maybe pushing a pram. Hang on, it'll come to me in a minute.'

But in the general opinion sufficient time had been expended already, and to murmurs about pressing commitments and with a cessation of eye contact, the ad hoc group dispersed.

In his bedroom, Alex Reece was tapping a message into his computer.

Hi, Uncle Jonathan. Mega thanks for getting the Saeko man to view my game. You know we thought the third route was a bit tame? Well I've worked out a really brilliant diversion . . .

Here he paused, hearing the arrival of his mother's car in the drive, then the car door slamming and her key entering the lock of the front door. He clicked on SAVE.

But this evening she surprised him. She did not charge straight upstairs to check whether he'd been correctly deposited in the house from school and had got himself upstairs in one piece. After a moment or two, hearing her voice and assuming she was using the phone, he continued: *. . . which would be easy to incorporate. Can you let him know, please? Also that I could probably make any alterations he wants . . .*

Again Alex paused, as his mother's voice rose to him in a passionate wail. The wail went on and on. He clicked on SAVE and then QUIT, then wheeled to the door and let himself out onto the landing.

The sound from his mother surged, became a screech which hurt his ears. It was quite difficult at first to pick out the words.

'Not *my* money, *my son's*. What? Yes it was in my name, but it was intended for Alex who is only fifteen. Then why the fuck don't you listen? My son is *handicapped* – that's what I'm trying to get over. The money's vital to take care of his future. Hell, if you saw my son you'd know why I'm upset. Any mother'd be upset with a son who can't walk, who's confined to a wheelchair, and just when the future looks bright for a change it all goes up in smoke. Wouldn't you be upset? I have all this to face on my own, you know. What d'you think it's like being a single mother with a handicapped son and nothing behind her? It's a nightmare, that's what. Having that money let me sleep at nights. Jesus, I can't believe it. I can't believe it. I can't believe he'd do this to me. I can't believe anyone would, but Richard, *Richard . . .*'

Swallowing, feeling sick, Alex wheeled to the top of the stairs and hoisted the body that his mother had disparaged into the chair lift. She's at it again, he said to himself. He'd assumed those bad old days were over, the days when she'd scream details of his problems down the telephone to strangers. And what money was she talking about? As far as he knew he didn't possess any money. And where did Richard come into it?

With excruciating slowness the chair descended. His mother let out an animal sort of shriek: 'But I can't hang on, I have to know NOW!'

'MOTHER!' Alex shouted, hoping to stop her. But instead of the authoritative baritone that was needed to do the trick, his larynx emitted a reedy croak. The sound depressed him. It seemed to place him in ugliness with his mother. At last the lift ended its run and Alex levered himself into the ground floor wheelchair.

He pushed into the living room. He thought she sounded demented. 'STOP IT, MOTHER!' The strain of shouting caused not only his blood to rise but also an unpleasant feeling from the past. He hated her for re-stoking that feeling with her abandoned noise, hated her for causing him to force out his own cracked cry. When it was plain his protest had had no effect whatever, he thrust forward and back with frustration and repeatedly banged the chair arms with his fists.

Turning her head, her face still attached to the wet and steamy receiver, Cressida at last took note of her son's agitation. 'I have to go,' she said. 'You got my number? Please ring the moment you know the position.' She slammed the receiver down and hurried over, knelt on the floor and wrapped her arms round her son's legs.

'Get off!' yelled Alex.

'Love,' she cried reproachfully, sinking back on her heels.

'What the fuck's going on?'

'Don't talk like that, Alex.'

'Why not? You do.'

'Only when I'm very, very upset. And I am upset, I freely admit it. But darling, there's a reason. And I'm going to have to tell you, though it kills me to give you bad news . . .'

'Why were you talking about *my* money? You know perfectly well I haven't got any money.'

'Yes you have. Well, technically I suppose it's mine – you know, the money I was awarded in compensation. But darling as far as I'm concerned that money is yours. For your future. That's why I let Richard invest it for us . . .'

'It-is-not-my-money!' Alex shouted.

'Sh, love. Of course it is.'

Oh, there was no talking to her! He thrust about more furiously than ever, wishing to do her violence, wishing to rise up and pin her down and force her to pay heed to his position on the subject.

'Stop it. Please, Alex. You might tip over the chair.'

'Then will you listen—'

'Of course I'll listen.'

'—to what I'm saying?'

'I am, love, I am.'

'Then get this: that money's *yours*. You got it 'cos a doctor messed you up. Which is typical – it'd have to be that sort of reason for you to get money. And if a doctor was going to mess anyone up, it'd have to be you. Know why? 'Cos you're pathetic. You're so pathetic you ask for it. That's why I don't want a penny of it ever touching me, right? I can get all the money I want with my brain. Or is that too tough an idea for you to get your head around?'

'Alex!' cried Cressida. 'Alex, Alex . . .'

'And what the hell's Richard got to do with it?'

Cressida fell silent. She wrung her hands, stared at him glassily, breathed through an open mouth. The thought occurred to her that he could, if he'd a mind, now say a thing that was very much worse than the hurtful things he'd just come out with. He could say, and probably would, that it was typical of her to pick a man who would double-cross her; that being a pathetic sort of person she asked for such treatment. She waited with her heart hammering.

'I want to know about Richard,' he croaked.

She got up and looked round and spotted the screwed-up newspaper on the chair where she had earlier tossed it. She smoothed the paper out and handed it to him.

He studied it in silence. Endless silence, it seemed to Cressida.

'So Richard miscalculated,' said Alex at last. 'Made wrong speculations with funds belonging to' – he referred back to the newsprint – 'Mrs Guisborough-West – rich old biddies like that. OK, maybe as a result, your money's affected like everybody else's money he handled. So what? Richard wouldn't do anything to hurt us deliberately.' He rapped the newspaper: 'I don't care what they say in here, we're Richard's mates. He cares about us, like we care about him.'

Cressida's breath came out in wobbly gasps. 'Oh Alex, you don't know what it means to hear you say that.'

'Say what? That Richard wouldn't hurt us? Well he wouldn't, would he? Not on purpose. But at least this explains why he stopped coming round. I hope he doesn't think we'd hold it against him. Gosh, I wish he'd get in touch.'

'Oh, love, so do I!' Her legs went weak, she sank down on the carpet.

'It'd be nice to be able to say we're sorry about his trouble and show we stand by him.'

Cressida swallowed. Then, 'I've given those people in his office our phone number. Maybe when they ring back I could ask them to pass on a message,' she suggested weakly. 'I wonder if they'd let me speak to his secretary, that Miss Orvanessy.'

'That'd be good, Mum.'

She noted with relief she was Mum once more. 'Sorry about the row I kicked up, son. Sorry to have embarrassed you. It's only money, I guess.'

'That's right. Richard being in trouble is much more serious.'

Cressida nodded, and they both fell quiet for a while, allowing their feelings time to settle. Then Cressida rose. 'I'll go and get us some tea.'

Alex wheeled after her into the kitchen. 'Mum?'

'Yes?' she answered wearily.

'Don't be always worrying about money. You know that game I've been telling you about? Well, Uncle Jonathan's persuaded this high-up executive in a big computer company to take a butcher's at it.'

'Has he, love? That's nice. Now let me see: what do you fancy eating tonight?'

'Um, dunno really.'

'Tell you what: why don't I go out and get us a Chinese?'

'Suits me.'

'It'd be nice, wouldn't it? Make a bit of a change? I'll just pop upstairs while the kettle boils. Can't go out looking like this. I must look a fright.'

'Yeah, OK, Mum. Great,' sighed Alex.

The woman who had run into Parkes the butcher's for a glass of water that afternoon was now busy in her kitchen preparing a casserole for supper. For the past two hours she had continued to puzzle over the identity of the woman who'd had hysterics in Market Square. Now the name came to her. Cressida Reece, she said to herself. And promptly sat down on the kitchen stool.

A copy of the *Chronicle* lay nearby on the counter. She pulled it closer and re-read every word concerning the Richard Brightly scandal. She recalled that a year or so ago Cressida Reece herself had made the front page. Cressida had been the victim of a surgical error and had been awarded damages. She'd felt a particular interest in the case because Mavis Hutton (a close friend since pre-marriage days when they'd worked together in the office of a local factory) was a near neighbour of Cressida's and often spoke of her struggles to raise a disabled son. Filled with presentiment, she unhooked the kitchen phone.

Mavis Hutton was also preparing that evening's meal. She was flaking fish for a pie when the telephone rang. Hastily she wiped her hands. 'Yes, hello,' she said briskly, intending to convey little time at her disposal.

'Mavis, it's me, Beryl.'

'Oh, Beryl. You've caught me in the middle of cooking.'

'Sorry; but can I just ask you something? Your neighbour, Cressida Reece: a biggish girl, isn't she, with a great mane of blond hair?'

'That sounds like Cressida.'

'Does she drive a gold-coloured car, newish-looking?'

'That's right. She hasn't had it long. They chose it 'cos the boot was big enough to take the wheelchair. Oh my goodness, there's nothing wrong, is there? She hasn't had an accident?'

187

'Nothing like that. But Mavis, didn't she get a large sum of money as a result of that case?'

Mavis Hutton grew impatient. 'You know she did, Beryl. It was in the papers, it was on the telly; we talked about it.'

'Have you read this week's *Chronicle* by any chance?'

'No, I haven't. Fred's reading it now while I'm supposed to be cooking his supper.'

Mavis's friend gave a brief account of the week's big story and followed by relating the scene she had witnessed that afternoon in Market Square.

Mavis's impatience melted. She reached behind her and drew up a chair. 'Oh my God,' she said, sitting down.

'I may be putting two and two together and making five . . .'

'No, I don't think you are. Oh Beryl, this is all my fault.'

'Yours? How can it be, Mavis?'

'I introduced them. I sent him round to her house. She was in a state over all the publicity she was getting and I thought she needed counselling. He was standing in while we hadn't a vicar,' she explained to her friend who was not a churchgoer. 'If it's true, then there's no justice in the world. Cressida's the last person this should happen to: after all her trouble and years of devotion to Alex. I won't ever be able to face her again . . .'

'Now stop it, Mavis, that's rubbish. You didn't send him round to steal her money. You weren't to know. The man's obviously a hypocrite, a con merchant.'

'Beryl, I really must go. I'll see you at lace-making.'

'I can't get to class this week. Come and have tea one afternoon. Give me a call.'

'All right. Goodbye, Beryl.'

'Goodbye, Mavis, and don't worry.'

Mavis Hutton went into the lean-to conservatory where her husband was reclining in a patio chair lined with floral cushions. 'Give me the *Chronicle*, Fred,' she demanded.

'What?' said Fred.

She snatched it from his slack and unsuspecting hand.

'Hey! I was reading that,' he cried. 'It's all about that Brightly chap you were so keen on. I always thought he was a smarmy git.'

'Is that so?' said Mavis, glancing at the place where her husband's shirt strained over his belly and at the cigarette smouldering between his fingers.

'Yeah. And seems I was right. It says in there . . .'

'Shut it, Fred. I can read for myself.'

'I thought you were getting supper. What time're we having it?'

For two minutes Mavis made no reply. Then she chucked the newspaper into her husband's lap and said, 'When it's cooked.'

Far too agitated to re-apply herself to the cooking of food, she did not return to the kitchen. She ran upstairs, and in the privacy of her bedroom where she would not be overheard, removed the receiver from the bedside phone and tapped out the number of Chedbury Vicarage.

Cressida lay in the dark in bed, staring at the fact of her lost money.

All evening she had forgotten it. She had dwelt instead on Alex's opinion of her. Knowing he did not include the encouragement of a confidence trickster and laying herself open to the work of a crook in the list of sins he held against her was a relief. To some extent this had kept her from the memory of his harsh words earlier; though during the evening she'd often half heard them again, briefly, like the sound of a curtain swishing, or someone coughing in another room. With them a stinging pain had come, which she'd soothed down by repeating to herself the welcome words he'd spoken later, words of being mates with Richard, of caring about him and missing him. With words such as these Alex had seemed to make himself her ally.

189

But now she was alone, her thoughts dwelt on the whereabouts of her money. She found she was not at all consoled by Alex's faith in Richard's intentions. Richard's intentions were nothing to her. All she cared about was what he had actually done. For however keenly she'd loved and yearned for him, Richard had figured in her life only briefly. Whereas half a lifetime had been devoted to Alex, to worrying about him, fighting for him. She remembered some of the campaigns she'd waged, and the way her heart had sunk as each tussle had become unavoidable. She was not a natural agitator; with every crisis she'd had to gear herself up all over again. For instance that time the authorities, out of convenience and cheese-paring and lack of care, tried to place Alex in an unsuitable school, a school where the majority of pupils were mentally retarded or emotionally disturbed: she'd seemed to rupture her heart's vessels arguing for his present place in a normal school with nursing assistance and transport laid on. She remembered the nights when she'd lain awake scheming to get money out of people and institutions in the event of Alex's health deteriorating, as doctors warned it might. Who would have thought that because of some other doctor's callous mistake the money would simply fall into her lap?

The miracle loomed in her mind and sweat broke out on her body as she remembered signing the money away. Nothing, she thought, turning her head into the pillow and sinking her teeth into it, not soft words from Alex nor proof of Richard's intentions being bloody marvellous, nothing could compensate if that money were lost.

She didn't need Alex to point out she was pathetic.

Arriving home on the following day Cressida was surprised to see a car parked in the road outside, and when she unlatched her front door to hear voices within.

In the sitting room Alex was chatting with a stranger. 'Oh, Mum, this is . . .'

But the stranger cut in. 'Detective Inspector Witty. You are Mrs Cressida Reece? I'd like a word with you, please.' He looked at Alex. 'It might be better in private.'

'Anything you have to tell me can be said in front of my son,' Cressida said airily, remembering that, on the surface at least, she and Alex were at one over the subject of Richard and her money, and intending to keep it that way.

The inspector hesitated. 'All right,' he conceded, and went on to confirm that he was investigating the business practices of Richard Norris Brightly.

Cressida listened tensely, expecting to be soon enlightened as to the fate of her money.

'How long have you known Mr Brightly, Mrs Reece?'

'Um, about a year.'

'And you know him well? Intimately?'

Cressida frowned. 'Mm, fairly. He called round about once a week. Didn't he, Alex?'

'It was a regular arrangement?'

'He did tend to come every Friday.'

The inspector nodded while keeping his eyes on her. It struck Cressida that his manner was cold. She had begun to puzzle as to why this should be, when he broke roughly into her thoughts.

'I dare say you knew how he earned his living? You and he being such close friends and in regular contact, I dare say he confided details of his operations?'

'No he didn't. He never mentioned business or investments again, once I'd been persuaded to give him a cheque.'

'But he did persuade you. Now how'd he do that, Mrs Reece?'

Cressida shrugged. 'Sounded like he knew what he was talking about, I s'pose. Made the investment plan sound like, well, good sense. Said I'd get a better return than from a building society. And . . . I trusted him. He may have gone into details at the time, but to tell you the truth I wasn't following too closely. I'd never had to do with investments before.'

'Oh come on, Mrs Reece. From what I hear he's been visiting you every week for a year. I bet he painted you a rosy picture, let you in on a few plans.'

'No, he didn't,' Cressida cried, exasperated and quite at a loss to understand why she should be questioned in this hostile manner. 'And I haven't a clue what you're getting at.'

Alex came to her aid. 'If you want to know, Richard came here to relax,' he declared. 'He came to escape from his business concerns, and his church work and his wife going on about her amateur dramatics. He was interested in my computer programs. He often brought me a computer magazine. And he liked hearing Mum talk about college, and to chat about his daughter. Ordinary stuff like that.'

'I see,' said the inspector, looking from Alex to Cressida.

'Aren't you going to say what's happened to the money?' Cressida demanded. 'That's what I want to know. That's what I presumed you'd come about.'

'You and a couple of dozen others,' sighed the inspector. 'But all that's to be unravelled, and it'll take some considerable time. In cases like this it can take years before people know if they'll get anything back: it's usually a percentage, if they're lucky. Fortunately, this case might be sorted sooner than most: Mr Brightly is being co-operative, which is something to be said in his favour, I suppose. So, Mrs Reece, you had no inkling at all about how our friend was operating your portfolio?'

'Operating my what? Look, I just signed some papers and signed a cheque and that was it. You don't imagine I *agreed* to him helping himself? – to money I thought was going to take care of Alex's . . . and my future?' (In the nick of time, for Alex's benefit, she remembered to include herself.)

'It's not quite as straightforward as helping *himself,*

Mrs Reece. As well as himself he seems to have helped some clients at the expense of others.'

Cressida gave an impatient sigh. 'What're you trying to say? Is my money OK or isn't it?'

The inspector shook his head. 'I can't comment on the position of any particular investor, I'm afraid. I was merely referring to what Mr Brightly appears to have done. It's going to take a lot of work to trace monies back to their rightful owners – whatever money's retrievable, that is. But at least, as I said, we're receiving his cooperation. Well' – he got to his feet – 'your account of the matter seems to tally with Mr Brightly's.'

'Oh,' said Cressida, thoroughly confused, yet somehow impressed by the news that Richard had spoken of her.

'In which case I must go and put in my report.' He turned to Alex and became suddenly affable. 'So, young man, you're a computer buff. My son's the same.'

Cressida sat with her mind racing as Inspector Witty exchanged further words with Alex, and at last said he would see himself out.

'What the hell was that all about?' she asked, when the front door had closed and the sound of footsteps died away.

Alex squinted at her. 'You didn't get it?'

'Get what?' The bloke on the phone yesterday promised to give me news of my money. So naturally I thought . . . No, I *don't* get it,' she cried crossly, thinking that hunched in his chair and scowling at her that way he resembled a wizened monkey. 'So why don't you tell me, Mr Clever Clogs?'

Alex's face cleared and took on a lenient expression. 'Reading between the lines I'd say Richard didn't so much deplete our account as augment it with funds from other clients. The inspector was trying to suss out whether you connived in this.'

'But that's just daft. What do I know about that sort of thing? Look: are you saying our money might still be intact?'

'I shouldn't count on it, Mum. Sounds like one big mess all round. I wonder what Richard was playing at? God, by the sound of it. And probably figured he could go on juggling these accounts any way he fancied for years and years. There'd be no day of reckoning because he could always take on new clients to make up a short-fall. Something like that.'

'My head hurts,' said Cressida. 'I think I'll go and lie down.'

14

Mrs Parminter, answering the doorbell one afternoon
and finding the Reverend Michael Nunn under her
porch, knew immediately what he had come to say.
Wishing fervently to forestall him, she tried to recover
a suitable phrase. Consequently, for a moment she was
tongue-tied. And the Reverend Nunn remained on her
step explaining who he was and when and on what
occasion they had previously met: perhaps assuming
that all ladies of a great age need to have their memories jogged; or perhaps unclear in his own mind, having
to do with so many old ladies in his professional life
and finding one virtually indistinguishable from the
next. Meanwhile, Mrs Parminter's brain was wilfully
unobliging. First, 'Not today, thank you' arrived, which
she soon recognized as the phrase one employed to
despatch door-to-door salesmen. Then, 'I would rather
not talk about Mr Brightly, if you don't mind' tantalized
her lips: which she kept firmly closed, knowing these
words to be presumptive and ungracious. (Though, had
she known it, they were the very words employed
yesterday by Cressida Reece before closing the door in
the Reverend's face, with no compunction at all.) Aware
that her silence was approaching discourtesy, Mrs
Parminter fell back on what is customarily considered
suitable to say when the vicar calls: 'Do come in. Will
you have a cup of tea?'

The visitor was shown into the sitting room and Mrs
Parminter went into her kitchen. Mr Nunn, who was on
matey first name terms with many members of his

congregation, would normally stay with his host or hostess at this point, and would even make himself useful, fetching out cups and looking into the fridge for a bottle of milk. But this afternoon in The Gables, having solemn news to convey, delicate matters to discuss, sympathy to bestow, he judged a different approach was called for; furthermore, Mrs Parminter struck him as a rather formidable old dame. So he sat where he was bid, and eased his dog collar by running a finger round the inside.

Mrs Parminter seized the opportunity afforded by the preparing of tea to collect herself. This was not an occasion, she considered, when it would shame her to tell an untruth. She anticipated certain questions the vicar might throw at her and likened these to Mrs O'Connor's demanding to know whether her employer had remembered to call up the plumber or to return her library books. In such circumstances one was almost duty-bound to lie, out of self-preservation and self-respect. By the time Mrs Parminter joined her guest in the sitting room, only Mr Nunn was still apprehensive.

She left it to him to direct the course of their conversation. He began by asking how long she had resided in Chedbury and murmured sympathetically on learning that her husband had died soon after they had come to The Gables. In return, he gave some of his own history and mentioned his wife and four young children. Then, clearing his throat and taking a grip of his knees, he brought out the name of Mr Brightly. It had come as a terrible shock to people, he said, the news of the things their former lay reader had got up to. No doubt Mrs Parminter had read an account of it in the papers? In a steady voice and with a steady eye, Mrs Parminter allowed that she had. She went further, and volunteered that for some years she and Mr Brightly had been warm friends, and therefore the news had not only shocked but greatly saddened her. Mr Nunn grew excited. Shocked and saddened amounted to only the half of it for many people, he declared. The Church Building Fund, for example, might well be at risk, a prospect which drove to fury those stalwarts on the church council and other good folk who gave generously of their time and money getting up whist drives and jumble sales and bring-and-buy coffee mornings. And some there were who were quite distraught: that conscientious soul, Mavis Hutton, for one. Mavis Hutton was distraught on behalf of Cressida Reece. Mrs Parminter was no doubt aware of the sad case of Cressida Reece? Mrs Parminter nodded, and Mr Nunn confided that the former lay reader had sunk so low as to make free with the unfortunate lady's court settlement. Apparently, Mrs Reece's first inkling that this might have happened had been obtained from a newspaper she had recently purchased: she had promptly gone into hysterics in the middle of Market Square. Mrs Hutton, at whose instigation Mr Brightly had counselled Mrs Reece during the stresses and strains of her court ordeal, had sobbed her heart out to the Reverend Nunn, blaming herself and begging that St Peter's might set up a fund to compensate this particular victim. Of course, Mr Nunn had outlined to Mrs Hutton the various reasons why this was impractical, and he repeated them now to Mrs Parminter. Nevertheless, his heart went out to those who had trusted Mr Brightly and been deceived. He then paused and directed a meaningful gaze at Mrs Parminter.

Unblinkingly, she met that gaze. 'Fortunately for me, I am not one of them,' she told him.

The Reverend Nunn let out his breath and drank some tea. Setting down his cup, he confessed that he had feared the contrary. Several people had mentioned a friendship between Mrs Parminter and Mr Brightly. Indeed, some had attested to the fact that Mr Brightly was a frequent visitor to The Gables. (Mrs Parminter stared into her cup and thought how disagreeable it was to be the subject of gossip and speculation.) 'So I was rather afraid you, too, had been taken for a ride – like some other friends of the Brightlys'; particularly those who reside in Framley Lane.'

'Indeed? Well, I'm most sorry for those people I'm sure, but your fears for myself are groundless. Matters of business were never raised between Mr Brightly and myself. Will you have some more tea?'

'Oh, no. No, thank you.' He rubbed his hands together. 'I must say, I'm relieved. I came expecting the worst, but . . . There now. Thanks be to God! We'll say a prayer together, shall we, before I leave?'

Whereupon, to Mrs Parminter's great horror, without waiting for her yea or nay, he closed his eyes and clasped his hands and proceeded to address the Lord in terms of uncomfortable familiarity and with frequent and embarrassing reference to named persons including herself.

She waited till he had done, then rose, and with a stiff back and a very stiff face went to her front door. 'Good afternoon, Mr Nunn,' she said severely, pulling the door open and failing to notice his proffered hand.

'Good afternoon, and, er, I'm so glad . . .' Finding himself on the outer step and the door closing, the Reverend Nunn, with a puzzled expression, turned towards the gate.

I have never cared for this new man, Mrs Parminter said to herself. From the start I couldn't take to him. She remembered saying as much to Mr Brightly – dear Mr Brightly who, for all that he was a man of God, would never intrude a word with his Maker into a conversation. Good taste would prevent him. Never in a hundred years, she told herself, would Mr Brightly behave as Mr Nunn had this afternoon.

Mrs Parminter, in her rubber gloves, was washing the Reverend Nunn's teacup. Now she abandoned it, and watched it sink in the foamy water. What right had she to cast judgement over this man, she wondered, when her judgement had proved to be such a lamentable instrument? She gripped the edge of the sink and forced herself to acknowledge that the Reverend Nunn, whatever his faults, would never behave as had Mr Brightly. Overcome by a shaky feeling, she stripped off the gloves and went to sit down at the kitchen table.

It was time to face up to things, she decided. And the first of these was the fond foolishness of her hopes when the news of this business first broke out: hopes that an innocent mistake had been made in Mr Brightly's accounting, or that Mr Brightly had of late become mentally ill; or that his lapse would prove to be a single lapse provoked by desperation to assuage a greedy wife. But time had elapsed and nothing had come of these hopes. She could only concede that her erstwhile friend was a practised fraudster. She thought of him sitting with her, twinkling his eyes at her, listening to her courteously, making intelligent comments in his beautiful voice, handing her a glass of whisky, sharing a joke, and once, ah once, putting manly arms round her to support her after her fall. Face it, cried Mrs Parminter to herself: it was a scoundrel performing these actions, a man who consistently angled to gain control of other people's money for his own use. And despite her assurance to Mr Nunn this afternoon, she herself was one of those people. Mrs Parminter wrung her hands and wondered whether her lie would be found out. She resolved to visit her solicitor and make a clean breast to him. She would offer her advanced years in mitigation and explain that her concern for the money was negligible compared to her horror of seeing the Parminter name connected to the affair. She would assert that vulgar publicity would finish her off. Her solicitor, a reliable man who had acted for her husband, would surely do his best to keep her name out of it.

During the following weeks several articles on the subject of confidence trickery drew the attention of Mrs Parminter; one in the *Daily Telegraph*, one in the *Sunday Times* colour supplement, and another in *The Lady*. No details were given of the Brightly case, for that was *sub judice*, but similar cases that had already been proved and dealt with were described. And Mrs Parminter learned of other small towns, other church organizations, other groups of trusting and respectable folk who had been taken in and relieved of their savings by a plausible rogue. And it was somehow made clear in these articles that the renewed interest in the phenomenon was due to an example in Warwickshire that had recently come to light. So there it was, Mrs Parminter reflected, plainly stated, accepted as fact: Mr Brightly was a rogue and a crook. Gradually, any lingering reservations that this could not be so, or at least not the entire story, were slowly dispelled by the written word telling her differently. The more Mrs Parminter read on the subject, the more her former feelings were undermined, and the more established became the new orthodoxy. Confidence trickster, authoritatively hinted the *Daily Telegraph*, and Mrs Parminter trembled to think of the ease with which she had been misled.

Though every day was bright and sunny, and the garden called to her, and Mrs O'Connor before she left for her cruise brought her a good stock of thrillers from the library, Mrs Parminter felt unusually low. She pruned back the early flowering shrubs and weeded the rose bed and religiously watered the precious tiny plants she had purchased last year on an outing to Hidcote, and yet her heart was not lifted. She began one of the thrillers and found her concentration wandering. And she remembered with amazement her insouciance when she first heard the news that come July of this year she would be deprived for a month of Mrs O'Connor's services. The regular dusting she had agreed would be of little trouble to her proved in the event to be surprisingly taxing: that is, when she remembered to do it. She even missed her private battles with Mrs O'Connor and the repetitive tales of the O'Connor family's doings. Worst of all was sitting in front of the television and turning the pages of the *Radio Times* to find out what was showing that evening, and being reminded that this evening was Wednesday. Wednesday: his evening off.

Oh yes, she missed him. There were times when there was no point denying it. Secure in their friendship she had never felt alone in the world. Deprived of it, she knew she was. But perhaps there was a worse effect than just her missing him. She had reason to believe a severe jolt had been administered, for sometimes she noticed her mind playing tricks. Dozing in her chair one evening, she heard her voice calling her son's name: Robert? Robert? And then her eyes opened, and she caught herself in the expectation of Mr Brightly responding: as if, for a moment, her mind had confused Mr Brightly with her son. A possible explanation was that the loss of her friend had re-awakened the pangs of maternal loss. Another, that it was symptomatic of a general confusion of mind. Certainly, she was very forgetful. When Mrs O'Connor returned, it would be harder than ever to disguise this fact. Mrs Parminter shuddered, and foresaw a time when she would be obliged to give herself over to the Mrs O'Connors of this world. She had thought it would never come to her, the feebleness of mind or body that led to acceptance of the childish role. Now it seemed not so very improbable that one day soon she would again respond to 'dear' and 'Clara' and 'there's a good girl'. She could imagine in her dependency having no alternative but to appease those with the upper hand.

One evening, retiring to bed, Mrs Parminter stared for some moments at the aspirin bottle. It was one way out, she thought.

But not a right or proper way. She swallowed the correct dose of half an aspirin and climbed into bed. I am suffering from depression, she said firmly to herself, which will eventually pass.

But 'depression' hung on in her mind, sounding empty, merely an expression in modern day jargon. In her heart Mrs Parminter didn't believe in it. She believed that people decayed bodily and in all their faculties; some sooner, some later; just as, in differing ways, plants in the garden decayed and died. She remembered how her father had deteriorated and believed she was going the same way.

15

'I suppose,' said Aimée's client, lying back on the bed and drawing deeply from his cigarette, 'what it is, you've had the busies sniffing round.'

Aimée at the dressing table didn't reply but continued with the task of repairing her make-up. Out of long habit she glanced surreptitiously at the carriage clock on the mantelpiece and estimated that he had five more minutes.

'Go on, you can tell me,' urged the man. 'In this business we know how to keep our traps shut. Wouldn't get the stories if we didn't.'

But Aimée had no intention of explaining why the house had again been closed for business; or why Aimée's room, and the rooms of the other girls also, were decked out like students' quarters with books and notepads prominently displayed, and their frilly bits and bobs and items of equipment all hidden away; or why Mrs Thompson had said they could start pulling punters again but only one or two per day and only the sort who would pass as boyfriends. Matthew qualified on this count, being the type of guy Aimée fancied for a boyfriend: mid-thirtyish, tall and dark, and in a glamorous job with Midlands TV.

To divert him from his line of inquiry, she asked: 'Working on anything interesting at the moment, Matthew?' and leaned closer to the looking glass to facilitate an application of mascara.

'Yeah. Am, as a matter of fact. Did you hear about that guy in Warwick, the solicitor who defrauded his clients? We're planning this prog on the case, to go out when the trial's over. He'll be sent down, no danger.'

Aimée sat back and studied her reflection. 'That's really interesting.'

'Yeah? You mean you know something about him?'

'I might,' said Aimée, putting her head on one side. 'Ask me next time.'

'Right.' Matthew stubbed out his cigarette and swung off the bed. 'Then let's not leave it too long, eh? How about Friday?'

'Mm, OK,' said Aimée.

Considering the feelings liable to rise in her at the very mention of the name Brightly – impotent fury, a violent craving to lay hands on the bastard and deprive him of certain body parts – Mrs Nanette Thompson had herself well in hand. 'Sit down, young man,' she said. And as Matthew obeyed, Mrs Thompson jerked back her head for the benefit of Aimée, who promptly departed. 'I'm interested to hear you're making a TV programme about this bent solicitor.'

'Richard Brightly,' said Matthew, 'is the name of our man.'

'That's him,' said Mrs Thompson, without a flinch.

Matthew hesitated. Keenness lighted his eyes. 'He wasn't a client of yours, by any chance?'

'Oh, I wouldn't say that,' Mrs Thompson said: with perfect truth, for it was her first rule of business never to own to a client's name. 'But I was one of his, more's the pity.'

'Ah. Well I'm really sorry to hear that, Mrs Thompson. Have you a great deal of money at stake?'

'If nothing's recovered, then I'm just about cleaned out. I put my life savings in that bastard's hands. He's a very smooth operator, you know. I should have seen the red light when he took up religion; they're always the worst in my experience.'

'To tell you the truth, I'm curious, Mrs Thompson. Was your potential loss at all connected with your

204

closing down the business for a while, and the girls acting so cautious?'

Frankness tempted Mrs Thompson. She recalled Aimée describing this man as a punter of long standing with the sort of tastes that would keep him loyal. 'Well now, dear: the short answer to that is yes. Last year I installed some very expensive security features: in the interests of clients, you understand. And I needed more cash than I'd got in the bank. With Mr Brightly, as I said, looking after my savings, it seemed a good plan to ask him to cash in one or two of my investments. So the way it turned out, just before this business blew up, I'd received a cheque from Mr Brightly for a quite substantial sum. Nice for me, you might think: a few quid saved from the plunderer. Unfortunately, the coppers investigating the Brightly business thought the timing of the cheque looked most suspicious. I had to convince them it was just a coincidence: show them receipts for the work I'd had done, prove why I'd needed the money. It was very awkward, dear, having the plod come round asking their questions. Caused me a heck of a lot of bother, as a matter of fact. Of course, they soon realized with the amount I stood to lose, I'd hardly have turned a blind eye to what the bastard was doing, much less been a party to his schemes. This lot soon backed off, but I dare say they mentioned my name to their chums in the Vice. So just for the time being we're taking things quietly, Mr, er . . .'

'Call me Matthew.'

'Well, Matthew, love: how can I assist?'

An outline of the programme, which was still at the planning and research stage, was described to her. It was hoped that some of Mr Brightly's victims could be persuaded to relate their tragic stories on screen. Those who required anonymity would appear in silhouette, and if necessary, actors and actresses would speak their lines.

'And what would be the fee for such an appearance?' Mrs Thompson enquired, 'bearing in mind not only do

I stand to lose my savings, but business has had to be drastically curtailed, what with the coppers showing an interest and all.'

'It might not be much,' Matthew admitted. 'But I'll see what I can do. Would it be all right if our researcher called round to see you? Pam's very sympathetic. She's not one of your hard-faced hacks; she won't put words in your mouth. I think you'll find her easy to talk to.'

'Just so long as the business is kept out of it, Matthew.'

'Certainly. That goes without saying. Far as Pam's concerned, far as the programme's concerned, you'll be one of our subject's victims, end of story.'

'Then I might be able to oblige. It's just a question of the fee.'

'I'll get back to you. I'll call round Monday.'

'It's always nice to see a handsome young man,' said Mrs Thompson. 'Take a snifter, dear, won't you, before you go?'

'Miss Cressida Reece?'

'Er . . .'

'Hi! Good afternoon! Pam Jamieson here from Midlands TV. Mind if I speak to you for a moment?'

'Mrs Reece.'

'Pardon?'

'It's Mrs Reece,' said Cressida. 'And I don't want any more to do with the media, thanks.'

'Oh Mrs Reece – *sorry*, but this isn't about you. We're making a documentary about recent events in Warwickshire. I'm researching some background for the programme and basically I'm looking to talk to people in the area. Could I call and see you, do you think? It wouldn't take up much of your time.'

'Call here? What about?'

'Well, what we're trying to do, we're contacting anyone who had dealings with Mr Richard Brightly. Basically, we want to hear their views on what happened . . . basically.'

'How'd you get on to me? No, don't bother saying, 'cos I'm definitely not interested.'

'Mrs Reece, I can promise you your name wouldn't come into it. Everyone who speaks to us can be assured of our utmost discretion. We've already spoken to some of Mr Brightly's former clients, but we'd like to hear from as many as possible. Basically, what we're after is how people who've been affected *feel*. You wouldn't be committing yourself by speaking to us, and if we did want to use you at all, your anonymity could be guaranteed. There'd be a small fee, of course, to compensate for your time and trouble.'

'Yeah? Well, I suppose, maybe . . . When would you want to come?'

'*Brilliant*, Mrs Reece. You won't regret it. Basically, we'll just have a chat and see how we go. Would Tuesday suit?'

'Wednesday'd be better. Wednesdays I'm home in the afternoon.'

'No problem. Shall we say Wednesday at two thirty?'

'OK. Do you want my address?'

'Oh, we have that, thank you. See you Wednesday then, Mrs Reece. Bye now.'

'Right,' said Cressida. 'Bye.'

Basically, said Cressida to herself, imitating the speech of the woman from Midlands TV, *basically*, I shouldn't have agreed. She was pressing brittle stalks of spaghetti against the bottom of a pan of boiling water. So what? she went on. A little chat won't hurt. No need to tell Alex. I wonder how much they pay by way of a fee? A fee if they use me, she corrected herself, so as not to bank on it.

Money had come to be something to fret over again, money in small amounts: the weekly housekeeping bill, the cost of a fill-up of petrol, the price of a new shirt for Alex and a pair of shoes for herself. There was probably no real need to worry, but the idea of a few thousand quid in a building society being all that remained of her compensation award was quite scary after twelve months of feeling rich. She tried to think back to the years before the award when she'd had little spare cash at all, and to compare that situation with her relative affluence now. But the year of plenty got in the way. Thank heavens Mum and Dad refused to take their three thousand back for Alex's stair-lift, she sometimes said to herself; and: There's bound to be something to come for the investors once the muddle's sorted out.

Thoughts about money always led her to Richard. She couldn't get it out of her mind that if it weren't for him, moneywise she'd still be carefree. This is all down to him, she'd think angrily when her mind got snagged up in worries over Alex's future.

But memories sometimes revived Richard in an alternative light. The other evening, for instance – she and Alex watching *The Fast Show* on telly, laughing together, each adding a contributory word now and then to the other's gleeful appreciation; and later during the evening, further chuckles as one of them came out with a catch-phrase from the show at an apt moment – when did we learn to be chummy and easy like this? Cressida found herself wondering, recalling that not so very long ago they'd been locked into their roles of over-anxious mother and resentful son. When Richard was with us, soon came the answer.

Yes, he'd certainly let her down over money, but she would never deny he'd left something positive behind.

A great whooping 'Yes!' burst from above and resounded in every room of the house. In the kitchen, unloading a carrier bag, Cressida very nearly dropped a jar of marmalade. 'Yes! Yes! Yes!' cried Alex again. 'Good grief, whatever is it?' called out Cressida, and abandoned the shopping and ran upstairs.

Alex, seated in front of his computer, was punching the air over his head in the manner of a football enthusiast. When he saw his mother he broke into a chant: 'Sold it, sold it, sold it, sold it.'

'Sold what, you daft loon?'

Alex leaned forward and tapped the computer screen. 'It's just come through from Uncle Jonathan. Saeko have bought my game. I get five hundred now, five hundred when it comes on the market, and royalties on top.'

'Five hundred pounds?' cried Cressida.

'Five hundred pounds,' said Alex.

'Let me see.' Cressida fell onto her knees by the side of his wheelchair. She frowned at the screen and read what her brother had written, while beside her Alex jigged up and down and thought of further ideas he might put into practice – his head was crammed with them.

'Hey! It says here, I mean, your Uncle Jonathan says he's going to take you to see these Saeko people.'

'Of course, so I can sign the contract. And because they want to know what other ideas I've got, find out if I'm creative, offer me a retainer – you never know.'

Cressida, feeling stunned, sank back on her heels. 'I can't believe it. That's a thousand pounds. Gosh Alex, how'd you do it?'

From where he was sitting he could see the top of her head; the yellow bush of hair streaming out from either side of the white central parting. A sudden tenderness filled him, a feeling he'd not experienced before, and he decided not to mar the moment by inflicting a detailed or technical account. 'Oh,' he said lightly, 'I tapped some keys, scrolled some space, zoomed up some images.'

'I dunno, son; I reckon you're brilliant.'

He put an arm round her and squeezed her shoulder. 'That's me, Mum,' he confirmed happily, 'your brilliant son.'

Mrs O'Connor, tanned to a turn, came home from her cruise with one ambition: to repeat the experience just as soon as she and Mr O'Connor between them had gathered the necessary cash. Never mind saving for your old age, life was for living while you still had the inclination. So if Mrs Parminter ever felt a need to increase Mrs O'Connor's hours, if the ironing was getting on top of her or the shopping too much, then Mrs O'Connor would see her way clear. Mrs Parminter said stiffly that this was unlikely to be necessary: the walk to the shops did her good, there was always the telephone, and the laundry took care of her linen. Mrs O'Connor seemed unconvinced. Laughingly, she advised her employer that the offer still stood, hinting with her knowing eyes at a time approaching when Mrs Parminter would be glad of it. Mrs Parminter stated her opinion that the windows could do with a clean.

In the autumn the exploits of yet another confidence trickster attracted the attentions of the press. The man in question, a bank manager in Gwent, was well known as a preacher in local chapel circles. People in Chedbury read the reports and drew parallels with their own experience. The words of the *Daily Telegraph* on the matter were closely studied by Mrs Parminter, her horror at the out and out villainy of these smooth-talking rogues reinforced by every paragraph. These men seem to be everywhere, she said to herself.

'Have you seen that case in the papers: a bloke in Wales been conning people out of their cash?' asked Mrs O'Connor one afternoon over tea and biscuits in The Gables kitchen. 'These fellows seem to be at it all over the place.'

'They do indeed,' said Mrs Parminter. 'My thinking was the very same. It makes one wonder what the world is coming to.'

'It makes you think,' agreed Mrs O'Connor. She chewed her chocolate digestive and considered the matter further. 'I'll tell you what beats me: the way sophisticated folk, with an education and a high class position in life, the way folks like these get taken in. Wouldn't you be suspicious if some smooth talker, never mind he was a friend or a neighbour, started dropping hints he could look after your money better than you could? Well, yes, we know *you* would, Mrs Parminter.' Saying which, Mrs O'Connor shot a discreetly knowing look to the far side of the table. 'I said to Patrick, isn't it nice Patrick, I said, knowing not everyone's just begging to be made a fool of? At least there's Mrs Parminter who was friendly and sociable with the chap and never saw occasion to get out her chequebook. Shows no-one was forced, I said to Patrick.'

Mrs Parminter made a soft parrying whinnying noise, which her companion took for an expression of modesty.

'Say what you like, Mrs Parminter, but it's a pity others weren't strong-minded like you. I was very shocked to hear he took in the Fieldings. Course, living right opposite the Brightlys, I expect they were in and out of each other's houses, which is a habit I've never condoned. And they say there's others in Framley Lane: that Mrs Maskill: though she doesn't surprise me, I've heard rumours of that one in other directions. And Mrs Wright, now she's another. Would you credit it, really? But the saddest case I heard was that poor woman up Symmonds Close, her with the deformed lad. Wouldn't it make you weep to think of him using his wiles on her, Mrs Parminter?'

'Yes, I did hear Mrs Reece was involved. It's quite deplorable.'

'Well thanks be to God he didn't catch everyone. I suppose there'd be occasions when he mightn't feel comfortable broaching the subject; some people would know how to prevent it cropping up. Would that be how it was, do you suppose, Mrs Parminter?' It was as direct a query as Mrs O'Connor dared venture. Sadly, Mrs Parminter on the far side of the table gave nothing away. 'Breeding,' declared Mrs O'Connor. 'Say what you like but it still counts.'

'Er-hem. Will you have another cup of tea, Mrs O'Connor?'

'Oo, no thanks. One is my rule.'

'Well . . . Please let me know if you discover any deficiency in the supply of cleaning materials.'

'Ah. Good you jogged my memory,' said Mrs O'Connor, rising to return to her tasks. 'I was thinking when I was doing the upstairs lav we could be getting low on Jeyes.'

When the whine of the vacuum cleaner broke out overhead, Mrs Parminter left the kitchen and went into the sitting room where, having quietly closed the door behind her, she sat down in her favourite chair. She closed her eyes and summoned the voice of Mrs O'Connor, listened methodically to the words and phrases Mrs O'Connor had employed in the kitchen earlier and paid studied attention to the facial expressions and body movements that had accompanied them. At the completion of the exercise, Mrs Parminter drew her conclusions.

There could be only one explanation. After representations from herself, Mr East her solicitor had forcefully impressed upon the investigators of the Brightly affair that his client's name was to be kept out of it. So forcefully had he done so that in response to a direct question – probably from some local reporter acting on knowledge gained from town gossip – the investigators had denied point blank that there was any victim of the debacle by the name of Parminter.

It was a huge lie and a public lie. Mrs Parminter visualized this lie: a shining blinding thing that widened and intensified as she dwelt on it. She felt her blood pressure rise. Guilty warmth livened her cheeks and she turned with an automatic childlike gesture to check whether she was being observed.

The foolishness of this action made her impatient. She levered herself up and went over to the bureau to gaze into the clear eyes of her son Robert. Feeling more calm, she opened the bureau lid and drew from one of the compartments inside a photograph of her husband. The communion with his face sent strength into her heart, and determination. She had acted for the best, she

212

said to herself; furthermore she applauded her action, was glad and grateful for it.

From her handbag, Mrs Parminter extracted the exact money to cover Mrs O'Connor's wages for her two visits this week, and took it to the kitchen and set it on a corner of the table. After a while, footsteps were heard descending the stairs, and the trundling hose of the vacuum cleaner.

Mrs Parminter was composedly washing the cups they had used earlier when Mrs O'Connor, buttoning her coat, came into the kitchen. 'Ta very much,' said Mrs O'Connor, picking up her money. Putting it away in her purse, she added: 'Now you won't forget the Jeyes, Mrs Parminter? Not like you kept forgetting the polish that time, till I had to fetch it myself.'

'I might very well forget it, Mrs O'Connor. Such things do slip my mind, particularly when I'm occupied by more important matters. However, you will find on the counter a notepad and pencil. Do you see? – placed just beneath the calendar. I suggest, whenever we start running short of a commodity, you jot it down. You could begin by putting down lavatory cleaner.'

'Isn't that an idea?' cried Mrs O'Connor, sounding amazed.

Mrs Parminter raised her head and gazed out of the window. But the figure of her cleaning lady was imprinted on her vision, and instead of lawn and roses and purple asters and golden rod, she saw Mrs O'Connor licking the point of a pencil and laboriously printing in capital letters the name of a household item. Something had changed between Mrs O'Connor and herself, there'd been a shifting of ground, a subtle re-adjustment of their relationship back to what it once had been.

'Don't your roses look a picture still?' commented Mrs O'Connor, coming up behind. 'I'm surprised the cold nights we've been getting haven't seen them off.'

'Good heavens, no. It will take a penetrating frost to do that. And so far we've had barely a nip.'

213

'Well, you'd know best, Mrs Parminter, you being the gardener. I'll be off, then. See you next week.'

'Thank you, Mrs O'Connor. See you next week.'

In the spring, Mr Brightly was found guilty of embezzlement and sent to prison for five years. The judge in handing out the sentence said it was less severe than it might have been, the accused's willing co-operation with the investigating authorities having been taken into account.

There followed in the press some discussion of the length of this sentence. A columnist writing in the *Guardian* invited readers to compare the sentence given Mr Brightly with others handed out that day. For example: to a single mother on benefit found guilty of stealing goods worth fifty-seven pounds ten, a jail sentence of three months.

Tony Colebrook, eating scrambled eggs in his flat in Warwick and reading this article, began to compute the sum. If fifty-seven pounds ten gets you three months in the slammer, he muttered to himself, how many years does a couple of hundred thou – give or take a few quid – get you?

'I reckon your old man got off lightly, my sweet,' he remarked to Ginny who was sitting on the other side of the table. 'There's a school of thought here thinks he ought to do time for going on a hundred years.'

'I wish you'd shut up on that subject. You've gone on and on about it ever since the trial started, and it's boring, *boring*,' cried Ginny, yanking together the two edges of her black satin wrap. She too was eating scrambled eggs, with reading matter placed to the side of her plate: though in her case the reading matter was a holiday brochure. 'The case is over and done with, so can we please forget it? Tell you what: I'll make some more coffee and we can cosy up on the sofa. Let's take a look at the holiday brochures, shall we, darling? Pick out somewhere gorgeous?'

'Can't, sweetheart, sorry. Time to go haul in the

shekels. One of us has to do it, and so far you've only shown talent for spending 'em, angel.'

As Tony Colebrook in Warwick kissed the turned-up tip of Ginny Brightly's nose, Mrs Parminter in Chedbury arrived at page twenty-eight of the *Daily Telegraph*. There she was advised that the sentence meted out to Richard Brightly was not over-lenient. It would be no picnic sharing a cell with a crazed drug addict or a foul-mouthed yob or a thug with a history of violence. For a man of Mr Brightly's background, a well-educated man used to a refined style of living, it would be hell on earth.

Mrs Parminter, when the sentence was announced yesterday on the six o'clock news, had considered it not harsh enough, her view of the miscreant's crimes having been honed and hardened by their daily exposure during the time of the trial. But now a nightmarish scenario came to her: she saw an iron door bang shut enclosing her former friend in a tiny cell, saw the two narrow bunks and the coarse villain lying on top of the upper one. She said to herself that he would never stand it, and foresaw that the very qualities she had found so attractive – sensibility, delicacy, taste – would prove his undoing.

But then, reading on, she learned that only the initial few months were likely to be served in such fearful circumstances. Usually this class of prisoner would serve the bulk of a sentence in the more civilized environment of an open prison. It seemed a very sensible arrangement, and Mrs Parminter was relieved to hear of it. Nearing the end of the article, reading its conclusion, she found herself nodding in complete agreement: in the case of Regina versus Brightly, justice would seem to have been served.

A letter arrived at The Gables, in a thin brown envelope with the name and address of Mrs Parminter inscribed on it in biro. Its cheap appearance struck Mrs Parminter at once, which she then decided was mitigated to a degree by the shapeliness of the handwriting. Nevertheless, she held the envelope a little away from her as she slit it open, and maintained the undistinguished notepaper she then withdrew at the same distance. No address headed the letter; there was just the date, *2 April*, followed immediately by *Dear Mrs Parminter*. Puzzled and a little apprehensive, Mrs Parminter decided to commit herself no further before ascertaining the letter's source. She turned to the final page and looked to the end. Her eyes met the words *Richard Brightly*.

'Oh, no!' cried Mrs Parminter, letting the letter fall. She stared in dismay at the intrusive presence on her white and primrose checked breakfast tablecloth; but after a while, attempting to be calm, she retrieved the letter and with some feeling of being imposed upon, began to read.

You may wonder at my long silence, wrote Mr Brightly to Mrs Parminter, who, as she read, felt only discomfited by that silence's ending. *This was due to a reluctance to communicate with my hand shackled, so to speak; I have been under strict instructions to remain guarded until after my trial. (I have asked my solicitor to post this to you in the event of my being sentenced to a term of imprisonment: as I write, my trial is nearing its end and I have no illusions.) During these past months I have devoted every waking moment to assisting the investigation into my clients' affairs. (More on this later.) However, dear Mrs Parminter, you have often been in my thoughts. I should guess not a Wednesday evening has passed without my thinking of you and fondly recalling past Wednesday evenings, and wishing they might come again.*

Mrs Parminter jumped violently at this. What on earth would she do if he were released early for some reason (for one did hear of such cases), and one Wednesday evening turned up on her doorstep, urbane as ever and twinkling his eyes at her? With her concentration somewhat impaired, she embarked warily on the next paragraph.

The name of Cressida Reece figured in the first sentence, and then again in the second, and again in the third and the fourth. Thinking this excessive, Mrs Parminter frowned and re-read these sentences. She gathered that Mr Brightly, as well as thinking of herself, thought very often of Cressida Reece. *You may be surprised to learn how very much Cressida has come to mean to me*, Mrs Parminter read, and was indeed surprised, uneasily so. Summoning up a certain detachment, she continued her reading at a brisker pace. But soon grew exasperated. What was all this about Cressida Reece in the rain, Cressida Reece trying to shield her son watched by Mr Brightly through his car windscreen? It hardly made sense. *I was inspired by her*, wrote Mr Brightly. *Can you understand? I was moved by some quality I discerned in her that is quite hard to pin down.* The man is obsessed, said Mrs Parminter to herself, as the letter, attempting in spite of the difficulty to define this quality, informed her that Cressida Reece although slipshod in her habits was brave-hearted as a lioness. He cannot be in his right mind, she cried. *Forgive my writing to you in this way, but I cannot allow myself to write any of it to Cressida. I am fearful of distracting her from pursuing her life in a positive way. Also, as an accused man facing a term of imprisonment, I am someone with whom it would alarm anyone who cared for her to see her associated. And you see, I do care for her deeply. It is my greatest sorrow to have brought pain and trouble to her when my intention was the precise opposite.*

And here I should say how grieved I am also by the pain I have certainly caused you, my dear friend. In fact, it was the knowledge of such pain that fired me to do all in my power to assist the straightening out of my clients' investment entanglements. Entanglements, suffice it to say, that would have proved insignificant in the fullness of time. But alas I was not granted the fullness of time, and therein lies the tragedy. This is not to say I always acted in strict accordance with the law: I know I did not, and that things were done that should not have been done, and that I succumbed to the temptation to take shortcuts with funds in order to satisfy and appease my wife. At the same time, if precipitate action had not been instigated by a certain cleric, I am clear in my mind that outstanding money would have been more than made up, with no loss or pain accruing to any one of my clients: indeed, with positive benefit accruing to many. I trust and pray this is understood by you, Mrs Parminter.

In fact Mrs Parminter was completely lost. Catching only the smack of self-justification in these words, Mrs Parminter, who had been guided and settled into an understanding of the situation by the authoritative words of the *Daily Telegraph*, felt disinclined to waste brain power on these with their dubious tone of excuse. *Let me bring you up to date with some news*, wrote Mr Brightly, and Mrs Parminter encountered with relief some plain statements of fact.

My wife, who left me when I was arrested, is in the process of obtaining a divorce. My son, who prefers contact between us to cease, is well, I believe, and successfully embarked on his chosen career. My darling daughter Harriet remains in touch and is as affectionate as ever. She has left her boarding school, where she was never particularly happy, and is now at college, training to become a nursery nurse, which you may remember was always her ambition. I understand her mother is now reconciled to Harriet's pursuing this line of work. Ah, thought Mrs Parminter, lifting her eyes for a moment and picturing Harriet as she had last seen her in St Peter's Chedbury: that is good news at least: I am glad about that.

I hope and pray life is treating you well. I will write as my situation allows. My chief feeling about incarceration is frustration at the delay in returning my attention to Cressida's financial affairs. To know it lies within my power to set these on a profitable path, and yet be prevented, is perfect torment; for since that occasion I described to you, I have yearned to make her secure.

With great affection, my very best wishes: Richard Brightly.

Dear Lord, cried Mrs Parminter, staring beyond the letter to her sensible everyday arrangement of toast rack and butter dish and marmalade pot, whose very orderliness seemed to highlight the bizarre nature of that final reference to Cressida Reece: the rogue evidently plans to lay hands once again on that poor girl's money, whatever remains of it. And in her head Mrs Parminter addressed her correspondent with dreadful severity: Then it is certainly to be hoped that you are kept out of harm's way for a very long time.

16

'Richard Norris Brightly,' the interviewer said, talking
directly to camera. And the hearts of three women
viewers jumped, as the hearts of other women also
jumped to whom the name was significant. They had
made certain of privacy, these three, not wishing to be
disturbed by anyone's thoughts but their own on
the subject. They watched and listened and did not
move: Mrs Parminter, Cressida Reece, and Mrs Nanette
Thompson.

It was not the most convenient time of day for telly
viewing for Mrs Thompson. Business being resumed as
usual, it was now in full swing all over the house. She'd
stood on the landing for a moment before coming into
her room and settling down to view, she'd stood and
listened and sensed the busy activity occurring; she'd
thought of the girls humping away and had visualized
her recovering finances; and she had warmly congratulated herself. For no-one caught good old Nanette sitting
on her backside, moaning and griping. Stuff Ricki
Brightly she'd said, soon as the initial shock wore off,
and had tarted herself up and got her finger out. She was
a resourceful woman. A trouper. With the loss of her
money she'd seen there was nothing for it but to start
tackling some of the donkey work herself once more.
Why, this very afternoon she'd devoted an hour to one
of those ginks who don't actually want to do anything
(the most wearing type of punter, those, with their
declining to provide evidence of any clear conclusion).

Buttoning her impatience and pretending to an interest, she'd smiled benignly as he fingered the pair of her panties he'd asked to borrow. With excellent good grace she'd responded to his request that she go and stand over him as he sat in his chair (doing bugger all, far as she could tell). Hours she'd seemed to stand there in her high-heeled sandals with her stomach only inches from his head, staring down at his greasy hair and its dandruff flecks; even when her feet started playing up she hadn't hurried the poor sod, but faithfully carried on obliging for every last second he'd paid for. And her day's work wasn't over yet. Later on she'd do her stuff at the party the girls always put on on Friday nights; she'd wink and pass the drinks, scold the guests and swap jokes with them, keeping a critical eye the while on the girls' routine. Yes, retirement had taken several steps further into the distance, thanks to Ricki Brightly. But did she moan? She did not.

She was tired though. Bloody tired. Her sandals, kicked off, lay apart on their sides on the carpet. Her purple dress lay spread on the bed. In her satin slip, supported by plump cushions in frilly cases, she sat bolt upright on the velvet chaise longue with the television control in her lap. Tired as she was, with the programme under way there was no danger at all of her nodding off.

'I suppose you'll be going back upstairs to get on with it now,' Cressida had remarked to her son when they'd finished their evening meal. She had spoken casually, almost lazily. 'Yep, Saeko calls,' Alex had happily confirmed, and Cressida had promised to bring him a mug of tea later on. She'd chosen to produce the tea exactly ten minutes prior to the start of the programme, and had found when she took it to his room Alex satisfactorily absorbed in front of his computer. 'Um . . . thanks, Mum,' he'd said vaguely, the words reaching her through the clicks and whirrs of his machine just before she closed his door.

In the sitting room she sat on the floor with her back

against a chair and the telly stand pulled up close. The remote control lay on the carpet beside her, ready to have its OFF button jabbed in the unlikely event of the stair-lift descending. It seemed a miracle that she'd got away with it: taken part in a TV programme, hidden the notices of its scheduled broadcast, all without Alex finding her out. Maybe she was developing cool at last.

But now thoughts of Alex and fooling him vanished, and the dread vanished that had been building all day of people who knew her watching the programme and guessing her identity; even awareness of her own self vanished and of the handy position of the remote control. 'How did you *feel*?' the interviewer asked. And Cressida waited suspensefully for the reply of the shadowy figure (who in this instance was not herself).

There had been little likelihood of an interruption to Mrs Parminter's viewing. Even so, she had closed the door of her sitting room and put the draught excluder in place (despite the weather being mild and the air still): this to ensure that the sound of her television would not travel to the front door, and in the event of someone calling to collect money on behalf of the NSPCC she could safely pretend to be out for the evening.

But with Mrs Parminter it was not so much a case of wishing not to be disturbed, as of wishing not to be discovered. There were times in the recent past when she had absently answered the phone or the door without first switching off her television. 'What? When? Excuse me one moment while I turn down the television,' she'd been obliged to tell her friend Mrs Foulkes, finding details of an invitation to lunch obscured by the screeching of Cilla Black. It had been bad enough getting caught with *Blind Date*: Mrs Parminter was determined not to be inadvertently caught with tonight's programme. So, unable to trust herself not to blunder up in response to the ringing of telephone or doorbell, there was a secondary purpose in her placing of the draught excluder: as well as a sound dampener, it would serve to remind her in the event of a summons that this evening Mrs Parminter was not at home.

In fact, in spite of being a little shame-faced about it, Mrs Parminter eagerly anticipated viewing the programme. She had endeavoured to read every word written on the Brightly case and catch every broadcast comment. How could I have been so misled? she would invariably wonder after the perusal of yet another article. So she searched the papers and the TV listings in the hope of further discussion, and, possibly, of enlightenment.

'What would you say to him now if you were given the chance?' the interviewer demanded of the silhouette Mrs Parminter had identified as Cressida Reece. 'If you happened to bump into him today: how would you respond?'

Waiting to be informed, Mrs Parminter suspended breathing.

Cressida could no longer bear to watch. As her ghostly self stuttered on screen, she clapped a hand over her eyes and waited in dread for the words that were coming, the words with which she had made a prat of herself. The silence, as her ghostly self hesitated, seemed to go on for ever. At length she parted her fingers and peeped between them, just as on screen her silhouette went right ahead and said it: 'Give him a hug. Give him a hug and a great big kiss.'

'Oh, Christ,' moaned Cressida, in the here and now.

Mrs Nanette Thompson had viewed her own contribution with satisfaction: that'll teach him, she'd thought, if the bastard's able to be watching. But now these words of Cressida Reece gave her a jolt. They brought back Ricki, not Richard Brightly the bent solicitor of media fame, but Ricki who had been a pal, the Ricki she'd always said was the handsomest fellow on earth, with his flawless voice and charming manner and his

223

eyes twinkling down at her with loving kindness. Her throat seized up, and a sob hiccupped out of her. But the noise of it going off like a bomb in her ears filled her with fury, and she reached out and snatched a tissue and blew her nose. Silly cow, she spat out, meaning both of them: the woman who'd said she'd give him a kiss, and herself for blubbing.

Mrs Parminter, blinded by tears, struggled to her feet and turned off the television. She wished to digest the cry that had come from Cressida Reece in absolute silence. Standing on her hearth rug with her head bowed, it came to her that she had at last received her enlightenment: but not the enlightenment she had expected, nor anything she would have recognized before viewing this programme as an answer to her question *How could I have been so misled?* She knew now that no answer was possible. The question itself was the difficulty, being based on a false premiss. The point being that I was *not* misled, she said to herself, and wobbled back to her chair and sat abruptly down.

It had taken the simple honesty of Cressida Reece to bring this home to her, Cressida Reece blurting out that her reaction to being presented with Mr Brightly would be to hug and kiss him. It was a confession that had been precipitated, thought Mrs Parminter, by Cressida Reece truthfully picturing the man she knew. Deeply moved, Mrs Parminter felt it now behoved her to do similarly: to summon up and consider the man *she* had known, her dear friend for over a decade.

Slowly he returned to her: in scenes remembered and measured conversations, in shared confidences and ironic remarks and knowing looks and smiles, in tumblers of whisky raised to the other's good health, in his arms about her after her fall, in his eyes reflecting merriment or concern, and in silences. This was her Mr Brightly. Having firmly re-established him in her heart and mind's eye, she recalled again the many words written of him in the *Daily Telegraph*. They were true words no doubt, but gave only half the picture. Part of the picture was the man who had impelled that cry of Cressida Reece. Part of it also was her own experience.

She rose up and went to the sideboard and poured a large measure of whisky. She felt in need of it, as if she had come in from a long journey. She stood on her hearth rug sipping the warming liquid and looking at familiar objects about her room, and wondered how next to occupy herself. Bed seemed like an anticlimax, yet she was in no mood for more television, nor for any unread columns of the *Daily Telegraph*. She wondered if Cressida Reece had also watched the programme, and thought this likely. She wondered if it wouldn't be a painful experience hearing yourself blurt out a confession like that, against the thrust of the programme and probably against one's own better judgement. Now she considered it, Mrs Parminter recalled a tell-tale note in that cry, the note of someone who perceives with a sinking heart that they are about to be judged a fool. Indeed, the programme makers had undoubtedly allowed the interview with Cressida to stand, in the belief that it illustrated just how low the confidence trickster was prepared to sink if he would set out to deceive such an impressionable creature. Poor, poor Cressida, said Mrs Parminter to herself, wishing heartily to comfort her. She wondered if it would be kind to write her a letter.

After some hesitation, Mrs Parminter laid out writing materials and drew up a chair. She began by describing her long friendship with Mr Brightly and her feelings for him, adding, so as to prevent misunderstanding, that she was eighty-three years old. She explained how muddled she had become, how her mind had been bent in another direction by all that she had read and heard. And she thanked Cressida for leading her to a rounded picture of her friend, and to restoring her peace of mind.

Suddenly, as she wrote, Mrs Parminter was visited by a sense of the quality Mr Brightly had discerned in the girl. *Brave-hearted as a lioness*, he had written. *Brave* said it exactly, Mrs Parminter thought, understanding that Cressida, having pictured the truth of how an encounter with Mr Brightly would go, had been unable to deny it however strongly pressured by the expectations of the programme makers or by her own wish not to be thought foolish. Brave-hearted, indeed.

On an impulse, wishing to give something in return, Mrs Parminter added that she had recently heard from Mr Brightly, that she had in her possession a letter in which he spoke movingly of Cressida. *I would like it very much if you would come to tea*, she added. *If this is agreeable, please give me a ring so that we can arrange a day*.

In case of daylight causing her to regret anything, she left the letter open so that it could be scrutinized in the morning. Then, tired at last, she turned off the lights, collected a glass of water, and went upstairs.

Daylight did not after all reveal her letter to be flawed. Before rising from her bed this morning, Mrs Parminter had gone over all the revelations and thoughts and emotions that had come to her on the previous evening. Feeling particularly clear-headed, she had come downstairs and calmly taken breakfast. Only then did she go into her sitting room and read over what she had written. It was excellent, she found. Before folding it into an envelope, she took up her pen and wrote beneath her signature, *I do hope you will come*. Then she sealed it and went to look up the Reeces' address in the telephone directory.

Thoughts of her letter, lying in the pillar box, then in the sorting office, followed her around all day, nudging her with hope and expectation. I do hope you will come, she said frequently in her head.

17

'Oh help,' said Cressida Reece, biting into a maid-of-honour tartlet baked earlier by Mrs Parminter, and spilling much of it down her front.

Mrs Parminter looked in another direction.

Cressida brushed herself down, then stooped to collect crumbs from the carpet and deposit these in her saucer. 'Trust me,' she cried. 'I always . . , Oh, there's another bit. Sorry. Actually, they're very nice these tarts.'

'Do have another one.'

'Thanks, I will.' This time Cressida ate with her plate jammed against her breastbone to collect any droppings. 'Thing is,' she said, when the tart was finished, leaning forward to dump her plate on the coffee table. 'Thing is,' she repeated, sitting back, 'I do tend to drop things when I'm feeling jumpy. And the reason I'm jumpy – I may as well come right out with it – the reason I'm jumpy is, I want to ask you something which you'll probably consider a terrific cheek.' She fixed her eyes on her hostess. (Big, blue and guileless, thought Mrs Parminter meeting their gaze.) 'I want you to show me that letter you got from Richard. I'd like a look at it, if you don't mind.'

Mrs Parminter watched with fascination the colour bloom in her guest's pale cheeks: bloom and flame. 'Of course,' she murmured faintly, and rose to go to her bureau. She had left Mr Brightly's letter in an accessible place foreseeing that she might have need to put her hands on it this afternoon.

'I wouldn't want you to think it's the only reason I've come,' Cressida called to Mrs Parminter's back. 'Hell, no, I really wanted to meet you, you being a friend of Richard's and all. And I've enjoyed it,' she said, as Mrs Parminter returned, 'having a nice chat, seeing your lovely house, and seeing, you know, where Richard's been coming all these years. Funny he never said . . . Oh,' she demurred, as the letter was handed to her, 'it feels awful, really, asking someone you've just met to see their private correspondence.'

'It's an understandable request.'

'Well, thanks,' mumbled Cressida, taking the letter. 'You did say there was something about me in it.'

'I think I'll make a fresh pot of tea,' Mrs Parminter said. And she collected the teapot and diplomatically left the room.

Mrs Parminter took her time over the tea making. She reached for the caddy containing the special tearoom blend that was sent to her regularly by post from Harrogate and that required a full five minutes to brew. The tea reminded her of holidays in the Dales taken long ago, and for a moment she imagined her husband with her, he and she sipping the aromatic liquid and gazing through the tearoom window over the broad Strays of Harrogate, hearing a background chatter of afternoon gossip and the plaint of a violin. She looked up at the wall clock and saw the second hand, which had been moving briskly as her eyes came to it, change speed and begin creeping between the numerals. She thought of her visitor reading Mr Brightly's letter, and reflected, as she had reflected many times before, that Mr Brightly had not intended it to be read by Cressida; a fact that had been present in Mrs Parminter's mind as she wrote to Cressida of the letter's existence. Nevertheless, she had referred to the communication quite deliberately, hoping thereby to lure Cressida Reece to The Gables. She had thrown her a tempting crumb, thought Mrs Parminter, wondering why she could not feel shocked at herself, and recalling how she had re-read her letter in the light of day, had understood her motive for writing as she had, yet still had sealed it in an envelope and carried it to a pillar box. Sometimes, she reflected, one is driven to commit a reprehensible act at the behest of an instinct. And an instinct told Mrs Parminter that it would be as well for Cressida to know of Mr Brightly's continuing ideas concerning her money, and to know also that Mr Brightly had not set out (as perhaps she feared) cynically to engage her affections in the manner of a practised confidence trickster. Cressida, therefore, had no real reason to feel shamed or humiliated by having spoken on television of giving him a kiss. The affection that existed was a shared affection, as anyone reading his letter must grasp. *You may be surprised to learn how very much Cressida has come to mean to me,* Mr Brightly had written. *I was inspired by her. I do care for her deeply.*

Composedly, the requisite brewing time having passed, Mrs Parminter took up the teapot and set off for the sitting room, confidently anticipating that during the intervening minutes, and as a result of her actions, peace of mind had been restored to Cressida, just as Cressida's frankness on television had restored her own.

On the sofa a third reading of Mr Brightly's letter was under way, hindered by dropping tears.

'Oh dear!' cried Mrs Parminter, spying the tears.

''S OK. I'm only crying because I'm happy.'

'Ah,' said Mrs Parminter on a note of triumph.

'And 'cos I'm sad.'

'Ah,' said Mrs Parminter on a different note.

Cressida swiped her nose with the back of her hand. 'Can you lend me a tissue?' she asked, the action proving ineffective. 'Mine's all used up.' As evidence she held out a ball of tightly wadded paper.

Mrs Parminter stared at it blankly. Then, suddenly tumbling to what her guest required, produced from a pocket a neat square of laundered linen.

'Oh I couldn't use that,' cried Cressida. She lurched

to her feet and thence from the room. 'I'll get some loo paper. Where is it?'

Mrs Parminter struggled up after her. 'Oh, the lavatory,' she murmured, as Cressida, having opened and closed the door to the dining room, now entered the correct room and gave the toilet roll holder a vigorous spin. A little dazed, Mrs Parminter returned to her chair in the sitting room, and Cressida blew her nose and pushed down the flush handle and broke off a long length of paper to keep with her in case of further tears.

Part of Mr Brightly's letter had fallen to the carpet. Cressida retrieved this and sat down. 'Slipshod in her habits,' she quoted with a grin. 'He got me bang to rights there.'

Mrs Parminter passed her a fresh cup of tea. 'I'm so sorry you've been distressed.'

'Not *distressed*,' said Cressida. 'A bit shook up. But in the main I'm ecstatically happy. I mean, you agree it comes over that Richard really and truly cares for me?'

Mrs Parminter conveyed her belief that it did.

'You see, I was never a hundred per cent sure. I was always on at myself: Richard wouldn't spend so much time with you and take an interest in Alex and go to all that trouble over the car and care what sort of grades you get at college, if he's not bothered about you, you dolt. He wouldn't smile the way he does, and act so tender . . . But then all this happened about the money, which was an almighty shock, and I didn't know what to think. I began looking back and wondering if I'd imagined it, or if he'd been putting it on. Well you can't help wondering. I expect you wondered too, Mrs Parminter. He did have money off you as well?'

The big blue and guileless eyes engaged her own in honest enquiry, and Mrs Parminter found herself unable to dissemble. 'Yes, I'm afraid he did,' she admitted, 'though I prefer not to have it known.'

'Yeah. Course,' said Cressida sympathetically. 'Well at least it doesn't look as black for us as it did. I had a letter saying we'll get 67p in the pound. Did you hear the same?'

'I believe that's the figure.'

'Not too catastrophic a loss,' said Cressida comfortably.

'Do bear in mind that one's purpose in making an investment is to see some profit.'

'Mm, I s'pose. Still, it's not as bad as it might have been. Hey, I see he actually imagines I'd let him have another crack at mine. He should be so lucky! Soon as I get the cheque, it goes straight in the building society and jolly well stays there. But you know, Mrs Parminter, reading what he said about that, made me realize something. He's an incorrigible dreamer. He may be clever and suave and know his way around, but he gets these ideas and they carry him away. What he desperately needs is someone down to earth, someone like me, who'd keep him in touch with reality. And to think all this time I thought it was just me needed him! We need each other – isn't that amazing? It makes me feel all sort of yearny. But he's going to be in prison for years and years.'

'Please don't distress yourself, my dear,' urged Mrs Parminter as Cressida's nose dived into the toilet paper. 'The situation won't last for ever.'

'I know,' said Cressida through a hank of hair. 'Tell you what,' she said, lifting her face, 'it's good about his horrible wife. Oh, pardon me if she's a friend of yours.'

Mrs Parminter disclaimed this hurriedly.

'Good. Because in my personal opinion she was a mercenary, miserable bitch, always badgering Richard for something or other, always complaining about their poor daughter. And Richard was always so loyal. "I can never be disloyal to my marriage," he said. I couldn't argue, I was too scared of losing the bit of him I'd got. So yippee, she's getting a divorce! That's one obstacle out of the way. Oh, if only I could see him. Or write to him, even, but he didn't put down an address. If he writes again, you will tell me, won't you?'

'Er-yu-es,' quavered Mrs Parminter, beginning to perceive that she had taken on rather more than she'd bargained for.

'Thanks. I suppose' – Cressida hesitated – 'I suppose it'd be possible to find out where he is. But I dunno. Maybe not giving an address is like signalling he's not ready to be contacted yet. What do you reckon?'

'It might be wise to wait for an indication that contact would be welcome.'

'Yeah. Anyway, thanks a million for showing me this. Here, you'd better have it back.'

The letter came towards her over the coffee table. Mrs Parminter saw that it had a mangled appearance.

'I can't tell you what a relief it is, having someone to talk to. I've had to keep the whole business buttoned up inside, terrified my mum and dad, or my brother Jonathan, or my friend Julie would start thinking, Oh lord, Cressida's landed herself in trouble again. Of course, there's my son, Alex; but you can hardly talk about loving someone and not being sure whether they love you to a fifteen-year-old kid. I hope,' she said shyly, 'I can come and talk to you again.'

'But of course, you must! You'll be most welcome.'

'Thanks,' said Cressida, 'that's really nice.' She looked about the room. 'So where did Richard usually sit?'

'In that chair,' said Mrs Parminter, indicating. 'He came to see me almost every Wednesday evening for over ten years. He liked to joke that it was his evening off.'

'Huh?' Hearing the familiar treasured expression casually on the lips of another gave Cressida quite a turn. She decided to let it pass. 'How did you get to know him, then?'

'Well,' said Mrs Parminter, settling back comfortably. 'I was in my front garden one evening I recall, dead-heading the roses. "Good evening," said a voice, a very melodious voice . . .'

'Oh yes, Richard's voice is lovely.'

'Indeed. I'd heard it in church and had been most struck. "Why, good evening," I said to him. "It's Mrs Parminter, I believe," he answered. "I'm Richard Brightly. I often pass this way and admire your roses. Are they scented at all?" I explained that these in the front lacked any discernible scent, but that some at the back of the house were strongly scented, in particular an old musk rose with the most glorious perfume. "You are most welcome to come round and judge for yourself," I told him. And there he was, striding ahead of me. I thought to myself that very first time how easefully and gracefully he carried himself.'

'Oh he does, doesn't he?'

'In another month that rose will be out, the one Mr Brightly was particularly fond of. I'll show it to you, if you like. I'll cut you a few.'

'Would you really? That'd be wonderful. You never know, if by then we know where he is and I can get to see him, I could even take him a bloom. "The rose you love from Mrs Parminter's garden," I'll tell him.'

'It's a dark crimson globular rose, so old, I'm not even sure of its name. But its scent is heavenly.'

'So then you asked him in?' prompted Cressida.

'Not on that occasion. We stood and chatted for a while in the garden. Then a week later – I think it was a week – there was a knock on my door, and there on the step stood Mr Brightly. "I'm delivering the church magazines," he said, "and on an impulse I thought I'd knock." "Do come in," I replied.'

Suddenly, as if recollecting herself, Mrs Parminter halted.

'Yes?' prompted Cressida.

'Oh, but you don't want to hear my interminable tales. The elderly do tend to go on, I'm afraid.'

'But I do, I do. So Richard came in, yeah?'

'Well, if you really . . . Yes, yes, he did. Let me see now.' And with a comfortable sigh, Mrs Parminter continued.

*   *   *

On learning that for every pound she had invested in Mr Brightly's special scheme she was to receive 67p, colour mounted the flesh of Mrs Nanette Thompson and joy pierced her heart. Perhaps because the investigators of the case had treated Mrs Thompson as they had not treated other distressed female investors (with undisguised pleasure at her apparent downfall) she had been led to conclude that she was unlikely to see even a penny back. *Been helping himself for years. Made off with it. Properly taken you to the cleaners, madam*, were some of the phrases employed by men in suits when explaining matters to Mrs Thompson. 67p compared to nothing at all seemed riches indeed. Her view of her future shifted a gear, from grinding labour to sunny coasting.

That evening, looking over the banisters, she spied Aimée collecting from the waiting room her client, Matthew. The sighting reminded Mrs Thompson of the television programme on the Brightly case. She recalled her own part in it and certain harsh comments she'd made about Ricki; and recalled also her fervent desire that somewhere, in Wormwood Scrubs or Pentonville Jail, Ricki Brightly would be viewing the programme and hearing her make them. Now, with the prospect of her money's partial restitution, she regretted those comments. *Smooth-talking wanker, Double-dealing bastard*, and *I hope the hypocrite rots in hell*, seemed on reflection to have been rather rough. Still, it was most unlikely that Ricki had been in a position to view. Her understanding of the facilities in jails and the rules governing their use was very hazy, but hadn't there been a row in the media recently about inmates being banged up for twenty-two hours out of twenty-four? Not a lot of scope for telly viewing there.

Poor Ricki, thought Mrs Thompson. And for the first time since learning of her financial loss she allowed him, as she had known him in the flesh, to enter her memory's senses. He was not so terribly wicked, she cooed, laying, in her imagination, her head on his chest.

After all, in some of these cases, the whole caboodle is gone before anyone gets wind of a swindle. Innocent people's entire savings can end up in some protected foreign bank account, or in the bricks and mortar of some paradise villa beyond the reach of extradition treaties. No, Ricki hadn't been viciously crooked. Just rather naughty, Mrs Thompson smiled, remembering how in the old days he'd relished playing the role of a naughty boy. And however much of a holy joe he'd become in later years, he'd never lost that naughty twinkle. Whenever he smiled, specially when he stood up close, that twinkle would be dancing down at you, making a girl remember things and wish like anything she could turn the clock back. He was a lovely man. Lovely to look at and lovely by nature. The only client, as she'd always said, she'd ever felt anything for. The only jack man of them she'd known she could trust.

Which was a bit of a laugh when you came to think about it.

Over the following days, the power of 67p to charm and console gradually waned for Mrs Thompson. It finally dissipated one overcast morning when she sat down with pen and paper and worked out exactly how much was coming to her, and how much was lost including an estimate of the profits that had been promised her. The latter sum made her grieve. And the more she grieved, the more 67p appeared like an insult. She thought of the extra years of work she must undertake as a consequence of Ricki Brightly's sticky fingers. And her mind's eye banished him from her boudoir to a hard chair in a smelly viewing room in some harsh jail. 'I hope the hypocrite rots in hell,' shouted her shadowy TV image. And she saw Ricki Brightly taking it in. That's poor Nanette, he said, recognizing her, feeling shaken to the marrow by her lust for vengeance, and racked by remorse.

18

'I've a confession to make,' said Cressida to Mrs Parminter. She banged Mrs Parminter's cushions then returned one to the hollow of her back and placed the other beneath her knees. She shook out a rug and laid it across Mrs Parminter and leaned over to secure it between the sofa's back and seat. 'That ought to stay put,' Cressida said, and sat down in a chair and stared about the sitting room with a considering expression. It was a look Mrs Parminter had learned to recognize. It would appear when Cressida had a difficult thing to say.

'Alex wanted to come and see you today. I told him there was no point because you were still too ill to come downstairs.'

'I see,' said Mrs Parminter. 'Well, it was very nice of him to want to come. It's quite some time since he was here.'

'Well, you know how I am,' said Cressida.

'Yes. But surely I am past the infectious stage.'

'I'm sure you are really. But it's such a virulent bug, this flu; half Chedbury's down with it. And this winter's been so lowering, dragging on and on. Alex should be extra specially careful; it's not worth taking a risk, however minute. Telling him you were still in bed saved ever so much hassle; he goes galactic when I fuss. Sorry,' she said, spreading her hands.

'I understand.'

'I thought Friday would be about right, which'll

be ten days since you went down with it. I'll say he can come then. You will play along?'

'Of course. I'll probably be up on my feet by Friday. I'll look forward to seeing him.'

'Thanks. Shall I make us some tea?'

When Cressida had gone from the room, Mrs Parminter leaned back and closed her eyes and smiled to herself. How amazing life is, she thought; how wonderfully full of surprises. Who would have thought a new experience could be in store for her, saved up for her eighty-fifth year? She had absolutely no authority for imagining she was discovering what it meant to have a daughter at last, but could think of no better way to describe the situation. Cressida was always popping in, ready for a chat, generous with her confidences, keen to swap reminiscences and speculate in a satisfying and female way about people's experiences and motives and reactions. During Mrs Parminter's bout of flu she was so very concerned, calling regularly to check on her and see if there were any errands to run. Daughterly or not, Cressida's manner was not quite like any other experienced by Mrs Parminter in the whole of her life. It seemed a gift from providence, and as remarkable in its way as her friendship had seemed to her with Mr Brightly.

No letter from Mr Brightly had come. 'It will have to be next summer's rose,' Cressida had sadly remarked when autumn came and there were no more buds on the bush that had been Mr Brightly's favourite. A card had arrived at Christmas, with his best wishes expressed inside but including no address; and the postmark on the envelope proved too indistinct to decipher however long Cressida held it to the light and pored over it with a magnifying glass. 'Never mind,' Mrs Parminter had said. 'At least he's keeping in touch. I'm certain a letter will come before long.'

At the height of her recent fever the thought had crossed Mrs Parminter's mind that Cressida called so regularly and tended her so diligently in order to prevent any communication from Mr Brightly escaping her. She is keeping a look-out, was Mrs Parminter's baleful thought upon opening her eyes one afternoon and finding Cressida shifting articles on her bedside table. But Cressida was not fazed by being discovered. 'Hi, you awake? Headache any better? I must say, that cleaning woman of yours leaves a lot to be desired, for all she's so thoroughly pleased with herself. This table's still sticky from where I slopped your medicine last night. I thought she was supposed to clean up in here this morning? I know I'm a fine one to talk, but when people paid me to clean a house, I did the job properly. I bet you find that hard to believe,' she'd added, turning to Mrs Parminter with such a disarming grin, her face shining with frankness, that Mrs Parminter had felt ashamed. 'Mrs O'Connor is very self-satisfied,' she'd agreed; 'you've hit the nail on the head there.' And later, recalling her unworthy thought, she'd blamed it on the flu.

'Here we are,' sang out Cressida, coming in now with a tray. 'I used the Harrogate tea, OK?'

'Perfectly,' said Mrs Parminter.

'Funny,' said Cressida, as she placed Mrs Parminter's cup on a small table beside the sofa, 'funny your husband refusing point blank to go abroad for a holiday.' The tea's provenance had reminded her of Mrs Parminter's account of her late husband's taste in holidays.

'He was in love with England: Yorkshire, the Lake District, Dartmouth, the Cornish coast. He said he could never have enough of it and that he knew in his bones it was the most beautiful place on earth.'

'But he couldn't really know. Not if he wouldn't go and find out.'

'I think, really and truly he just didn't want to. He was insular in that respect, I'm afraid, like a lot of Englishmen of his years and background.'

'Perhaps he didn't want to be proved wrong: to discover some places are even more beautiful.'

'Perhaps. I must say, I did rather resent it. I longed to see the Alps. Oh, and the Italian cities: Rome, Venice, Florence, Verona; I should love to have seen those.'

'Men are funny,' sighed Cressida. 'They get an idea and won't let it go.'

'That is very true,' said Mrs Parminter. And she shuffled into a more upright and alert position on the sofa, as an incident occurred to her that would aptly illustrate Cressida's comment.

Dated 4 February, and clearly headed by a notorious address, the longed-for letter arrived at The Gables. Any remnant of suspicion concerning her young friend's motive, of the sort that had been provoked by her influenza, was now wholly expunged, as, to Mrs Parminter's surprise, Cressida showed no inclination to rush off and commence prison-visiting but continued to call at The Gables as usual. 'You write to him,' she urged Mrs Parminter when a week had elapsed. 'I'm too scared. It's been such an age. Maybe he's forgotten about me. I hardly get a mention in this one.'

'He hardly mentions a thing other than his present circumstances,' offered Mrs Parminter in riposte. 'He sounds like a rabbit dazzled by headlights. All he can see is prison, prison.'

'Maybe it's a bit like being in hospital,' said Cressida reflectively. 'It takes you over. All those books you brought in, all the letters you thought you'd write: there's never time; and the world outside gets dimmer and dimmer; visitors are like people from another planet, and you bore them to death by going on and on about what's been happening in the ward.'

'It seems you have an excellent understanding of Mr Brightly's position.'

'Maybe I do. Doesn't help me much, though.'

'I think you're a bit down. It's not surprising. You've been anticipating a letter for such a long time. Yes, I will write to Mr Brightly. I'll tell him about our friendship, and how you and Alex are getting on. It will please him to know that.'

'Don't forget to tell him about Alex's contract. He'll be amazed to hear what Alex has been doing.'

The next letter from Mr Brightly was very different in tone. *You have woken me up,* he wrote to Mrs Parminter. *Your news about Cressida and Alex, the thought of you and Cressida striking up a friendship, has fired my imagination. One can become utterly obsessed with day-to-day trivia in a place like this. Since your letter arrived, I have found myself picturing the scene at The Gables. Cressida is such a marvellous girl, I am not at all surprised you've fallen in love with her. Please give her my affectionate best wishes.*

'You see, he is scrupulous. He is afraid of saying too much. He thinks, in the circumstances, it would be wrong of him.'

Mrs Parminter expressed this opinion to Cressida, hoping to forestall any sense of disappointment or let-down. She need not have worried. When Cressida looked up from the letter she was smiling broadly.

'I know. I'll have to go very carefully. You must help me, Mrs P.'

'Softly, softly catchee monkey?' suggested Mrs Parminter, surprising herself.

'Yeah? That's very good! That's the way exactly.'

It was so strange to be in this place which was unlike anywhere she could have imagined, and events, after hours spent on the road and then kicking her heels outside, were now proceeding at such a lick, that when Richard strode to the table and took the chair on the opposite side, Cressida was dumbfounded. Unable to get out a word, she stared at him, his pallor and harsh navy-blue shirt adding to her sense of unreality. She was not even clear whether he'd spoken; her ears were overwhelmed by noises in the room: chairs scraping the floor, a couple on the far side of the room already arguing, someone cursing a child who persistently charged up and down the aisle.

'You look lovely, Cressida.'

This she heard, and thought it a mad thing to say. She felt most unlovely: sweaty, her stomach churning and her throat dry, and a vile taste in her mouth.

He let her silence hang a while, then asked, 'How are you, Cressida?'

'Hurt,' she blurted, as the many facets of her disorientation fused in hostility towards him. 'Really hurt,' she cried out again, then was overcome by a fit of coughing.

He, meanwhile, lowered his eyes. He had not expected to be scolded, her letters had not suggested she bore a grudge.

'Hurt you tried to stop me coming,' she got out at last. 'Hurt you made all those difficulties.'

'Ah.' He waited as a fellow prisoner loped up to a neighbouring table: 'What you come for?' the prisoner snarled; 'Christ knows,' retorted his visitor.

Mr Brightly craned his head nearer Cressida's. 'Soon after I was put in here, Harriot came to see me. It was a grave mistake, I should never have allowed her to come, she was dreadfully, most awfully upset. I didn't want that for you. I couldn't face your being distressed.'

'But I can handle it,' she blazed. 'I'm a grown woman, Harriet's still a girl. Anyway, she's your daughter; that's got to make a difference. It must be really undermining seeing your father in jail, specially when he's been your protector, the one you've always relied on, the strong person in your life. It'd give you a shock finding him stuck in a place like this. But see? – for me it's not like that. I've been through the mill. I can take it – I can take *you* – warts and all.'

At this he broke into a smile. And his eyes lighting up and twinkling at her restored the missing element of familiarity. 'Oh Richard,' she said softly, and reached a hand across the table. He hesitated, then took it and held on, and a warder who had been standing unobtrusively at the side of the room strolled towards them, paused by their table, then strolled on by.

'What was that about?' she hissed.

'Just doing his job. But I'm sure he knows in his heart I'm not in the drugs market. I'm a trusty, you see,' he told her with humorous pride.

She looked dubiously down at their linked hands. 'Don't worry about it,' he said, not letting go.

'Anyway,' she went on, feeling her sense of grievance was not exhausted, 'you should've written. All that time without a word: it wasn't fair.'

'If I'd got in touch it might have landed you in trouble. As it was, the way I'd arranged your affairs was enough to make them suspect you were implicated.'

'That's true,' she conceded, recalling the afternoon when she'd returned home to find an investigator waiting, and his unpleasant manner and the questions he'd asked. But then she recalled the months that had followed with still no word from Richard, and the doubts that had plagued her and the misery. 'But later on you could've written.'

He looked at her, and remembered how he'd sometimes pictured her: bombing about in her car, attending lectures, sprawled on the floor in front of the television, presiding over a dinner party in her smart black frock with her hair piled up and ruining her elegance with giggly squiffiness; and had also pictured Alex: rapt in his own wizardry, sharing his enthusiasm over a find in a magazine or a development in one of his computer games, jigging with impatience at an enforced stately descent of the stairs; and pictured the small house in Symmonds Close: the bedroom stuffed to the gills with electronic equipment, the dining room table smothered in books and files, the disordered kitchen, the bright warm sitting room. 'I wanted you to get on with your lives,' he explained. 'I couldn't be the cause of them being disrupted. And you had enough on your plate, Cressida, with Alex and your studies; getting involved in things that were happening to me would have done you no favours.'

The child who had been running up and down was now caught and slapped. An outburst followed. Clasping hands and looking eye to eye, they suffered the screams and yells in silence, until a female warder intervened and took the child from the room.

'I wish you'd stop always trying to work out what's best for me, Richard,' said Cressida. 'Don't you think it's a tiny bit arrogant? I mean, who are you to judge? Why shouldn't I know myself? From now on I wish you'd pay attention to what I actually want.'

'And what do you want, Cressida?'

A grin came on her face and widened ear to ear. She squeezed his hand. 'You know damn well what I want,' she hissed. 'It's just a shame you can't give it me here.'

He found that her grin was catching, and also that he was unable to utter a word in response. She brought up her other hand to be held, and when he took it, squeezed both his hands and gave them little encouraging shakes. 'Oh, Cressida, Cressida,' he said after the lapse of some minutes.

'I love you, Richard.'

'I know. I don't deserve it.'

'I'll be the judge of that.'

A buzzer sounded. Chairs scraped and people stood up. Cressida was unable to believe their time could be over. 'Is that it?' she cried, as all the stressful hours leading to her arrival here and the weary hours of travelling that lay ahead loomed disproportionately on either side of their brief coming together.

'I'm afraid so. And visitors must remain till the prisoners have left. I'm sorry, darling. Please don't move.'

She hung on to his hand as he rose, feeling there was much to be settled and they had barely started. 'There'll be no objections about me coming again, I hope?'

Smiling, he shook his head, then loosed her grip and was gone.

Closing her eyes, Cressida saw blackness upon

which she soon imposed Richard's eyes twinkling down at her. All around her harsh noises continued: bangings, last minute messages called across the room, a woman crying, a woman uttering oaths. A warder arrived at her side: 'Miss?' he said. Cressida neither saw him nor heard. He touched her arm. Jumping, staring wide-eyed from her reverie into the room, she heard him say, 'Time to go, love. Come along.' And she lurched to her feet and went to join the departing throng.

Mr Brightly in his prison cell could not stop thinking of Cressida smiling at him over a table and holding his hands, Cressida smiling in a particular way and applying pressure with her thumbs to the tips of his fingers, Cressida saying, 'I love you, Richard.' And later these things stayed with him as he travelled from his cell via gangways and flights of steps to his duties in the prison kitchen; spreading margarine on a thousand squares of pre-sliced bread he thought of them still. 'Lofty looks happy tonight,' commented one of his colleagues. 'He should, he's had a visitor,' called another. 'What you grinning at, *nark*?' a prisoner collecting food growled menacingly. Mr Brightly ignored every remark, both kindly and otherwise, and continued to think of his hands being lovingly and suggestively squeezed and shaken.

Later, when he returned again to his cell and lay down on the upper bunk, he reflected that Cressida's visit had brought him a few moments of pure joy. He couldn't positively pinpoint when he had last tasted such happiness, but certainly it would pre-date the occasion when the bank had intimated its dissatisfaction with various matters Mr Brightly had a hand in and Mr Brightly had foreseen correctly that one morning soon he would be preceded at his office by men with warrants to examine the files. Through all this time Cressida's love had continued, he marvelled. His mind flew back to the evening when she'd first declared it, he and she in the small kitchen, she clinging to him, he forcing himself to resist.

On the bunk below him, Mr Brightly's cell-mate began noisily pleasuring himself over a magazine, cursing as he did so the woman whose photograph engaged his attentions, promising to rip off her nipples with his bare teeth. Against this background, Mr Brightly reflected on Cressida's devotion and his own motives for resisting her. As well as the wish not to compromise his religious convictions, nor to take advantage of a vulnerable person, he had hoped to send Cressida into the arms of a more suitable lover, a fellow student, perhaps, or a youngish lecturer, someone nearer her own age. Now, staring at the ceiling of a prison cell, with his nostrils full of prison's smell and his ears contending with its sounds, it was more than their age difference concerning his mind. Caring for her as he did, he balked at the thought of her tied for life to a fifty-two-year-old jailbird with a murky past. Such a man was no partner for Cressida.

Deciding he must write and tell her so at once, he swung down from the bunk, collected paper and biro, and sat at a ledge that served as a table.

'Sorry about that, mate,' came gruffly from the lower bunk.

'Oh, I was engrossed in my thoughts,' said Mr Brightly tactfully, thereby offering reassurance (for he was obliged to live with the man) without condoning a distasteful expression of violent intent. Such accommodation had become second nature. 'And now I must write a letter. I shan't disturb you, I hope?'

'Nah, not me,' replied his companion, rolling onto his side and preparing to sleep.

Mr Brightly thanked Cressida for coming to see him. He described the joy her visit had brought him. He also, after some perusal of the stained wall in front of him, confessed to loving her in return. Then, gathering his courage, he set down honestly and frankly all those things that made him the sort of person he shuddered to imagine her associated with: their age difference, his criminal record, the degradation of his present circumstances, and sins from the more distant past including regular visits to a disorderly house. He regretted the need to shock and disgust her, he added, but feared he had given a falsely virtuous impression of himself and it would be better if she knew the entire truth.

Snores were now coming from the lower bunk; and angry sounds from along the corridor, which Mr Brightly recognized as prisoners kicking up because a period of association was overdue and a favourite television programme about to start. Suddenly there were different sounds: feet clattering, eager shouts, and the jangle of keys, and Mr Brightly looked up expectantly just as the door to the cell flew open. 'Simmonds, you lazy git,' cried the warder – at which the man on the bunk sat up: 'Cor what a stink! Gerrout of here.' Simmonds staggered out, and the warder looked across at Mr Brightly.

'I'd like to finish this letter if I may.'

'Personal, is it?' the warder asked, having adapted his tone to suit an exchange between members of the human race.

'It's to a friend of mine, a young lady. I'm trying to collect my thoughts. I'd welcome a few minutes' peace and quiet.'

'Sounds reasonable. By the way' – he came further into the cell – 'I've heard you'll be moving on very shortly,' he confided, and went on to mention the name of an open prison. 'So don't go blotting your copybook, eh?'

'I'll do my very best,' smiled Mr Brightly. 'Thanks for telling me.'

'Leave you to it then.' And the warder hurried away to unlock further doors that were being impatiently hammered on.

Soon it was pleasantly and unusually silent. Mr Brightly again took up his pen, but after a moment laid 't down. Ever since arriving in jail – in the battering

noise of jail, its unpredictable moods and pervading
squalor – he had felt in two minds about what he should
do, bereft of a sense of direction, unable to glimpse his
best course of action either now or in the future.
Sometimes he told himself that the moment he was free
he'd buckle to and make good every penny of his
clients' losses, and he dreamed up various ways and
means of accomplishing this, but always ran into the
stumbling block of the restraints that had been placed
on his future business practice. At other times,
becoming involved with some of his fellow prisoners –
the inadequates, those who were here mainly as a result
of being unable to cope alone in the outside world and
who were pathetically grateful for the small measures
of support he found he could give them – he wondered
whether he ought to do something on these lines when
he was released. Was this part of God's purpose for him?
But somehow, since he'd been in prison, God didn't
appear to be directly in touch. He was there, all right.
God had been present in a protective way on many an
ugly occasion, saving Mr Brightly from feeling intimi-
dated, lending him the confidence to remain himself
rather than trim to the callous norms that operated here.
There was just no discernible special call: at least, none
that Mr Brightly had managed to catch, no sign of the
sort he'd experienced in the past. Picking up his pen,
he asked himself whether there was any point in
explaining these difficulties to Cressida. At length, he
began to write, giving a brief account of his lack of direction, and going on to point out what a drag it would be
on a promising new career if she were involved with
an aimless individual who hadn't a clue how he'd
support himself in his late middle years: for, as he
begged her to remember, in a few years' time she would
be a graduate and – if her ambitions were unchanged –
a qualified teacher. In all conscience he couldn't permit
himself to be that drag. This was not to say he wouldn't
continue to supply friendly support, if and when she
requested it. But he hoped most sincerely that the

emotional satisfaction she craved would soon be supplied by someone worthy. Think of Alex, he pleaded, the son you love so fiercely. You cannot saddle Alex with a jailbird. At last, with his spirits flatter than they had been for months, he added love and good wishes and signed his name.

'It went fairly well on the whole,' Cressida said, addressing Mrs Parminter as though in response to a query. 'After a dodgy start it ended up more or less OK.' But Mrs Parminter, who would never dream of asking a direct question of a personal nature, continued with her pruning of the rose bushes. 'At least I think we ended up all right: time will tell.' Cressida broke off to ask if Mrs Parminter wasn't being rather hard on her rose bushes, for the secateurs were snipping ruthlessly, and Mrs Parminter's gauntleted hands were pulling out branches and tossing them onto a tarpaulin sheet with a will, leaving naked-looking forked twigs in the ground little more than a foot high.

'The more severe the pruning the better will be the blooms.'

'So why haven't you been equally tough on Richard's rose bush?

'Because that is a shrub rose and requires different treatment.'

'Right. I guess I don't know too much about gardening, really.'

'No, I'm afraid you don't,' said Mrs Parminter, who had been brought up with the idea that a knowledge of gardening was an essential ingredient of a lady-like upbringing.

'Actually, to be honest, walking into that jail was one of my worst experiences ever. It knocked me out. It made me forget things I'd been planning to say, and say things I hadn't. I could kick myself for that.'

'It will be so much easier next time you go.'

'I suppose. Hey, aren't you tired, Mrs P? How long have you been at it?'

'I began straight after breakfast. It's a tricky job and requires some stamina, so I was determined to make an early start. It's rather late in the year to be doing it, with April almost upon us; but these night frosts we've been having made it unsafe to prune earlier.'

Cressida surveyed the rose bed and estimated thirty or more bushes; and there were more roses at the side of the house and more at the front. 'It would finish me off having to clip all those,' she said, recalling how fed up and exhausted half an hour's weeding made her. 'You must be fantastically strong.'

'If you'd like to make yourself useful, you can go and make some coffee. I'm almost finished.'

'Right-oh,' said Cressida. But before she went, she looked again at the bush she thought of as Richard's. She stared at it sternly, willing it to produce many fragrant purplish blooms. By the time one's ready to pick, she thought, making a silent vow, setting both the bush and herself a target.

After a while Mrs Parminter straightened up and examined her handiwork. Yes, I suppose I must be strong, she reflected with a degree of pride. Her eyes fell on the rose called Lili Marlene, and she remembered an afternoon when she had lain on the ground beside it with no idea of how she came to be there. That incident had shaken her confidence, it had set her worrying about blackouts and strokes and whether she was going the way of her father. She had gone on to experience one or two bouts of giddiness and more of emotional silliness. Then at some point all that had stopped, and she no longer kept watch on herself for signs of physical decay. When this change had occurred, Mrs Parminter couldn't recall, but if she were asked to say why, she would guess it had something to do with her attention's being held by affairs of the present moment rather than memories of the past. The shock of Mr Brightly's wrongdoing had certainly given her plenty to think about; and then Cressida had come on the scene, and ever since Mrs Parminter had been thoroughly engrossed in the ups and downs of the Reece household. Deterioration and dying no longer seemed imminent for her. How could she possibly die, thirsting as she was to know whether Cressida's hopes would materialize, involved as she was with the uphill progress of Cressida's dreams?

Stripping off her gauntlets, Mrs Parminter went carefully round the pile of rose cuttings (which must lie on their tarpaulin sheet until the gardener came to dispose of them), and with her secateurs in hand proceeded towards the house, eager for refreshment. Mrs Parminter also anticipated, keenly but reticently, up-to-the-minute news on the state of play between Cressida and Mr Brightly.

'Thank goodness you're up,' cried Cressida, flying past Mrs Parminter a few days later without invitation. Mrs Parminter closed her front door and raised eyebrows to herself, for she had been up since half past seven that morning and it was now a little after nine. In the centre of the hall Cressida was doing a sort of jig. 'I've had a letter,' she cried, waving it about. Her eyes were huge, blotches of colour stood in her cheeks, and her mane of hair standing out almost at right angles to her head put the word *shock* into Mrs Parminter's mind. 'You've had a shock,' she said. 'Come and sit down. Where would you like to be?'

'The kitchen,' said Cressida, leading the way. She flopped onto a chair and flung her arms over the table. Mrs Parminter sat opposite.

'He actually admits to loving me,' she reported. 'At last! I thought, and was so happy I started kissing the very words. He says my visit brought him pure joy.' She looked across at Mrs Parminter, who, sensing a downturn in the story, reserved her congratulations.

'Then, what d'you know?' wailed Cressida. 'He only goes and uses loving me as an excuse to spite me. Like it gives him the right to judge what type of bloke I should have for a partner. Because naturally he concludes he's not that type, for various reasons. Can you credit it?'

'I'm afraid I don't follow . . .'

'Here, I'll read you the bit.' Cressida opened the letter and hunted through it. 'Yeah, here we are: *Loving you as I do, Cressida, the very last thing I would wish to see is my darling tied for life to a fifty-two-year-old jailbird with a murky past. You deserve someone very much better.* See?'

'But isn't that just like Mr Brightly – scrupulous to the very last? My dear, he is thinking of *you.* He is putting your interests before his own.'

'But who asked him to?' roared Cressida. 'I sure as hell didn't. I told him specifically to lay off that sort of thing. "Stop trying to decide what's best for me, Richard, and start paying attention to what I actually want." That's what I told him.'

Feeling out of her depth, Mrs Parminter forbore to comment.

'Then he goes on and on about everything that makes him this unsuitable candidate, like being older than me, and doing time, and . . . Oh, all sorts of stuff,' she ended lamely, taking a swift decision to leave out any reference to a disorderly house. She turned the page over and scanned the second side. 'Then there's lots about not being sure what he ought to do when he gets out. Oh, but wait! It's this bit at the end that's the real punch in the guts. *I beg of you to think of Alex, Cressida, the son you love so fiercely. You cannot saddle Alex with a jailbird.* What d'you think of that?'

Mrs Parminter thought the words had a ring to them. She told herself she had never considered this aspect of the situation, and began to wonder if Cressida was failing in her maternal responsibilities not to consider it also. Just as words printed in the *Daily Telegraph* had undermined her attitude to Mr Brightly, these words written by him caused her view of Cressida's attachment to wobble. 'There is that aspect,' she began.

But the question had been asked rhetorically, and Cressida, after drawing breath, was already embarked on the correct answer. 'Alex *adores* Richard,' she cried.

'After all this time he still talks of him, remembers things Richard said and little incidents that happened while he was with us. He was pleased as punch I'd been to visit him. "How was he? When will he get out, Mum?" he asked. "Did you tell him about my Saeko contract? What did he say?" You know something?' demanded Cressida, directing a look of such intensity at her that Mrs Parminter quailed. 'When Richard was with us – those evenings when we sat or ate together, or Alex and Richard were doing something and maybe ganging up on me a bit, or Richard and I would be grinning together over Alex getting enthused . . . Times like that were the only times ever when our family didn't consist of just Alex and me. 'Cos it's always been us on our own. Always. From Alex's point of view, if someone comes to see us, then we've got Grandma staying, or Mum's friend Julie, or Uncle Jonathan's called for some reason. But as far as proper family goes, for Alex I'm it. Just like he's it for me. It was different when Richard was with us; somehow, with him, we expanded. I don't know how it happened, what it was: Richard's natural-ness, maybe. Tell you something, though: it felt fantastic. Alex and I had been grating on each other's nerves, feeling sort of claustrophobic. Then Richard came and let in air, allowed us to breathe. Alex and I still have the odd row or tussle, but that time with Richard showed us a nice way to be with one another. And when one of us gets edgy we can still manage to pick up on it. Couldn't half do with a booster, though.'

'Oh my dear,' cried Mrs Parminter tremulously. 'You must write and tell Mr Brightly that. Every word of it, just as you've told me.'

'I know. But when? I've got lectures. I've got an essay . . .' Cressida looked up at the wall clock and scrambled to her feet. 'Hell, I should be there already.'

Mrs Parminter reminded her that the weekend was almost here. But the weekend was no help to her, wailed Cressida, with the shopping and cooking and cleaning and washing of clothes it brought, not to mention an

252

essay due to be handed in on Monday morning. Mrs Parminter, desperately anxious to help, ran her eyes over her kitchen as though in search of inspiration. 'I have it,' she cried. 'You and Alex must come to me for Sunday lunch. That will mean less shopping and no cooking on Sunday or clearing up. Alex can help me with the washing up, and you can have a nice quiet room upstairs and devote Sunday afternoon to writing your letter. How would that be?'

'Oh Mrs P, it'd be truly marvellous. You're an angel. Whatever would I do without you?' asked Cressida, flinging herself on Mrs Parminter and embracing her so roundly that on her release Mrs Parminter was obliged to clutch at the table.

'What time, Sunday?' shouted Cressida, charging through the hall.

'Twelve thirty?' called Mrs Parminter, and heard Cressida reply 'Fine!' just prior to the front door slamming. Upon which a small tremor passed through The Gables.

Mrs Parminter, feeling very vigorous, rang up her butcher and ordered a joint to be delivered. Then she went upstairs and looked into the garden-facing room she had in mind for Cressida to write in. Mrs O'Connor would be coming later on, and Mrs Parminter resolved to ask for her assistance in shifting some furniture: the writing table to go under the window, for instance, so that Cressida's eyes being raised from her work would take in scarlet tulips and greening shrubs and creamy magnolia blossom; and one of the straight-backed chairs with the padded seats from downstairs to go under it. She felt the radiator to see whether it required to be burped, but found a warmth that was evenly distributed and satisfactorily robust. Arriving once more in her kitchen, she took down a cookery book and turned to the pages under the heading *Puddings*. A cold one and a hot one, thought Mrs Parminter. And a Victoria sponge for tea at five o'clock, for no doubt Cressida would be peckish again by then after her letter writing. She wondered whether Alex would prefer something savoury for tea; in her experience men often preferred savoury things to sweet. Altogether there was a great deal to be done, and only two days to do it. Careful planning being indicated, Mrs Parminter took the notebook and pencil she kept on the counter for Mrs O'Connor's use, and began to draw up a list.

19

Driving the tractor, looking frequently over his shoulder to check the progress of the drill, Mr Brightly was reflecting on the astonishing speed of the turn in his circumstances. He was still a prisoner but no longer felt like one. His aimlessness had been replaced in a matter of days by a sense of well-being and purpose. How amazing it all was. Drawing in the keen air, he savoured the full expansion of his lungs, lungs that for months had functioned only minimally in sour cramped rooms. His hands on the wheel were already brown. Strength was reflected in the movement of sinews and muscles in his bare forearms. When the tractor met the edge of the field he switched off its engine and jumped down to examine his handiwork, and on an impulse crouched in the fine tilth. He took up a handful of earth, crumbled it and sniffed it, and thought of its slow composition from rocks and plants and shells and bones over billions of years. The earth was pervasive; it was on his clothes and under his fingernails and its odour was filling his nostrils. 'Earth,' he said aloud, drawing the word out and dwelling on the sound and thinking it beautiful: exulting in it.

This was Mr Thornwood's land. Mr Thornwood was a farmer and market gardener who relied solely on organic aids to production. He was also a man of philosophical bent. He and Mr Brightly had hit it off at once. Mr Thornwood treated every prisoner sent to work on his land with courtesy and consideration, but did not confide to every prisoner the theme underpinning his way of life. 'Respect Nature and she'll respect you. Abuse her and it'll rebound on you,' said Mr Thornwood. 'There's a rhythm and a cycle to Nature, and there are basic laws. Man should work with them, never against.' Mr Thornwood would plant his feet a little apart and stand massively, keeping his chest free from encumbrance and resting a hand on a gatepost or workbench in order to deliver these truths. His manner of speaking was slow, and as he warmed to his theme his eyes grew dreamy and he gently smiled. Now and then he paused to nod and look at Mr Brightly directly.

None of this might have seemed impressive were it not for the frequent opportunities Mr Brightly enjoyed to observe his mentor conducting a variety of tasks. The sight of Mr Thornwood transplanting seedlings made tears start to Mr Brightly's eyes—the deftness of the stubby fingers, the infinite patience, the little grunts of satisfaction, the stoop of the body describing tenderness. And Mr Thornwood pacing out a plot, making his calculations and weighing matters, cut as substantial a figure as Mr Brightly had seen. Watching him and working under him, the talk of cycles and rhythms and respect for Nature began to make simple yet revelational sense. An old excitement stirred. And his limbs began, though at first unconsciously, to assimilate Mr Thornwood's professional manners. Soon, pots and trays and secateurs and pieces of string were impossible to manipulate in any manner other than Mr Thornwood's; and somehow Mr Thornwood's walk insinuated a little into Mr Brightly's legs; even a pause for reflection felt more enjoyable with his feet placed a little apart and his chest kept free from encumbrance and his hand resting on a convenient object. Catching himself in Mr Thornwood's hoeing posture one day, Mr Brightly told himself it was not surprising. No doubt the methods of Mr Thornwood had been inculcated from observing his father, and the methods of that father from observing his; they were tried and proved, each the most appropriate for a particular job. What was rather surprising, perhaps, was how naturally these methods and manners had come to him. And how satisfying they were to perform, as if in tune with his new frame of mind.

One morning, driving a load of dung to a field, and feeling particularly happy and satisfied with life, a question startled Mr Brightly's mind. Was it possible that something had occurred to him here of similar nature to a past experience? But then he smiled and shook his head, and told himself he was feeling the effects of sudden liberation. What could be more exhilarating, after months of cramped and unpleasant confinement, to find himself out in the open air with thoughtful and civilized company and the stimulation of new ideas? It would impact on the dullest person. And yet: there was no doubt of his sense of aimlessness being gone; no doubt of a new sense of purpose. He laughed at himself, admitting only that it was an intriguing question.

Later on he asked Mr Thornwood if he might borrow some books on organic husbandry.

'Aye, I can lend you one or two. But you'll not find much in books you can't learn better out here getting your hands dirty.'

'I'm sure that's right. But it's a fascinating subject and I'm keenly aware of large gaps in my knowledge. By the way, it's probably not my place to make the suggestion, but I'd be very glad to work late in the evening if it'd be useful to you – and acceptable to the powers that be, of course. I know you're anxious to get those carrots thinned out.'

'That's very obliging, I'm sure. I could certainly do with the extra help. I've not been knocking off myself these past few nights while eight o'clock or later. Tell you what: I'll give Bob Deakin a ring; see if he's got any objections. If it's all square with the folk at the prison, we'll take a bite to eat in the kitchen around five, and then carry on.'

'Excellent,' said Mr Brightly.

Mr Brightly had been an inmate of the open prison for ten days when Cressida's letter caught up with him, belatedly re-addressed from his former prison. By this time the letter was a fortnight old. But the date at the top did not immediately register with Mr Brightly who was impatient to read her news.

In his new mood of optimism, and with her words – I wish you'd pay attention to what I actually want – hovering somewhere at the back of his mind, he began to read. He was soon chuckling appreciatively at her reaction to the news that he'd once frequented a disorderly house: she wasn't in the least bit bothered, she wrote, being perfectly certain he'd have nothing going spare for prostitutes once she got her hands on him. And then he was touched by her remarks about age: *Never mind about your age, Richard. All I know is, I'm thirty-three and so far haven't struck lucky with a single bloke. For Pete's sake give me a break*! And he enjoyed the forthright way she handled his worries over her being linked with a jailbird: *OK, so maybe I'll get grief from Mum and Dad, even from Jonathan. But to the two people (apart from you, that is) who matter most in my life right now, Alex and Mrs Parminter, you are simply you. They know I love you and they want me to be happy. Anyway, I heard this chap on the car radio saying, the way the Home Secretary's going, everyone in the country will soon know someone who's been in prison. So get yourself in perspective, Richard.*

Then he came to a passage describing Alex's and Cressida's feeling of being a proper family when he was with them. *So you see, Richard, we need you, we really do. We long to have you with us again. It will make such a difference, you just don't know.* Tears sprang as he read this, and obliged him to go over the following sentences twice. *But I do realize, darling, it will be very difficult for you, showing your face in Chedbury again. It's a lot to ask.*

Cressida had composed these last two sentences in

what she told herself afterwards was a fit of inspiration. She had glanced up and looked out of the window, and her eyes, after staring so long at sheets of note paper, had been dazzled by the vibrancy of Mrs Parminter's garden. And the sentences had simply jumped into her head. With them had also jumped an intuitive knowledge of her beloved's response. He'd picture himself striding along Stratford Road or arriving in Symmonds Close and becoming the subject of looks and nudges and nasty whispers. Then pride would enter him, and he'd be bursting to demonstrate that he could handle it gracefully, that for her sake he would bear it gladly. I do believe I'm getting the hang of this man, she'd congratulated herself.

And now, though she was not present to witness it, Cressida's foresight was proved spot on. A great keenness filled Mr Brightly to show himself again in Chedbury. He thought how he would welcome the chance to stride up to Cressida's door and under the eyes of neighbours take a key from his pocket and let himself into the house. Sadly that must wait for a time in the future. He folded up the letter and was about to return it to its envelope when his eyes fell again on its heading. The significance of the date hit him like a blow.

'Cressida?'

'Richard!'

'Darling, I've just got five minutes. Your letter's only this moment arrived. They've moved me, you see, to another place; evidently they took their time sending it on, the rotters. The set-up here's quite different; much more reasonable and sympathetic. When I explained you'd be worried, not having had a reply, they said straight away I should give you a call. I ought to have sent you my new address days ago. I am sorry, my love, but things have been moving at such a pace, and it's made such a deep impression, I hadn't noticed how the time was flying. Are you and Alex all right?'

'We're fine, Richard. But I've been ever so miserable. I thought . . . Oh it doesn't matter now; it's just wonderful to hear your voice. I can come and see you, wherever you are?'

'Of course. I'll write this evening and give you the address and directions, and the dates when I'm allowed a visitor. You'll find visiting here very much nicer, Cressida.'

'As if I care about that, you idiot! I'm just dying to see you. Make it soon, Richard.'

'I'll do my utmost, darling.'

On a Saturday afternoon in April, a day as the forecasters promised with plenty of sunshine and a gusty southwesterly but no precipitation, Mr Brightly was leading Cressida on a walking tour of the Thornwood farm. 'I can't believe we're here,' said Cressida. 'I hadn't imagined anything like this.'

Mr Brightly hadn't imagined it either, until the day before. He'd heard from other prisoners of the possibility of a private visit. The regime was enlightened; for a prisoner with a personal problem to sort out or intimate matters to discuss, arrangements could generally be made. Accordingly, when the date of Cressida's visit was fixed, Mr Brightly put in a request. 'That'll be all right,' said the deputy governor. 'I'll make my office available. Two o'clock on the twenty-sixth,' he said, making a note of it. But then Mr Brightly began visualizing the scene: the small room, the two basic chairs, the desk with the photograph on it of the deputy governor's wife. It was difficult to imagine an easygoing encounter in this setting; strained conversation came more readily to mind, and the misunderstandings that can occur when two people are thrust together in unfamiliar circumstances. And there was something else. When he reported the arrangements for Saturday afternoon to the warder who would then be on duty, a waggish but well-intentioned chap, the response was a wink and a promise: 'You'll be all right there. You'll not be

disturbed.' At which an unwelcome image rose in Mr
Brightly's mind of Cressida being eyed in a speculative
fashion. He wondered how to prevent it. During a break
for tea the following day, he mentioned the problem to
Mr Thornwood. 'Bring the lass here,' said Mr
Thornwood at once. 'You tell Bob Deakin, if it's all right
with him, it's all right with me. No, better still, I'll
mention it. Me and the missus'll be seeing Bob and Dora
tonight; there's a do on in the village hall. Leave it to
me. I'll have a word.' So here they were, the
wind billowing Cressida's skirt, slippery grass and a
rutted track presenting an occasional challenge to her
unsuitable shoes.

During the half-mile walk along the lane between the
prison and the farm, Cressida, in response to Mr
Brightly's questions, had reported Alex's latest doings
and her own. Arriving at the farm entrance they'd met
Mr and Mrs Thornwood driving out in their Land Rover.
Introductions were made, and the Thornwoods said
they were off to town to find an outfit for Mrs
Thornwood to wear at a forthcoming wedding. Then the
Land Rover chugged away, and Cressida and Mr
Brightly started along the farm track. In the distance the
cowman passed through a field, calling up the herd for
milking. Otherwise, they had the whole of the
Thornwood acres to themselves. Mr Brightly knew this,
but it did not occur to him to tell Cressida. Cressida,
while listening to her beloved's enthusiastic account of
his work hereabouts, was eyeing the landscape for some
feature that might provide them with privacy.

Mr Brightly outlined the basic principles of organic
husbandry. Now and then he pointed out examples of
these in practice.

'You've been bitten by a bug,' said Cressida,
observing the gleam in his eyes. 'A new one.'

'Oh – you mean a new enthusiasm. Mm, I suppose I
have. I've been in a state of high excitement since the
moment I arrived. It's elation, I suppose, at the release
from confinement. Though I must say, I feel drawn to

this life. And drawn to its possibilities.' His arm was around her and he squeezed her into his side. 'There's a feeling in the air, Cressida, a new sense of concern. People are waking up to the way their food's been contaminated; they're worried about the consequences. But it's not just a matter of health; people yearn for food to taste as it used to . . .'

Yeah, he's been bitten, all right, said Cressida to herself. And it's going to need watching. It was lovely to see him more like his old self; and if he'd latched on to something that had given him back his lost sense of purpose she was pleased for him. But it would be as well, in the future, to keep an eye on where this bug might be leading – discreetly, of course – in view of where some of his enthusiasms had led in the past. 'It's good to see you all fired up,' she said, wondering whether she was counting her chickens since she hadn't yet made sure of him.

'Take these carrots,' said Mr Brightly, and stooped down to rub away earth and gently expose the green-streaked top of a moon-coloured tuber.

'Yeah,' said Cressida, riveted by his pose: the one leg outstretched, the other bent at the knee with the thigh straining against the trouser seams. He brought out a handkerchief and rubbed the carrot free of soil. 'Like to taste?'

She bit off the carrot's tip.

He watched her face as she chewed, then took a bite himself.

'Mm. Fantastic,' she declared.

He laughed and returned his arm to her waist, drawing her onwards. 'I can't tell you what a treat it was to stretch my eyes when I first arrived.'

'I can imagine. You look incredibly fit, Richard. I can see the life suits you.'

'It does, darling. I've never felt better.'

He smiled down at her, and she thought his eyes were even more twinkly than she remembered and very blue against his tan. When they came to a five-bar gate, he removed his arm and placed a hand on the gate and looked over it. 'See the shoots coming? That's a very old type of wheat. Mr Thornwood's growing it specially for the Seed Conservation Society. It'd be a dreadful mistake to allow the older varieties to die out. The new ones that have been bred for their prolific yield could easily fall prey to some pest, or a disease we don't even know of yet and haven't a clue how to eradicate. That's why seed banks are so important. There's wisdom in Nature's rich variety,' he said, turning to smile at her. 'Save the seeds! – now there's a rousing call.'

Oh God, but he's gorgeous, inwardly groaned Cressida. So gorgeous it was perhaps fortunate for her that he was confined to the company of men for the time being, bearing in mind his divorce had come through. The thought engendered panic. Wouldn't it be just her luck if he were nabbed by some classy svelte-looking type the moment he was free? She glanced rather desperately about. 'What's over there?' she asked, spying a dip in the land.

'Ah, now over there is the site of my first attempt at muck spreading. Come on, I'll show you.'

Disappointingly, the dip flattened out as they approached, and cowsheds and barns and the rear of the house sprang into view. 'Amazing,' commented Mr Brightly, looking over the field. 'You'd never guess the pig's ear I made of this, turning a simple morning's work into a two-day job. Fortunately for me, Mr Thornwood's a placid man and the earth is forgiving. My goodness, look at it.' He gathered a handful of earth in his hand and held it out to her. 'A few weeks in the open with the rain and the sun and the worms doing their job, and it's all integrated. Wholesome, eh?'

Cressida lowered her nose to it. 'Lovely,' she said, looking up at him, thinking she would gladly swallow the stuff if he'd find it exciting. While Mr Brightly rubbed the dirt from his hands, Cressida, shielding her eyes, made a further search of the skyline.

'There's the orchard,' he said, pointing towards a high

hedge with the tops of blossomy trees beyond. 'The hedge was planted by Mr Thornwood's father. It encompasses the entire orchard to provide shelter – most important at this time of year, protecting the blossom from icy blasts; and pretty useful later on – saves against windfalls.'

'I'd like to see it,' said Cressida, setting off at a brisk pace. She clung to his arm, ostensibly for support on the rough ground, in fact to savour the jostle of hip against thigh.

'Now, those apple trees over there are a case in point,' said Mr Brightly, taking high strides through the longer grass of the orchard. 'What would you guess is the age of this tree here?' he asked, coming to a halt and raising a hand to a gnarled bough.

'Tell me,' said Cressida, as her mouth went dry and her heart dinned in her ears: for the thought was burning her brain that the extensive hedge surrounding them provided perfect cover. She heard his reply, but failed to register its nature. 'Fancy that,' she murmured, stepping forward. She wrapped her arms round him and laid her head on his chest.

'Cressida,' he said.

It was his heart now she heard in her ears. As his arms came round her, she tilted up her face, and after a moment he leaned down to kiss her. This is it, she warned herself. Now or never.

'Cressida!' he cried indistinctly. And then, 'Cressida, darling!' as her hand grappled with his trouser fastenings. 'Cressida, will you marry me?' he cried out, knowing that nothing could stop what was about to happen.

'Yeah,' said Cressida, with her mouth full.

At least we're promised to one another, he offered up in urgent silent mitigation, before abandoning himself to the pleasures of satisfying his companion.

'How's that rose bush coming along?' Cressida asked Mrs Parminter, some weeks later. She stepped out through the French windows and went across the lawn. 'You know the one I mean: Richard's rose bush. Any sign of buds?'

'Good heavens, no,' said Mrs Parminter, following after her. 'That bush is late flowering. It won't bear buds till July.'

Cressida, stopping in front of it, found Mrs Parminter was quite correct: buds were not even hinted at. 'Well, I can't hang about,' she said, turning round. 'Richard and I are getting married in three weeks' time. I'd hoped for a rose from this bush for his buttonhole. But there you go,' she shrugged.

'Married?' cried Mrs Parminter. 'You mean . . . Is Mr Brightly to be released?'

'Oh no. He won't be eligible for parole for months. We're getting married in a register office, quite near the prison. It'll be a quiet affair, just him and me and a couple of warders. Oh, and Mr Thornwood: that's the farmer Richard works for. I'm sorry you won't be there, Mrs P, but neither will Alex or Harriet, or any friends or relations. It's the way we want it. In and out, and no fuss. When Richard comes home we'll have a proper celebration. You know, maybe it's good about the rose,' she said, turning again to look at the bush. 'We'll have no adornments at all; just our big daft grins. Say you're glad for me, Mrs P. Say you're happy that for once in my life I've actually got what I've set my heart on.'

'Oh my dear, I am! Come along, you and I shall have a small celebration this very minute.' And Mrs Parminter headed back to the house and the drinks cupboard.

'Great idea,' said Cressida, giving the rose bush a final glance, telling it under her breath: Beat you to it.

Ten months later, due to his exemplary behaviour, Mr Brightly was informed he had been granted parole. Cressida and Alex drove straight to The Gables after receiving his phone call, eager to share the glad tidings with Mrs Parminter. Monday 12 March would be the day of his homecoming. Mrs Parminter was overjoyed by the news. Delighted, she declared. Thankful. Quite overcome.

And so she was, all of those things. But also, to her shame, a little downcast. She told herself it was the fault of the time of year, she was always under par in the early spring. And this, after all, was only to be expected: old bones ached worse in the cold.

During the days of preparation Cressida seemed to call at The Gables more frequently than ever. She came to borrow something, or for a respite, or to ask for advice or a favour. 'I have the most enormous favour to ask you, Mrs P,' she announced one day. 'You must promise to say no if you'd rather not. Thing is, Richard's coming on Monday, as you know, and the following weekend we'd thought we'd have a restricted family get-together: me and Richard and Alex and Harriet. Then I got thinking. Well, you know how small our place is. (I'm not moving Alex out of his bedroom, by the way. Richard will come in with me and he can keep his personal stuff in the little room over the garage.) There's a camp bed I could put up for Harriet, but gosh we'd be awfully on top of one another. And the poor girl might be the teeniest bit embarrassed: you know? – close quarters with Daddy and his new wife? So I wondered . . .'

'Harriet must stay at The Gables, of course,' cried Mrs Parminter. 'It will be lovely to have her. You must always say if I can be of use to you in that way, Cressida. There are all these empty rooms here.'

The arrangement was made, and also that Sunday lunch would take place in Mrs Parminter's dining room, all hands assisting. Mrs Parminter worried to herself about Harriet feeling shy at The Gables, but decided Cressida's hunch was probably sound; the girl might well feel relieved to have a convenient bolt-hole, somewhere near her father's new domestic set-up but not cheek by jowl with it. The important thing was to make Harriet welcome. Mrs Parminter spurred herself to achieve this end, and with mounting excitement and Mrs O'Connor's assistance, began making a bedroom ready. There were as well all the preparations for the Sunday lunch: precise instructions to be issued to the butcher, and a comprehensive shopping list drawn up for Mrs O'Connor's attention. There was simply no time at all for silly ideas, thought Mrs Parminter to herself.

But one night as she lay in bed, weary of shopping lists and Mrs O'Connor's opinions, tired to the bone, she was unable to resist a gloomy cast of mind. She imagined a time beyond the first heady days of reunion. It won't be quite the same, she acknowledged. The intimacy she had enjoyed with Mr Brightly, and then later with Cressida – that particular cosy intimacy two people can forge – would as a general rule be lost to her. Visits from a married couple, and from a married couple and their grown children, however informal and affectionate, would have a different quality. No, it would never again be the same.

'Are you nervous, darling?' asked Cressida, who was driving her husband home to Chedbury at eighty miles an hour.

Mr Brightly said no, he wasn't nervous, but she was going at rather a lick. It might be better to stick to the speed limit.

Cressida's foot came off the accelerator, causing her passenger to lurch forward. 'No, no, silly. I meant, do you feel nervous now you're almost back? Though I suppose nervous isn't quite the right word. Apprehensive would be better.'

There was a short pause as Mr Brightly examined his feelings on returning to the place where presumably he was notorious. He found, on this score, that he was not in the least apprehensive. He found it hard to associate his present self with the Richard Brightly or the Dick Brightly (much less the Ricki Brightly) who merited the opprobrium of the good folk of Chedbury. He felt totally renewed. Set on a new path with a clean slate. Though he did have one or two worries. He wondered how soon he would find a job, and what sort of job, and whether the testimonial in his pocket from Mr Thornwood would impress the National Centre for Organic Gardening that was situated a few miles outside Chedbury; and whether he could earn sufficient money to support and not be a drain on Cressida. But taken over all they were minor worries: his heart wasn't in them. His heart was in building a life with Cressida. 'Well perhaps just the tiniest bit,' he said, turning his head to smile at her.

'Poor darling,' she said, removing her left hand from the wheel and clasping his right one. 'It's going to be fine. You'll cope. I know you can rise to any occasion.'

'Thank you, Cressida,' he said, giving her hand a quick squeeze and returning it to its proper place.

Silence between them fell again. After a few miles, a sign indicating Warwick appeared and put Miss Orvanessy into Mr Brightly's mind. And now he did feel a pang. The poor woman had endured a very difficult year, labouring to assist the inquiry into the mix-up of his clients' affairs. He had insisted on Miss Orvanessy being paid a salary for her trouble, and on severance, her innocence having long been established, had secured for her a sum of compensation. But this wasn't enough, he knew, seeing in his mind the plain woman with the outstanding wart reverently approach him with a cup of coffee, seeing her holding back her body as she leaned forward with a taut arm across her waist, as if reining in passion. 'I shall have to call on Miss Orvanessy in the next few days,' he said. 'I feel badly about her; she was put through the hoop rather dreadfully, you know. I must check on how she is.'

'Your secretary, huh?' asked Cressida, grinning. 'Of course, I've only got your word for it that she's a poor old stick with a hideous blemish. Could be she's a raving beauty.'

'I'm afraid she's not. No, there's only one raving beauty of my acquaintance, and she's sitting beside me at this very minute.'

Cressida's smile deepened. She did not dispute the description as once she would have. She leaned back her head and looked quickly at her reflection in the driving mirror. She saw a broad face and lively eyes and a quantity of wild hair. Yeah, she did look good. Probably because she was so darn happy.

That afternoon, Cressida and Mr Brightly arrived at The Gables. They could barely have had time to unpack Mr Brightly's belongings, Mrs Parminter knew. 'It's just a flying visit, but we had to pop in,' Cressida said. Mrs Parminter was touched. She knew their purpose was to show they meant to include her. She would not be left out, she had a place in their hearts, their smiles confirmed over the teacups.

It was gratifying. It brought a lump to her throat. She had so much to be thankful for and to look forward to. There was just that small, rather selfish regret. For which she ought to be thoroughly ashamed, decided Mrs Parminter, administering a mental shake.

'I must be off, my love. Sadly, I must leave you for a while.'

'Off? What d'you mean?'

'Just for two or three hours.'

'Christ almighty, Richard, it's only your third night home.'

'Think about it, Cressida. What day is this?'

'Wednesday.'

'Wednesday,' he repeated.

'Oh, I get it,' laughed Cressida. 'Go on then, off with you. Give her my love. Tell her I'll probably call in tomorrow after lectures.'

269

She watched him leave, then suddenly thought of something. 'Hey,' she cried, pulling the door open. 'You can take the car, you know.'

'I'd rather walk. It'll do me good.'

'OK. See you later.'

With an easy stride and a hand in his pocket, Mr Brightly walked round the curve of the close. If any curtains twitched, he didn't notice. He turned into Stratford Road, where once angry mothers had brandished placards demanding traffic calming measures (much to the annoyance of Jason Wright who had disparaged the action in the pub one Saturday lunch time to the Framley Lane set). The demonstration had brought no discernible results, observed Mr Brightly, as cars rushed by breaking the speed limit. Soon he came to the traffic lights where he had once been moved by the actions of the woman who was now his wife. Fondly smiling at the memory, he turned into the square.

It was late-night opening at the self-service grocery. A woman was just leaving it, wheeling a wire trolley to a parked car. She was smartly dressed and middle-aged with solidly lacquered hair.

'Good evening, Nesta,' said Mr Brightly.

'My God,' cried Nesta Wright. 'It's Dick Brightly. Bold as brass. Dick Brightly.' Recovering from the initial shock, she made little shoving motions at him with her trolley. 'You deserve to have your face slapped,' she ground out through her teeth, and he could tell from the way she looked quickly to her left and right that she was seriously contemplating administering the punishment herself, and was only held back by the uncertain consequences, given that there were witnesses. Adopting a contrite expression he moved on smartly to spare her further provocation.

And now he was in Sheep Street, on the part of the route he had always taken to The Gables. Here were his feet striding as ever along the same pavement to the familiar gate. As if nothing had intervened since that last Wednesday evening.

A SELECTED LIST OF FINE WRITING
AVAILABLE FROM BLACK SWAN

99313	1	OF LOVE AND SHADOWS	*Isabel Allende*	£6.99
99630	0	MUDDY WATERS	*Judy Astley*	£6.99
99619	X	HUMAN CROQUET	*Kate Atkinson*	£6.99
99687	4	THE PURVEYOR OF ENCHANTMENT	*Marika Cobbold*	£6.99
99730	7	FREEZING	*Penelope Evans*	£6.99
99624	6	THE COUNTER-TENOR'S DAUGHTER	*Elizabeth Falconer*	£6.99
99721	8	BEFORE WOMEN HAD WINGS	*Connie May Fowler*	£6.99
99657	2	PERFECT MERINGUES	*Laurie Graham*	£5.99
99774	9	THE CUCKOO'S PARTING CRY	*Anthea Halliwell*	£5.99
99681	5	A MAP OF THE WORLD	*Jane Hamilton*	£6.99
99771	4	MALLINGFORD	*Alison Love*	£6.99
99392	1	THE GREAT DIVORCE	*Valerie Martin*	£6.99
99688	2	HOLY ASPIC	*Joan Marysmith*	£6.99
99506	1	BETWEEN FRIENDS	*Kathleen Rowntree*	£6.99
99325	5	THE QUIET WAR OF REBECCA SHELDON	*Kathleen Rowntree*	£6.99
99584	3	BRIEF SHINING	*Kathleen Rowntree*	£5.99
99561	4	TELL MRS POOLE I'M SORRY	*Kathleen Rowntree*	£6.00
99606	8	OUTSIDE, LOOKING IN	*Kathleen Rowntree*	£5.99
99608	4	LAURIE AND CLAIRE	*Kathleen Rowntree*	£6.99
99732	3	A PRIZE FOR SISTER CATHERINE	*Kathleen Rowntree*	£6.99
99777	3	THE SPARROW	*Mary Doria Russell*	£6.99
99753	6	AN ACCIDENTAL LIFE	*Titia Sutherland*	£6.99
99700	5	NEXT OF KIN	*Joanna Trollope*	£6.99
99720	X	THE SERPENTINE CAVE	*Jill Paton Walsh*	£6.99
99723	4	PART OF THE FURNITURE	*Mary Wesley*	£6.99
99642	4	SWIMMING POOL SUNDAY	*Madeleine Wickham*	£6.99

'I said to my wife,' he told Mrs Parminter, when she, looking startled, opened her door, 'I must be permitted one evening off a week.'

'Mr Brightly!' cried Mrs Parminter. 'Oh do, do come in.'